A Bid for Romance

A Bid for Romance

The Ladies' Wagering Whist Society, Book 5

Meredith Bond

Copyright, 2020, Meredith Bond. All rights reserved.

No part of this book may be reproduced or transmitted in any form by any means—graphic, electronic or mechanical—without permission in writing from the author, except by a reviewer who may quote brief passages in a review.

Cover Art by QuarterbackTB, https://qtbdesign.wixsite.com/qtbdesign

Logo by Anjali Banerji

Edited by The Editing Hall, http://theeditinghall.com

Published by Anessa Books,
For more information please visit
http://anessabooks.com

Dramatis Personae

Christianne Ayres (previously Lady Norman): Founding member of the Ladies' Wagering Whist Society

Lydia Welles née Sheffield: member of the Ladies' Wagering Whist Society

Diana Crowther, Lady Colburne née Hemshawe: member of the Ladies' Wagering Whist Society

Claire Tyne, Lady Blakemore: member of the Ladies' Wagering Whist Society

Alys Russell, Duchess of Kendell: member of the Ladies' Wagering Whist Society

Mrs. Penelope Aldridge: member of the Ladies' Wagering Whist Society

Cynthia Montley, Lady Sorrell: member of the Ladies' Wagering Whist Society

Ellen Aston, Lady Moreton: member of the Ladies' Wagering Whist Society

Joshua Powell, Lord Wickford: owner Powell's Club for Gentlemen

Tina Bronley, Duchess of Warwick née Rowan: Christianne's natural daughter

Robert Bronley, Duke of Warwick: Tina's husband

Lady Margaret Bronley: Warwick's sister

Liam Ayres, Lord Ayres: Christianne's husband and Tina's father

John Welles, Lord Welles: Lydia's husband

Andrew Crowther, Lord Colburne: Diana's husband

Beatrice & Isabelle Kendrick: Lady

Blakemore's nieces

Edward Pike, Lord Conway: Bel's fiancé

Paul Adler, Lord St. Vincent: fiancé

Elizabeth Adler, Lady St. Vincent: Paul's young step-mother

James Douglass, Marquess of Rossburk: Lady Margaret's romantic interest, school friend of Joshua Powell

Chapter One

~March 24, 1807~

"Get your hands off her!" James Douglass commanded as he strode into Lord Coningsby's library. There were more pictures than books in the room, but his lordship liked the pretension of calling it the library. Jamie just thought the man an idiot.

It was exactly as he'd feared when Mary hadn't come back down to the kitchen after sweeping out the fireplaces. The fourteen-year-old maid always left the library for last, in order to avoid Lord Coningsby, but sometimes he returned in the afternoons instead of going out to his club. Jamie, a footman in the household, had warned her that his lordship was home, but Mary hadn't had a choice—she had to do her work.

And now, Jamie didn't have a choice but to rescue the girl from their employer's wandering hands.

Lord Coningsby's hand froze on the girl's budding breast as Jamie now came to a halt in the center of the room. His lordship still stood by the fireplace place where he'd accosted the scullery maid. His eyes widened for only a moment before narrowing in anger. He deliberately continued what he was doing, squeezing hard enough to elicit a squeak from the girl as if daring Jamie. The man's other hand gripped Mary's upper arm, ensuring that she couldn't move away.

"I said, get your hands off her," Jamie repeated. He felt his nails biting into his palms, but it was Coningsby who he'd like to hurt more than anything.

"And just who the hell do you think you are commanding *me* to do anything," his lordship spat.

"I am looking out for her welfare—something that should be *your* responsibility," Jamie replied.

A cruel smile grew on Lord Coningsby's face. "Yes, she is my responsibility, and I can do whatever the hell I want with her. She belongs to *me*."

"She belongs to nobody," Jamie said, trying to control the volume if not the tone of his voice.

"She is in my employ, as *were* you, now get out!" His lordship shouted before turning back to Mary. Tears were streaming down her small round face even as her big brown eyes implored Jamie.

"Don't lose yer job over me, Jamie," she cried.

"Oh, don't worry, my dear, he already has," Lord Coningsby said, giving her a cruel smile. "Now get out of my house and don't *ever* return!" he yelled at the former footman.

"I am not leaving without her," Jamie said, his voice quietly dangerous. If Coningsby had any intelligence, any sort of experience with a man like Jamie, he would have known that nothing good happened when he lowered his voice in that way. Sadly, Coningsby truly was an idiot. Jamie gave a brief nod to Mary.

"The hell you are," his lordship said loudly, pulling the girl closer.

It took two long strides before Jamie stood directly into front of the man. "Duck!" he said, keeping his gaze directed at Coningsby.

Luckily, Mary knew exactly what he meant and dropped to the floor. His lordship let go when her movement and then Jamie's fist took him by surprise. Jamie connected with the man's nose the moment Mary was out of the way.

As Coningsby screamed, Jamie grabbed Mary's hand and pulled her from the room. He started toward the front door with her in tow.

"No! We can't go out that way," she said, pulling back.

"Who's going to stop us?"

A rather rotund, older lady was standing in their way, assisted by the butler in pulling on her pelisse, when Jamie excused himself and slipped past her, dragging Mary behind him.

They hadn't taken two steps away from the house before Mary stopped Jamie, throwing herself into his arms and bursting into tears.

He could do nothing but rub her back consolingly. "It's all right, now. It's all right. He won't ever hurt you again." She was such a little thing. Her head didn't even reach his shoulder. She rested it against his chest, making such a brave attempt at containing her fright.

"Thank-thank you," she said, but a moment later, she gasped. "What are we gonna do now? We's lost our jobs."

"I don't know," Jamie admitted. "I'll, I'll think—" But he honestly didn't know what he'd do now. He couldn't go back to being an artist. It was that which had left him with only three options: go home, go into someone's employ, or starve to death—and he *wouldn't* go home. And then there was Mary...

"Young man!" a woman's voice called from the carriage standing just in front of the house.

Jamie turned toward her. It was the same woman who he'd just passed in the Coningsby's entry hall.

She crooked her finger at him.

He disentangled himself from Mary and approached.

She handed him a card. "Holton is my butler's name. Tell him I told you to come 'round." She sat back inside her carriage and rapped on the ceiling, giving her driver the go ahead to move forward.

Jamie stepped out of the way of the wheels and looked down at the card in his hand. *The Duchess of Kendell* it said and gave an address on Grosvenor Street.

He turned back to Mary who stood on the sidewalk with streaks from her tears dripping down her cheeks, her brown eyes wide. "It looks like we have an answer," he said as shocked as she.

~*~

Alys Randall, the Duchess of Kendell hated men like the Earl of Coningsby. She hated them with a passion. She sat back against the well-padded seat of her carriage and forced herself to calm by taking in deep breaths. She was positively shaking.

She'd had a very pleasant visit with Lady Coningsby to discuss some charitable work they would be engaging in, and was just preparing to leave, when she'd heard shouting coming from the room just off the foyer. It was most disturbing—not just the language but the implication. It was evident that someone had discovered his lordship doing something inappropriate with one of his staff.

Sadly, this was common enough. What wasn't, however, was a man brave enough to confront a nobleman and stop such behavior. Silently, Alys applauded the man, whoever he was.

When the footman strode from the room, dragging the scullery maid behind him and out the door, Alys was even more impressed. What a brave, idiotic thing to do, she thought as she made her way out the door to her carriage. Noticing the fellow standing nearby with the weeping girl just a few yards away, she simply had to do something. She could not, would not, stand by while these two innocent lives were destroyed by a horrid man like Lord Coningsby.

As her carriage pulled away, she knew she'd done the right thing. Never did she interfere in her butler's handling of the staff. She knew him to be fully capable of managing it, along with the housekeeper. But this was an extenuating circumstance. She just hoped these two were not only brave but good at what they did. She would hate to have them fired soon after rescuing them from this awful, awful situation.

~*~

Jamie and Mary didn't waste a moment but went straight to the duchess's home. Jamie handed the card over to the skeptical footman, who answered their knock on the servant's entrance door.

"We're here to see Mr. Holton," Jamie said. "The duchess sent us."

The fellow looked at the card and then back up

at Jamie with raised eyebrows. "Er, yeah, just a moment and I'll get 'im."

They stood in the back hall for about ten minutes waiting until, finally, a commanding-looking gentleman limped toward them. He was a good six inches shorter than Jamie, nearly bald, and probably no younger than forty-five or fifty years old. For all that, he lifted his chin into the air and said, "Yes?" in such a way that Jamie felt nervous. This was ridiculous, he thought to himself. If he could punch Lord Coningsby in the nose, he could speak with this butler, no matter how self-important he seemed.

"We're here for jobs. I'm Jamie Douglas and this is Mary…" He looked to her. He didn't know her last name.

"Brown," she supplied. "Mary Brown, sir," she curtsied.

"Yes, she's a scullery maid, and I'm, well, I *was* a footman at the home of Lord and Lady Coningsby."

"And would you care to tell me why you are no longer employed there?" the man asked with a suspicious tone to his voice.

Jamie cleared his throat. "Er, his lordship was taking liberties with Mary, and I, er, objected."

The butler's eyes bugged slightly from his head. "I see."

He paused to look Jamie over. "Tall," he said, as if checking off a mental list. "Broad. Blond. Good looking enough."

Jamie wondered if the man was going to ask to inspect his teeth next; he felt like a stallion being examined for purchase.

"The duchess is a widow," Mr. Holton said, finishing his examination. Jamie supposed he'd decided he would do. "The current duke resides at the Kendell estate—one of five holdings in the dukedom," the butler continued. "This household is tightly run, maintaining the highest standard. I, er, assume you have no letters of recommendation."

"No, sir, we do not. However, we would be willing to come on for a probationary period. If you are not happy with our work, we will seek employment elsewhere," Jamie said with a great deal more confidence than he felt. He imagined Mary felt the same way, but she nodded her agreement.

The butler nodded. "Very well. You may see Mrs. Holton, the housekeeper, to be measured for livery." He stepped back to allow them farther into the house.

CHAPTER TWO

~March 26~

Lady Margaret sat on the comfortable Grecian sofa in the Duchess of Kendell's drawing room. She pulled forward the menu for Lady Norman's wedding celebrations she and her sister-in-law, Tina, the Duchess of Warwick, had put together the last time they'd met.

Lady Norman was close to Tina and marrying her father, so she had volunteered to help organize the wedding. Margaret was very happy to assist, and quickly, the two young women found themselves to be the sole organizers of two rather large parties, the wedding breakfast and the ball the following day. Tina had even offered to host the ball in her home, which was one of a few houses in London with a ballroom large enough for such a crowd.

The menu still needed a lot of work, though, and they probably needed to discuss it with Tina's cook, who would be overseeing everything first hand. Much would depend on what was in the market and in what quantities.

For the wedding breakfast, the number of guests would be kept small—only the fifty or so people who were invited to the ceremony itself. The ball the following evening, however, would have hundreds of guests, and they would all need to be fed supper as well as smaller finger-foods throughout the evening.

They would start today by going over the dishes for the wedding breakfast, Margaret decided. One thing at a time. She looked down the list of possible dishes and started pairing them for each course.

"You are always hard at work when I come," Tina said, entering the elegant gold-hued room. Her voice made Margaret jump. She laughed at her own silliness as she stood to give her sister-in-law a quick curtsey.

"You don't have to do that, you know," Tina said, sitting in a matching chair opposite Margaret.

"Of course I do. You're the duchess," Margaret said.

"And you're the duke's sister."

"And *you* need to get used to people paying deference to you," Margaret added with a little laugh.

Tina scrunched up her face in disgust at that. "I don't need people—"

"You may not *need* it, but you should expect it and receive it," Margaret interrupted.

"I think we'll agree to disagree on this one," Tina said finally. "Now, tell me how your search for a husband is going."

"Oh! I thought you were here to go over the menus," Margaret said.

"I am, but honestly, I'm much more interested in you and how you're doing. The wedding isn't for another three weeks."

Margaret sat back and smiled at her sister-in-law. Now that she was happily married, Tina was determined to see Margaret in the same happy state. Margaret didn't even think her sister-in-law gave a thought to the fact that there was a set deadline by which Margaret had to marry or lose her inheritance. Tina just wanted to see Margaret happy and settled.

But finding a husband was currently the bane of Margaret's existence. She hated being on the marriage mart. She'd hated it last season, and she hated it even more this one. She was too shy to laugh and flirt and attract gentlemen like most girls her age. If she had a choice, she'd never go to another society party ever again. Sadly, she *didn't* have a choice.

Even as her smile faltered, Margaret lifted a shoulder negligently. "I'm doing my best."

"By which, I assume, you mean you're not doing anything," Tina said, reading through her words.

"No! I'm going to parties," Margaret said defensively. Tina didn't go to many parties. She didn't need to, and since she hadn't yet learned how to dance to her satisfaction, she avoided most engagements unless they were a soirée where dancing wasn't expected. Margaret envied her sister-in-law to no end.

"Are you encouraging gentlemen to dance with you, spend time with you, flirt with you?" Tina asked.

"I don't know how to encourage a man to flirt with me," Margaret said slightly aghast.

"By flirting with them!"

"But I don't know how to flirt." Margaret tried really hard not to whine.

"I know. It's not easy," Tina said, finally letting up on her. "Just please, try."

Margaret looked at her sister-in-law and then narrowed her eyes. "Warwick put you up to this, didn't he?"

"What? *Your* brother?" Tina asked, widening her bright green eyes. They were very pretty. Margaret had always thought so, wishing her eyes were as bright as Tina's instead the watery, washed-out blue of her own eyes.

Margaret laughed. "Yes, *my* brother. I know him, if you remember, and I know he's desperate for me to marry."

"He's worried," Tina admitted.

"I have this entire season to find someone."

"And you had all of last season too," Tina pointed out, making Margaret wince. Tina sat forward. "Please, Margaret, can you try just a little harder?"

Sighing heavily, Margaret nodded. "I will try, but you know how difficult it is for me."

"I do. Truly, I do. But I also know that you can do it if you put your mind to it. My goodness, you danced with the prince at your own debut ball! *And* you made him laugh! If you can do that, you can certainly attract other gentlemen. You just have to put your mind to it."

"But you see, that's the problem. I was *trying* with the prince. I was trying very hard. But I don't want to marry a man I have to always be trying to impress—it would be too exhausting. And besides, you were there supporting me as was Warwick. I don't have that anymore."

"You have the duchess."

"Yes, but she's not as…" Margaret lifted a shoulder and dropped it again. "She's very sweet and so kind to chaperone me this season but.."

"*Please*, Margaret," Tina said, looking at her imploringly.

"Yes, yes. I promise," Margaret finally relented. "*Now*, can we look at the menu?"

"Yes. Let's go over the menus."

~*~

Margaret walked Tina to the door after they'd finished with their work.

"Now, don't forget, you have promised to do your best at the ball this evening," Tina reminded her.

"Yes, I remember," Margaret said. She hadn't forgotten. How could she when it filled her with such trepidation. Flirt? Her? She hadn't a clue as to how to do so. But she'd promised because there really had been no other choice—and she wanted to make her brother and Tina happy.

"Good. I'll see you then." Tina gave a nod to the footman who opened the door for her.

"Oh! Will you be there?" Margaret asked.

Tina scowled. "Yes. Warwick is insisting I attend more parties. I think he's hoping to convince me to actually take the leap and dance—in public!"

Margaret laughed at her sister-in-law. "Well, if I can put myself forward with the gentlemen then you can dance."

Tina scoffed but gave her a smile and a wave and went out to her waiting carriage.

Margaret started to return to the sitting room when she suddenly noticed the footman. She stopped. She didn't recall ever seeing him before.

She would most certainly have noticed such an Adonis.

All footmen were easy on the eyes. It was one trait which all employers looked for, although Margaret did have to admit that the duchess wasn't especially particular in that regard. But this man... He was tall, blond, and blue-eyed, and the way he filled out his livery made it difficult for Margaret to keep her eyes above his shoulders—his very, broad shoulders. Somehow, they kept straying down his long regal neck, broad chest, narrow hips ,and well-turned calves encased in white stockings.

Her eyes flew back up to his face. He'd raised an eyebrow at her inspection of him and seemed to be trying very hard not to smile. Just before her gaze met his, he quickly reverted to staring blankly over her shoulder as a good servant should. Margaret felt her face heat with embarrassment.

"Are you new?" she asked the man. "I'm sorry, but I don't recall seeing you before."

"Yes, my lady," he said, in a soft baritone with a refined accent. What footman had such impeccable diction? "I started the day before yesterday, but today is my first day at the front door, er, the butler insisted. I believe he doesn't like taking the position?"

"It's difficult for him with his lame leg," she explained briefly. "What is your name?" she asked because she always liked to address people by their correct names. She knew some people simply called all their footman the same name so they didn't have to actually notice who was serving them, but Margaret thought that a horrid practice.

"James, my lady. My friends call me Jamie," he added.

"James," she said with a smile—she didn't dare presume friendship. "It's very nice to meet you. I hope you enjoy working here."

"Thank you, my lady." He bowed slightly and continued to stare over her shoulder.

How odd it was that Margaret wished he would look at her instead. She shook off her fancy and turned to go back upstairs. She paused with one foot on the first step unable to get past his refined accent. "Where are you from, James?"

He'd returned to his station, a chair just inside the door, but hadn't yet sat down again. Margaret had always been happy that the duchess allowed her footmen to sit while on duty. It was so ridiculous to insist they stand for hours, doing nothing but waiting for someone to knock on the door. "The north, my lady," James said without elaborating further.

"Oh. You don't have an accent. You speak very well, in fact," she commented.

He looked startled, even worried for a moment, but then quickly schooled his face into impassivity. "Thank you, my lady. I've been told I'm a good mimic. I pick up accents quickly."

"I see," she nodded. That made sense. "What a wonderful talent."

"Yes, my lady."

~*~

Jamie watched Lady Margaret slowly float up the stairs, her filmy sprigged white muslin gown flowing around her. Why didn't he have his sketchbook when he needed it? On the other hand, he didn't know if he would be allowed to have a sketchbook while on front door duty. He'd have to ask.

But my word, she was even more beautiful up close than he'd realized.

Mr. Holton had pointed the young lady out as he and Mary had been given a tour of the house and informed of all the rules and expectations. Holton had informed them that Lady Margaret was the duchess's charge for the season and a guest in the house. She was to be treated with the utmost respect, they'd been told, as if she were a duchess herself, which made sense since she wasn't too far off, being the sister to one.

Seeing Lady Margaret in passing through a doorway and having her stand directly in front of him couldn't have been more different than sketching with a pencil to using a paint brush to create a portrait. Seeing her at a distance she could have been dull, one-dimensional, but in person, face-to-face, she was vibrant, beautiful, soft and—what really surprised Jamie—kind.

A duke's sister didn't usually notice footmen, and they certainly didn't speak to them asking their names. Whoever heard of such a thing? Perhaps, the sister of a baron or a baronet might recognize a servant, but a lady of her stature? It wasn't to be expected. And yet she had been there, standing in front of him, smiling at him, making his heart pound and his skin prickle with awareness at her closeness.

He just couldn't get her image out of his mind.

She was...ethereal. Angelic. Soft, gentle, and oh-so lovely. She was like a waif or what Jamie had always imagined the fae folk might look like—slender and delicate with big blue eyes and rich, mahogany-colored hair. Just imagining her, Jamie began to feel warm and aware of parts of his anatomy he'd tried his best to forget.

And so he should! He was a servant in this house, nothing more. He had no right even thinking about Lady Margaret, let alone imagining her anywhere near his bedchamber. He nearly groaned as the image flashed in his mind's eye—Margaret stretched seductively on his bed with nothing but a sheet covering her...

No! He wouldn't, *couldn't* go there.

He quickly imagined the duchess in the room with him and Lady Margaret. Oh, yes, that was much better. His ardor cooled immediately. That look of shock and disgust in the duchess's eyes would be enough to keep a man celibate for a good long time.

Much better, Jamie thought. No more imagining Lady Margaret anywhere but in the drawing room.

He shook his head in disgust at himself. He wasn't normally the kind to think with his nether parts. Well, it wouldn't happen again. He was a footman, and he would maintain a proper distance and do his best to keep his thoughts about its occupants correct as well.

Chapter Three

~March 28~

Margaret and the Duchess of Kendell entered the beautiful home of the Marquess of Danby. Lord and Lady Danby greeted them, but Margaret quickly moved forward to her good friend Diana, the Danby's daughter-in-law.

"Margaret, it's so wonderful to see you this evening," Diana said as she curtsied.

"And you," Margaret said. She then leaned forward and asked, "Is it going to be a crush, do you think?"

"I'm sorry to say I do think it will be. It's Lady Danby's first gathering since she regained her health, and there are a number of people who wish to pay their respects."

"They couldn't do that in a smaller setting? In her drawing room?" Margaret asked, drawing her eyebrows down.

Diana gave a little laugh. "No. There are far too many."

"Margaret, we've taken up enough of Lady Colburne's time," the duchess said gently.

"Oh, yes," Margaret said, turning to look behind her to see the number of people lined up to enter and speak with the hosts.

"We'll speak later," Diana said with a smile.

Margaret gave a nod and then followed her chaperone and dear friend into the ballroom. Truly, she didn't know what she would do without the duchess.

Her Grace had been a good friend to Margaret's mother, the Duchess of Warwick, when Margaret had been a child. The one thing the two women had never agreed upon was how Margaret had been treated. Naturally, the Duchess of Kendell hadn't been able to say much to her friend at the time, although she had spoken up for the girl on occasion.

Now, however, she was doing a great deal to atone for years of staying quiet. She had accepted Margaret into her own home, agreed to chaperone her for the season, and was helping her to find a husband. It was much more than Margaret's own mother would have done for her, or anyone else, to be honest. Margaret would be eternally grateful, but for now, she would simply do what was expected of her, which was a great deal more difficult than anyone realized.

Margaret took in a deep breath and tried her best to still her pounding heart as they paused just inside the ballroom door. All her instincts told her to turn and run, or shrink back and find someplace to hide. But she couldn't. She'd promised Tina that she would try, and so try she would.

Taking in another breath, she forced her lips up into a smile. She could do this. She could do this.

What was she saying? *She was ugly! She was too skinny. She had no conversation. No intelligence. She would never be anything but a burden! Why would anyone want to speak with her, let alone dance with her, let alone marry her?* Margaret's mother's voice filled her head.

All her life she'd been told these things; of course they were true. She knew Warwick had always said otherwise, but he was her brother. Tina had told her that she was pretty, but she'd just wanted to befriend Margaret. At first it was to get work since she'd been Margaret's modiste, and then, later, to get close to Warwick. Tina claimed otherwise, but Margaret knew the truth.

"Lady Margaret, how wonderful to see you this evening," Lydia Welles said, coming up to her and the duchess.

Lydia was such a sweet girl. She was always laughing, making jokes, flirting with gentlemen—well, she'd mostly stopped doing that in the last year, ever since she'd met and fallen in love with Lord Welles. They'd married at the end of last season. But marriage hadn't changed the fact that she was a lot fun to be around. Yes, she was the perfect person to pull Margaret from her doldrums.

"Lydia, you look beautiful as always," Margaret said, trying to keep the envy from her voice. Her friend was fair and pretty, but it was really her smile that made her attractive. Margaret recognized that and tried to do her best to emulate her. Now that Lydia was married, she could wear the bolder colors that truly became her. This evening she was in a bright green gown that brought out the color of her eyes and made her cheeks look flushed and pretty.

"As do you, Margaret. I love the cut of your gown. It makes you look so willowy and elegant. I envy you your figure," Lydia said with a bright smile.

Margaret was certain she was just saying that to be kind. She truly was a good friend. Willowy was just a nice way of saying skinny, which indeed, was what Margaret was. No matter how much she ate her proportions just stayed the same. "You are too kind. Of course, Tina designed this dress. She has such an incredible talent."

"Yes, she does," Lydia agreed. She turned to face the room. "So, who do you have your eye on tonight?" she asked with a giggle.

"Me? Oh! No one, I'm sure," Margaret said, slightly taken aback.

"But why not? You should pick two or three men you want to dance with and then make sure they ask you. How else are you going to find the one man who is right for you?"

"I...I thought I'd wait for them to come to me," Margaret said. She'd never heard of such an outrageous idea! Persuading a man to ask her to dance? How did one do that?

"Well, I suppose you could do it that way. I always preferred to make the choice myself, but then, I do like being in control," she said with another laugh.

"And you have no qualms about hinting that a gentleman should ask you to dance?" Margaret asked curiously.

"No, not at all. It's actually much easier for the gentleman. He believes that you're interested in him, when in fact you just want to get to know him a little better to see if you would suit."

"That's an interesting way to look at it," Margaret said, considering her words. "If I had the nerve to be so bold..."

"It doesn't take much, to tell you the truth. A

flutter of your fan or a bat of your eyelashes and they'll come running. Try it, you'll see," Lydia said.

"I have to say, she's right," the duchess said, joining in their conversation. "I used to do the same thing when I was young, and I have seen Lydia and a number of other ladies do so. You might consider giving it a try."

"Oh, I don't think…" Margaret could feel her cheeks grow warm. "No, I couldn't."

"Try it," Lydia said, putting a hand on her arm, encouraging her.

"Good evening, Your Grace. Lady Margaret. Lady Welles," Mr. Hershawn said, coming up to them, accompanied by Lord Roseberry. The two men were almost never seen without the other. They both bowed to the ladies.

"Good evening, gentlemen," the duchess said, nodding her acknowledgement while Margaret and Lydia curtsied.

"What is it that must be tried, Lady Welles? Some new confection, perhaps? Or a fascinating new book?" Mr. Hershawn asked, turning a smile on to Lydia.

Lydia giggled. "I was just telling Lady Margaret that some gentlemen prefer it when a lady lets it be known that she is interested in dancing."

Margaret wished she could simply sink through the floor. Never had she been so embarrassed! It had to be completely clear Lydia was telling them that she was interested in being asked to dance. She wondered if she appeared to be desperate.

"Oh, you mean with a look or a flutter of a fan," Mr. Hershawn said with a nod.

"I appreciate it. It is nice to know when a young

lady is interested," Lord Roseberry said.

"Yes. What's disturbing is when a young lady looks at you from across the room, and then by the time you finally get over to her she's agreed to dance with someone else," Mr. Hershawn said.

"I can see how that would be disheartening," the duchess agreed. "But on the whole, you like to know when a young lady is interested?"

"Absolutely," Mr. Hershawn said quickly.

"It does make things easier," Lord Roseberry agreed.

"Not that anyone would turn down an offer to dance from either of you gentlemen," Margaret said quietly.

Both men turned smiles on to her. "Not yet, Lady Margaret," Lord Roseberry said.

"I say, Lady Margaret, has anyone asked you to dance yet this evening?" Mr. Hershawn asked.

"No," Margaret said, looking for that hole in the floor she'd wished for earlier.

"Would you care to dance with me, my lady?"

Her cheeks burned again, but in her heart, she was grateful to the gentleman. "Why, thank you, sir. That is most kind. I would enjoy that a great deal."

"I don't think it's kind at all. It's for my own enjoyment, I assure you. I'm a terribly selfish fellow," he said with a smile.

Margaret gave a little laugh and nodded. As if on cue, the orchestra began warming up for the first set of dances, and Mr. Hershawn held out his arm to lead her to the floor.

She was trying, she told herself. She was definitely trying harder, just as she'd promised Tina.

~*~

Mr. Hershawn was such a thoughtful man, Margaret thought as he entertained her with silly small talk throughout their dance. When he returned her to the duchess, Diana was there, chatting with the older lady.

Mr. Hershawn stopped to have a pleasant word with the two ladies before going off to find a partner for the next dance.

"You looked like you were having fun," Diana commented with a smile.

"He is a very nice man," Margaret agreed.

"I see Lord Rexford looking in this direction," the duchess said, looking off to their right pointedly.

"Well, before you get whisked away again," Diana said with a laugh, "I just wanted to invite you to join me, Lydia, and Miss Kendrick for a ride tomorrow."

"Oh, I would love to join you!" Margaret said with feeling. It so wonderful when her friends invited her to join them. It made her feel welcome and as if they truly *were* friends. "And I would appreciate the opportunity to get to know Miss Kendrick better. I've only spoken with her once, but she seems to be a very nice girl."

"Yes, that's exactly what I was thinking," Diana said.

Lord Rexford hovered just beyond Diana until the duchess gave him a nod, allowing him to come forward. He was a quiet man, Margaret thought approvingly. She really didn't know him well at all, but he seemed as if he would be a pleasant companion. It was lovely that he'd worked up the courage to join them and perhaps even ask her to dance.

Later that evening, as they were on their way home, the duchess turned to Margaret. "You did very well tonight. I'm proud of you. You danced and chatted, and I only had to pull you away from the wall once—no, twice. Still, it's an improvement."

Margaret's pride faltered only a little at being reminded of her lapses. "Thank you, Your Grace. I did try harder this evening."

The lady gave a nod. "And it showed. Keep it up and you'll have quite a few beaux chasing after you and, hopefully, a number of proposals before the season is through."

The thought of that coming true had Margaret shaking in her slippers, despite the fact that it was precisely what she needed. Well, they would see if that actually came to pass—if she *was* able to keep this up. It was exhausting and hard work being social. "One step at a time, I think," Margaret replied.

The duchess gave a little laugh and patted Margaret's hand.

Chapter Four

~March 29~

Jamie was enjoying a break below stairs, getting a breath of fresh air while standing in the open doorway, when Mary suddenly appeared at his side. She smiled up at him with her wide mouth and round cheeks looking adorable.

"Jamie! I haven't seen ye in forever!" she said, mimicking him by leaning against the opposite door jam.

"So, where have you been?" he asked with a laugh.

"Workin'. They don't like the upper servants mixin' with the lower ones here. It's funny," she said with a shrug.

It was true, though. At the Congingby's household there was much more opportunity for the different classes of servants to mix, but there was a much stricter hierarchy here. Jamie supposed it had more to do with the butler and housekeeper than the master and mistress making the rules.

"Well, it's great to see you," Jamie said, putting his hand on Mary's shoulder. "How are you doing?"

"Real good!" she said with enthusiasm. "I's made friends, and there's no lord here ta bother me. Mrs. Holton makes sure the blokes are kept away from the girls too. She keeps a close eye on us girls. It's kinda nice."

"I'm really glad to hear that. And she doesn't work you too hard?"

"Naw. Just the regular sweepin' and cleanin'. I'm used to it," she said with a negligent lift of her shoulder.

"James!" Mr. Holton's voice boomed from the other end of the hall, making Jamie jump.

He spun around. "Yes, sir."

"You would not be fraternizing with the scullery maid." It wasn't a question, more of a command.

"No, sir. Just checking in on my friend," Jamie answered.

He received a frown, but before he could be reprimanded any further, Jamie gave Mary a quick wink and moved toward the butler saying, "I have a question, sir, if I may?"

The man lowered his eyelids suspiciously. "What would that be?"

"I was wondering if I might keep a book or something else to occupy myself when I'm on front-door duty and there are no guests expected?"

Mr. Holton's eyebrows rose on his forehead as he thought about it. "You own your own books? There's to be no borrowing of those in the library, they are strictly off limits to the likes of you."

"I do own one or two, sir, and I would never presume to borrow one of the duchess's," Jamie answered.

"And it would only be when there are no guests."

"Absolutely, sir. And if either of the ladies of the house or a guest were to appear, my book would disappear as quickly if not faster."

The butler nodded slowly. "All right, then. The duchess has said that she approves of activities to better ourselves. I suppose reading counts."

"Thank you, sir. I greatly appreciate it." Jamie bowed and then left to go up the back stairs to his room and create a small sketchbook for himself that would fit into his pocket. He had some paper he'd bought with his salary a few weeks earlier. It should do nicely.

He still had his paints and brushes, but those would have to stay at the bottom of his portmanteau until he could afford to buy a canvas. He didn't imagine anyone would mind if he painted in his room so long as it didn't smell too strongly. First, though, he needed a subject and a sketch, then he'd be able to think about getting back to his art. He wondered if it would be too presumptuous to sketch the woman who'd been haunting his thoughts nearly every day, the lovely Lady Margaret.

~*~

Lydia and Diana were already at the park when Margaret joined them. Diana was on her enormous thoroughbred that, truth be told, made Margaret a little nervous. She knew that Diana could control the beast, but it was still so large and intimidating.

She put the thought out of her mind, however, and focused on the woman on top of the horse rather than the animal itself.

"Margaret, how wonderful to see you. Why do I feel like I haven't seen you in so long?" Lydia said with a laugh.

Margaret laughed. "I don't know. We just saw each other last night."

"I know what it is," Diana said. "It's because we've only seen each other at parties where we don't get to actually talk."

"It's true," Lydia said with enthusiasm. "But we won't really be able to talk this afternoon either. We're going to have to meet at one of our houses sometime soon."

"I'll speak with the duchess about perhaps hosting a little dinner party just for close friends," Margaret suggest. "That way Tina could join us as well."

"I love that idea!" Diana said, sounding quite like Lydia in her enthusiasm.

Margaret couldn't help but laugh.

Miss Kendrick joined them at that moment, and the four women started off on their ride around Rotten Row.

"So, tell us how you're liking the season so far," Lydia asked, turning to Bel as they rode.

"Oh, I'm enjoying myself even more than I had imagined," Miss Kendrick said.

Margaret was amazed and not a little envious of her ability to just slip into society so easily. Even after a year, she herself was still having troubles. Miss Kendrick was clearly an outgoing person like Lydia. "Well, you are extremely lucky to have Lady Blakemore to bring you out. She knows absolutely everybody," Margaret commented.

The duchess was a wonderful sponsor. She was invited everywhere and was a well-respected member of society. She wasn't quite as active in society as Lady Blakemore, but Margaret certainly would not complain of the number of invitations they received.

"Yes, it's been wonderful. She has introduced me to a great many people," Miss Kendrick agreed.

"She mentioned at our last meeting that you

have a sister who will be making her debut next season?" Lydia asked.

"Yes, Bee, er, Beatrice. We were both very disappointed that our parents decided not to bring us out together," Miss Kendrick said.

"But it must be nice to stretch out on your own. I've never had a sister, but I can imagine if you're always with them, it might be nice to do something entirely on your own," Diana said.

"I don't know. I couldn't imagine what I would have done were my brother not with me last season. And Tina was absolutely essential as well," Margaret said, thinking fondly of Warwick and his wife. She wouldn't have had a season last year without them, and never could she have faced going to parties without their support and encouragement. Truly, Margaret thought, she was incredibly lucky. Poor Miss Kendrick was without someone she obviously cared about deeply.

"It is interesting," Miss Kendrick said hesitantly. "We've never been apart and I have to admit I miss her terribly. On the other hand, it has given me the opportunity to make new friends, which is very nice."

That she was able to do so on her own was what Margaret greatly admired. She was about to say so when Lydia spoke up.

"Speaking of friends, you must call us by our given names," Lydia said with a broad smile.

"Yes! We decided long ago that it was silly of us to be on formal terms when we're all just about the same age. The same goes for you," Diana said.

"Thank you, and of course you must call me by mine," Miss Kendrick said.

"It's Isabel, isn't it?" Lydia asked.

"Yes, but all my friends call me Bel."

"Bel it is," Diana said. "Now, you have to tell us who you have danced with and who you wish to dance with again."

"And who you absolutely do *not* want to dance with again," Lydia added with a laugh.

Margaret wondered if she'd even be able to answer such questions for herself. Well, she knew who she'd danced with—she could probably count that number on one hand. Because of that, she didn't think she had the luxury of picking and choosing among them. She needed to take what she could get, she thought with a little internal laugh.

"Well, *there* is one gentleman whose company I have enjoyed a great deal," Bel said, nodding in the direction of a carriage approaching them. Margaret squinted a little at the people occupying it but didn't recognize either the man or the woman there. "I'm not entirely certain how much he's enjoyed mine, however." A little sadness touched her voice. Margaret was shocked. How could anyone not enjoy Bel's company?

"Who is that?" Margaret asked.

"Lord St. Vincent and his step-mother. They've just returned to London. Apparently, he was here the year before last, but not last year as he was in mourning for his father," Diana said. "Lady St. Vincent hasn't been in town...well, I don't know for how long," she finished with a laugh.

"I don't know him either," Lydia said to Margaret, making her feel a little better.

"Well, come, you should be introduced. We can't possibly have you, Margaret, unaware of one of the most interesting gentlemen of the season. You need to find a husband as well," Diana said.

Margaret could feel her heart speed up at just

the thought of meeting an eligible gentleman. She took in a deep breath. This was good for her, she reminded herself. Just as Diana had just said, she needed to meet as many men as she could.

"Good afternoon, Lord St. Vincent," Bel called as they all pulled their horses to a halt by his carriage.

"Good afternoon." He nodded to them all with a pleasant smile as he pulled his horse to. He was a handsome gentleman but so dwarfed the lady by his side, Margaret wondered how large he would be standing up.

"You remember my friend, Lady Colburne?" Bel asked, indicating Diana.

"Yes, of course, my lady. Lovely to see you again," he nodded.

"And have you met Lady Welles?" Bel continued.

"No. It's a pleasure." He smiled.

"And this is Lady Margaret," Bel finished.

Margaret nodded to the gentleman, not minding at all being the last to be introduced.

Lord St. Vincent nodded his greeting to her as well.

"Lady St. Vincent, it is delightful to see you again as well," Bel said, cutting off his greeting to Lady Margaret.

"And you, Miss Kendrick. Ladies, it's very nice to see you all again," Elizabeth said, nodding at them all. "I'm not sure I've met Lady Margaret, but it's a pleasure, I'm sure," she added with a smile.

"Lady Colburne, what a very impressive horse you have there," Lady St. Vincent said.

"Thank you. I'm trying to give my Nike a little exercise, but I'm beginning to think this isn't really the place to do so," Diana said with a laugh.

"No, I can't imagine that it is," Lord St. Vincent agreed. "And Miss Kendrick, may I say what a very pretty hat you have on?"

Bel giggled in that way men found attractive but Margaret had never been able to pull forth. "Why, thank you, my lord."

"Is that something else that the Duchess of Warwick assisted you with?" Lord St. Vincent asked, smiling.

"No. Actually, I got this in Lincolnshire before we came to London," Bel said.

"We?" Lady St. Vincent asked.

"Did I say 'we'?" Bel laughed. She flushed. "I meant me, er, before *I* came to London. I'm so used to saying 'we' because it's so rare that my sister isn't with me—and she and I bought the hat together."

"It must be so difficult for you to be here without her," Lady St. Vincent said.

"Yes, yes, it is, my lady," Bel said. "Do you have a sister you are close to?"

"Me?" Lady St. Vincent laughed. "No, just my brother. But we were friends as children. We're very close in age, so we spent a good amount of time together."

"Well, you are very lucky to have Lord Conway," Bel said.

"Yes, I must agree," Lady St. Vincent said.

Margaret was just building up the nerve to comment on how wonderful it was to have a brother to whom one was close when the driver of the carriage behind Lord St. Vincent started shouting for them all to move on.

"I'll look forward to seeing you all at Lady Sorrell's soiree," Lord St. Vincent said as he gave snapped his reins, giving his horse the go-ahead to continue.

"Yes, see you there!" Bel called after them.

They continued on as well as they had also stalled traffic on their side of the road.

"I haven't met either of the St. Vincents," Margaret commented.

"They are very nice," Diana said.

"And they are good people to know, I believe," Lydia said, agreeing with Diana.

"Very kind," Bel added. She turned and looked behind them to catch another glimpse. Margaret figured there was more interest there than Bel was probably willing to admit to.

"Are you going to Lady Sorrell's party too, Margaret?" Lydia asked.

"I...I don't know. It's not the sort of thing the duchess usually attends, but she is determined that I meet as many gentlemen as possible, so perhaps we will," Margaret said. It would be an excruciating evening if they did, of that Margaret was certain. Doing nothing but standing about talking to people she didn't know? She couldn't think of a more unpleasant way to spend an evening.

Chapter Five

~April 1~

Never had Alys played whist so poorly. She looked at the measly one trick she had won in the last hand and just shook her head sadly.

"An off day, Duchess?" Lady Colburne asked as they stood at the end of their game.

"It seems so." Alys gave the girl a little smile. She liked Lady Colburne. She was a very sweet girl. Most of the women of the Ladies' Wagering Whist Society were. It was really only Mrs. Aldridge who she had problems with—her and that dog! Duchess, indeed! Who ever heard of naming a dog Duchess?

Alys shoved the bothersome idea out of her mind and allowed her thoughts to return to where they'd been all afternoon.

"Lady Moreton," Alys began, calling the attention of the lady before she moved too far.

"Yes, Your Grace?" the young woman asked, turning a smile back toward her.

"Might I ask you a, a personal question?"

Lady Moreton looked a little surprised but said, "Of course."

"I cannot help but notice that you are a quieter person. I find that extremely calming and pleasant, but it can't be easy for someone who is on the lookout for a husband. How do you manage?" Alys asked. It felt so odd asking for advice, and especially from someone so much younger than she. But she was feeling rather overwhelmed by her duties regarding poor Margaret. She had no idea what to do with the girl.

"Oh! I, er, I don't try very hard, I'm afraid. I'm not actively looking for a husband, I'm afraid," Lady Moreton said with an apologetic smile.

"Of course. You are comfortable with your current situation. It is an enviable one for someone so young," Alys said, understanding immediately. Why look for a husband when there was no financial need to do so. Lady Moreton's husband had died in the war, but her in-laws had been so kind as to bring her to London with them. She supposed they weren't pressuring her to find another husband, which was very good of them.

"Your Grace, I noticed that neither you nor Lady Margaret attended my soiree last night," Lady Sorrell said, joining them.

"Yes, I do beg your pardon, Lady Sorrell. I didn't feel it would be a very pleasant evening for Margaret. She is so terribly shy," Alys explained.

"I know. Poor thing! I figured that was the reason," Lady Sorrell said.

"You wouldn't happen to know how I might help her find a husband, do you? I... I find myself at quite a loss," Alys admitted. No matter how much it pained her to appear anything less than perfect, she had decided before coming here today that if the opportunity arose, she would try to ask for some assistance.

"The duchess doesn't know how to go on?"

Mrs. Aldridge asked, interrupting their conversation.

"I beg your pardon?" Alys said in her most repressive tones.

The woman blanched but held her chin high nonetheless. "You always seem to know what everyone should and shouldn't do."

"I most certainly do not. I may have my opinions on things, but they are not definitive," Alys said. She did not like where this conversation had turned, so she swung it back to where she wanted it. "Do *you* know how to bring a girl out of her shell?" she asked Mrs. Aldridge.

The woman frowned. "No. I never had any girls, only my Charles, and he was always an easy child. He's not the easiest man, I have to admit, but he was most definitely an easy child."

"Young men are very different from young ladies," Alys commented as she turned back to Lady Sorrell. "You don't have any ideas, my lady?"

Lady Sorrell thought for a moment and then shook her head. "I think simply being encouraging," she said. "Guide her with a gentle but firm hand. Insist that she do all she can to speak with gentlemen and to dance with them, but if you see that she's in distress, well, I wouldn't push too hard. That might only make things worse."

Alys nodded. "Yes, yes, I understand. Perhaps that is the problem. Maybe I've been pushing her too hard. She did do slightly better last season after she had made her debut. This season she's been quiet again—more nervous." It was probably because she knew her deadline for finding a husband was approaching. It wasn't unheard of for people to freeze at the worst possible time.

"I think you did the right thing in not pushing her to attend my soiree last night. She would not have done well," Lady Sorrell said.

"No. I just didn't see the point, I'm afraid," Alys admitted. "Well, thank you." She gave all the ladies a smile except Mrs. Aldridge, who was standing there holding that dog of hers—disgusting creature with her tongue hanging out and her little black nose twitching.

~April 2~

Margaret had been sitting and working all morning on Lady Norman's wedding breakfast and the ball that would be held the following day. Her hand hurt from writing out invitations, but it would be well worth it. It was definitely going to be the event of the season, just like Tina and the duchess had said.

She stood up from the desk in the library where she'd been sitting for the past three hours. Stretching out her arms and legs and finally giving her hand a good shake made her feel so much better. A cup of tea and something to nibble couldn't hurt either, but the thought of calling for it to be delivered to her while she continued to sit just made all her muscles cry out. No, she needed to move, to walk. She'd go down to the kitchen herself to get what she wanted.

She opened the door and glanced to her left where James was sitting. Her own face stared back at her from his lap. She gasped.

"Lady Margaret!" James jumped from his chair and pulled the paper that had been sitting in his lap a moment ago behind his back.

"May I see that?" she asked, holding out her hand.

"Oh, it's, er, nothing. Honestly, it's nothing," he stammered out.

"But it's not nothing. It was a picture of me," she said, looking up into his expressive light brown eyes.

Just at the moment, they were filled with embarrassment at having been caught drawing a picture of her, but the first time they'd met, they'd been filled with something else, something that had made Margaret both uncomfortable and intrigued, hot and cold at the same time. She had done her best to hide her reaction to him that day and the few times she'd seen him since then, waiting on her and the duchess in the dining room, or when he'd been on duty at the front door, but it wasn't easy. She simply needed to keep reminding herself that he was a footman.

Clearly, however, he was a great deal more than that. He was an artist!

"I do beg your pardon, my lady. It's just scribblings to pass the time," he said, still not bringing forth the paper as she'd asked.

She didn't let up though. She continued to hold her hand out for the paper. "Please?" she asked as kindly as she could. She even managed to give him a hopeful smile.

He relented and handed her a booklet of paper.

Her face looked back at her, sketched out in black and white. But it wasn't just the likeness that had caught her eye, she realized now as she looked at his drawing. In fact, while the features were very like her own, the young woman in the sketch *couldn't* have been her. That person was strong, bold, and determined. The angle of her chin, the look of confidence in her eyes, the slight smile of satisfaction—it all added up to a woman of beauty and self-assurance. It was a picture of the woman Margaret wished she were.

She swallowed. "It's, it's very well done," she managed.

"Thank you, my lady. I, er, I came to London not to be a footman, but to be a portrait artist," he admitted. "As you can see, that didn't work out."

She looked up at him. This tall, strong man was embarrassed! It was so odd; she'd only ever seen men be self-confident and bold. His humility touched her. "I'm very sorry that it didn't. You have a real talent, James." She looked back down at the drawing. "May I keep this?"

"No. I mean, I do beg your pardon, my lady, but, but it's mine. I couldn't part with it."

"But it's a picture of me," she pointed out needlessly.

"Yes, my lady. But it's *my* picture of you." He seemed to not only be embarrassed by his refusal to give her the picture but rather steadfast in this decision.

"Do you have pictures of everyone here in the household? Is that what it is?" Margaret asked, trying to discover why he was so determined to keep this drawing.

"No. I mean. I've done a few others."

"Then why will you not part with this one? You could just sketch another," she said.

He shook his head, a little smile lifting one corner of his slender lips. "It wouldn't be the same. Every picture is different. I like this one very much. If you wouldn't mind," he said, holding out his hand for his booklet.

"But so do I."

"I'm sorry, my lady, but I really can't part with it."

"Margaret, there you are!" the duchess interrupted their conversation as she came down the stairs.

James slipped the booklet from her hand as she reluctantly turned away from him. "Yes, Your Grace. I'm here."

"Where have you been all morning?" the lady asked, coming closer.

"Writing out invitations to the wedding ball." She gave a little laugh and held up her right hand. Her fingers were stained with ink. "My hand is aching, I wrote out so many."

"Oh, you poor dear," the duchess said. "Well, come, I've ordered a light luncheon to be served in the breakfast parlor. I'm sure a little food will make you feel much more the thing."

The lady turned and led the way. Margaret followed, but looked back at the footman who was now looking very relieved. Was he also laughing at her? Margaret couldn't tell. He certainly looked amused.

Chapter Six

~April 4~

This evening should be so much easier than other social occasions, Margaret told herself as she got dressed to attend Lady Blakemore's musicale. It was going to be a smaller gathering, not an enormous ball or even a large soiree. The duchess had assured her that there wouldn't be above forty or fifty people in attendance, probably closer to thirty. It would be much easier to manage.

Margaret dressed in one of her pretty evening gowns designed by Tina the previous year. It was simple and elegant with very few ribbons or flounces. She liked Tina's designs so very much. They made her feel happy and even gave her a touch more confidence than she would otherwise have.

Picking up her fan, reticule, and gloves, she made her way downstairs to await the duchess.

James stood as she entered the foyer. "May I adjust your shawl, my lady?" he asked.

The offending garment had slid off her shoulders as she was attempting to walk down the stairs and put on her gloves at the same time. She nodded and turned her back to him. With gentle hands, he resettled her shawl on her shoulders. It was such an intimate gesture. She could feel his warmth at her back, the soft touch of his fingers against her arms, even his breath on the nape of her neck. She realized she'd stopped breathing when he stepped away.

"Thank you," she whispered, her voice suddenly not working quite right.

"Happy to be of assistance. May I say that you are looking lovely this evening? That gown is—"

"Ah, you are there, Margaret. Excellent. Shall we go?" the duchess interrupted as she came down the stairs. "Has my carriage arrived, Thomas?"

"It's James, Your Grace. His name is James," Margaret said.

"Oh, yes, of course, James." The duchess gave him a fleeting smile.

"Yes, Your Grace. It is outside waiting for you," James said, opening the door for them, once again the perfect footman.

He helped the duchess and then Margaret into the coach, then stood back as it started forward. He was the most unusual footman Margaret had ever met.

"I believe this is going to be a very pleasant evening," the duchess said, pulling Margaret's mind back from her thoughts of James.

"Yes, I was thinking the same thing earlier. It should be much easier with so few people there," Margaret said.

"Indeed. I do expect to see you conversing the entire evening," the duchess reminded her.

"Yes, Your Grace."

"There are going to be a number of eligible gentlemen present, and you need to make yourself as agreeable as possible. The intimate nature of the evening should make it easy enough," she continued.

"Yes, Your Grace," Margaret repeated, beginning to feel a slight churning in her stomach. Maybe it wasn't better for it to be a smaller party. At a ball, she could easily disappear in the crowd, but this evening it would be obvious if she weren't talking with someone. Oh dear, she thought with a sinking heart.

"Margaret, I'm so happy to see you," Bel said soon after they'd entered the Blakemore's drawing room. Her enthusiasm seemed a little tempered, Margaret noticed.

"And you," Margaret said. She took hold of her friend's hands. "How are you doing? Are you all right?"

Bel giggled. "Of course! I'm just...a little nervous, that's all. Goodness, is it so obvious?"

"Just a little—to those of us who know you," Margaret said. "Is it your performance this evening that's upsetting you?"

"I've only just learned the piece I'm to play," Bel said with a nod.

"I'm sure you've been working hard at it." At least, Margaret assumed as much.

"Oh yes! Every minute I could spare in the past three days." Bel gave a true giggle of amusement. "Honestly, I pity everyone in the house who's had to listen to it again and again."

"Then you've got nothing to worry about. You know it by now," Margaret said.

Bel cocked her head a little. "You don't play the pianoforte, do you?"

"No, why?"

"Just because I've been playing it over and again, doesn't mean I know it. It may take me months to really know the piece. I've only just started to learn it. I may be able to play it with some competency, but it won't shine after just a few days, as it will once I *truly* know it."

"Oh." Margaret didn't quite know what to say to that. Now her platitudes of "you'll do just fine" seemed woefully inadequate. "Who else is here this evening?" she asked, changing the subject.

"So many people! But you're referring to the gentlemen, aren't you?" Bel asked with a giggle.

"Yes, I'm afraid I am. The duchess reminded me that I was to try to speak with each and every one of them."

Bel burst out laughing at that. "Oh dear!"

"I don't quite know how I'm going to do that," Margaret admitted. "And I'm certain I'm not the only young lady here on the lookout for a husband."

"Well, I have to say, my aunt was rather strategic in that regard. Only you, I, and Lady Blackglass are actively looking. Most of the other ladies present are either already married or not so very interested in getting married."

"Well, that is advantageous, I suppose."

"I believe it will be." She was called away to attend to another guest, leaving Margaret alone.

It would have been so tempting to stand against a wall and try to disappear from sight, but she'd promised the duchess—and also realized that she would look odd and out of place if she did so. Instead, she approached Lord Bertram, who she'd met once or twice before. He was pouring a glass of wine for Lady Blackglass.

"I do beg your pardon, Lord Bertram, but would you mind pouring one for me as well?" Margaret asked.

"Of course, Lady Margaret. It would be my pleasure," he said, giving her a welcoming smile.

By the time dinner was over and everyone had retired to the music room for the musical portion of the evening, Margaret was mentally exhausted, but proud of her self. She managed to speak with about half the men—both eligible and not—in attendance. She was more than ready to sit down and enjoy some beautiful music—and not say a word to anyone for a good hour or more.

The duchess chose seats for them toward the front of the room and arranged it so that Margaret was sitting in between Lord St. Vincent and Tina. Her brother was on Tina's other side and the duchess next to him. Margaret supposed the duchess was hoping for something between her and Lord St. Vincent.

Lady St. Vincent started the evening off with a few very pretty pieces. When she sat back down between her step-son and her brother, who was sitting at the very end of the row, Margaret shared a smile with her. The lady looked very relieved, and Margaret didn't blame her one bit. For once, Margaret was happy her mother hadn't thought her intelligent enough to learn how to play—sometimes being a quiet child had its advantages.

Two more young ladies performed, and then it was Bel's turn. She appeared to be trembling as she seated herself at the instrument. She paused, wringing her hands, and then stood back up.

"As my aunt mentioned, I just received a new

piece of music—a Beethoven sonata. I have been working very diligently on it, but it is not yet as perfected as I would normally like before I play it in public," Bel said.

Despite the fact she didn't play an instrument, Margaret immediately knew what Bel was feeling. The poor thing was feeling exactly the same way Margaret always felt whenever she went out to a party: nervous and terrified she was going to make some horrid mistake.

"Perhaps it would help you to relax if you were to play something first that you already know very well?" Lady St. Vincent called out.

"That's an excellent idea, my lady. But what I know best are the songs I've always played for my sister to sing and as she's not here..." Bel said, her voice trailing off sadly.

"Well, I'm certain my brother knows any songs you might wish to play," Lady St. Vincent said, turning to look at Lord Conway.

"It would be a great honor if he were to sing for me—us. I meant us, of course." Bel stammered.

Lord Conway shook his head. "I'm sorry, but I haven't sung in months."

"Oh, come now, Conway," his sister goaded him and even gave his arm a little playful shove.

"Please, my lord?" Bel begged.

He looked around and then gave a little shrug of his shoulders. "For you, Miss Kendrick, only so you can relax a little."

Next to her, Margaret could feel Lord St. Vincent tense even as Lord Conway got up and joined Bel at the instrument. After a minute of whispered consultation, Bel sat down and began to play.

Lord Conway's voice was magnificent. It was a rich, full tenor and filled the room with its gentle notes. It was clear that he was well trained. But it was also equally clear that the gentleman next to Margaret wasn't happy at all with what was happening at the front of the room.

Margaret, herself, was shocked as Lord Conway and Bel stared at each other with such open longing. They looked like the lovers Lord Conway sung about as his voice rose to a crescendo and softened toward the end of the piece. They continued to stared at each other even as the last notes from the pianoforte hung in the air and then faded away. It was almost uncomfortable to be witness to the intimacy of the moment.

Margaret stole a look at the gentleman to her right. His face had turned red, and he looked like he was ready to pummel someone. She felt Tina's gaze on her other side and turned to share a look of shock with her sister-in-law. Someone started clapping, and soon everyone had joined in.

It was a short applause as Lord Conway regained his seat. Bel then turned back to her instrument and proceeded to amaze everyone in the room with the piece she claimed not to know. If this was how she could play when she *didn't* know the music very well, Margaret couldn't imagine how good she would be when she'd had enough time to really study and learn it well.

What surprised Margaret most about the evening wasn't necessarily the incredible display of talent, but the fact that no one, not one person, said a word about what had happened between Bel and Lord Conway.

As Margaret climbed into bed that evening, she wondered if a man would ever look at her with such longing. Yes, she had managed to say a few words to nearly every gentleman present, but not one had looked at her with anything beyond politeness. She didn't know that she would want any one of them to do so either.

Chapter Seven

~April 5~

Jamie was happy to find Mary in the kitchen on Sunday afternoon after church. It looked like Sundays would be the only day he would actually get to see her. He quickly pulled her outside into the garden, so they could talk without the glare of the butler who didn't like them "fraternizing."

Mary smiled up at him, saying with a little laugh, "I don't know why that nasty Holton doesn't like us talkin'."

Jamie shrugged. "I can't say I know either. We were interrupted the other day—you said you're happy here?"

"I am," she said with some hesitancy to her voice. "Ye know, since ye asked, I's been thinkin' about it."

"And?"

"An' even though there ain't no lord tryin' to get up me skirt, I still... I still think I'd like to start savin' my money to go home."

"So, you're *not* happy here?" Jamie asked. She'd sounded so sure of herself the other day, but now...

"No, no, I *am*. It's just that I'd be happier at

home, that's all. Don't you want ta go home, Jamie?"

He paused, trying to imagine his home in his mind's eye, but all he could see was his father's grave marker next to that of his mother's. The two stones had been leaning close to each other, almost kissing, when he'd visited just before he'd left to come to London. He supposed it was fitting. They had been close in life, why not in death as well? They had each other now, forever. It was wonderful, but it left him...alone. "No," he said finally. "There's nothing for me there."

"Ye ain't got no family?" Mary asked, looking up at him, her forehead creasing with concern.

He tried to give her a reassuring smile. "No, not really. My parents are gone, and I don't have any siblings. There are the people in...in my village, but..." He suddenly found his voice not working quite right. How ridiculous. They were probably better off without him, is what he'd meant to say. The only problem was that he didn't know if it was the truth or not. But he couldn't think about that. Not now. Perhaps not for some time to come. He just couldn't.

"I'm sure they miss ye," Mary said gently.

He gave a little shrug. "It doesn't really matter right now, does it? What matters is that you have a home that you'd like to get back to, right?"

"I would," she agreed. "And now that I been workin' for a duchess, I'm sure I could get another job—a better job—at another manor nears ta my family."

"So, when do you think you'd leave?" he asked, sad to be losing his only friend in the household. He'd enjoyed being friends with Mary. She felt like the little sister he'd never had.

"Ugh, not fer some time. I's got ta save the money for my ticket home, don't I?" She patted his arm. "Don't ye worry, Jamie, I ain't leavin' right away."

He gave her a warm smile. "That's good to hear. I'd miss you. I *will* miss you when you go."

She reached out and gave him a quick hug. "I'll miss ye too! Yer a good'un!"

~April 6~

James came into the drawing room with the tea tray the following day and set it down on the center table.

"Oh good, thank you, James," Margaret said. She put down her pen and shook out her hand which was cramping again.

"If you stretch out your hand like this, my lady, and then close it into a fist, it will feel a bit better," James said, demonstrating by opening his hand wide and then closing it a few times.

Margaret tried. It did make her aching hand feel much better.

"If I may?" he said, coming forward and putting out his hand. Margaret put hers into his a little hesitantly, not sure if that's what he'd wanted. Apparently, he did, because he immediately began to massage each of her fingers in turn, ending with pressing his thumbs into her aching palm.

Margaret couldn't stop the moan of ecstasy that escaped her throat. "Oh, my goodness that feels good."

He just smiled and then manipulated her wrist, gently pressing it backward and up and then down before returning to massaging her fingers and palm.

"How do you know how to do this?" she said, her eyes closing involuntarily.

"I'm an artist. I have a great deal of experience with an aching hand and wrist."

"Ah, yes, of course." She reopened her eyes and was treated to the footman's handsome visage smiling down at her. He looked so happy to be helping, making her feel better, but there was something else in his eyes. Margaret didn't know what it was, but the longer she stared up into them, the softer they became. Heat ran up her arms and down her spine at his look.

"There was no one at the door," Tina said, coming into the room. She stopped suddenly just inside the door. "Oh!"

James quickly dropped Margaret's hand and stepped back.

"Tina! Welcome," Margaret said. She realized her heart was pounding and put a hand to her chest. Laughing, she said, "You startled me."

"I do beg your pardon, Your Grace. I was just on my way to the door. I stopped to deliver tea to Lady Margaret. I shall, er, my apologies for not being there when you came in," James stammered. He quickly bowed to them and got out of drawing room as quickly as he could.

Tina laughed as she watched him exit. "Did I interrupt something?"

"No!" Margaret couldn't help the giggle of embarrassment. "He was just massaging my hand and showing me some exercises I could do. It's been aching terribly because of all the invitations I've been writing out."

"Oh, of course." Tina came and sat down on the sofa across from Margaret, putting a bag down on the table next to the tea tray. "Here are the one hundred and fifty I wrote out."

"Wonderful. I'm nearly finished with my half," Margaret said, moving to pour the tea.

After she handed Tina a cup, she pushed forward the planning book she had bought just for Lady Norman's wedding.

"I think we've nearly completed the menu. What do you think?" Margaret asked, sitting forward with her own cup of tea.

Tina took a sip and pulled the book forward to look over the list of dishes Margaret had written out. "How many are there?"

"Fifty, but I think we need to strike about ten from list," Margaret said.

"Yes. Fifty *is* a bit too much," Tina agreed. "What did you think of the fish ragout that Lady Blakemore served last night?"

"It was good, but I like the turbot dish we have already, and I don't think we need another."

Tina nodded, continuing to look over the list. "You did very well last night, by the way. I only saw you standing alone once the whole evening."

"I might have done so a few more times, but I was trying my best to be social," Margaret admitted.

Tina nodded. "You've been trying very hard. I think both myself and the duchess have noticed. Good for you!"

"Thank you. I only wish it were easier," Margaret admitted.

"I'm not sure what I can do to help," her sister-in-law admitted with a slight frown.

Margaret reached out and took her hand. "You

are too wonderful! I don't know how Warwick and I got to be so lucky."

Tina blushed and shook her head. She quickly turned back to their planning. They happily worked on the menu, debating which dishes would go well together and deciding on those they could do without.

The clock chimed three, making Tina jump. "Oh goodness! How does the time go by so quickly! Warwick will be waiting for me." She stood.

"Let me walk you to the door, then. Maybe I can catch a glimpse of my elusive brother," Margaret said with a smile.

"Elusive? You just saw him last night," Tina laughed.

"Saw him, yes, but I hardly spoke two words to him."

"Well, you needed to be concentrating on others," Tina said. "Actually, I asked him to keep his distance, I'm afraid, so you wouldn't get distracted or talk to him instead."

Margaret felt momentarily upset by Tina's machinations but then realized she was doing it for Margaret's own good. She had a tendency to only speak with those who she knew and with whom she felt comfortable.

~*~

Jamie was just opening the door as the two ladies came down the stairs.

"I am coming," the young duchess called out, hurrying down.

"There you are," said a man walking into the house, who Jamie assumed was the Duke of Warwick.

"I promise, I was coming," his wife said with a laugh, looking up at the duke with such open emotion. Jamie was surprised. It was rare that a noblewoman not only felt such love for her husband but that she should show it in public. He was equally shocked with the duke when he responded likewise. What sort of peers were these to so openly show their love for each other?

"And good afternoon to you, dear brother," Lady Margaret said, smiling at the duke.

"Good afternoon, Margaret," Warwick said, coming forward and giving her a peck on her cheek.

"Oh, Warwick, Tina, you should see what James has drawn." She turned toward Jamie who was standing off unobtrusively in the corner. "Do you have your sketchbook with you, James?"

He was surprised by the direct request but quickly pulled himself together. These *truly* were the oddest people. They went against everything he'd ever been taught. "Yes, my lady, of course." He pulled the book from his pocket and opened it to the page with the drawing of her and handed it to the duke.

"My goodness, that's incredible! You've got a wonderful talent," the Duke of Warwick said, taking it in.

"Let me see," the duchess said, moving closer to her husband. "Oh," she breathed, once she caught sight of the drawing. "That *is* good! Not only is it an excellent likeness, you look..." She paused.

"Confident," Lady Margaret filled in as her sister-in-law struggled to find the right word.

"Yes! That's it precisely. You look happy and confident," the duchess said, looking up.

"I asked James if I could have it, but he

refused," Lady Margaret said, looking at him. If she thought the slight pleading in her eyes would get him to give her the picture, she was sadly mistaken—no matter how adorable she looked.

"Well, I can certainly understand that he would do so," the duke said, much to Jamie's surprise.

"Thank you, Your Grace," he said, appreciating the support.

"He shouldn't just give away his work. I'll give you a guinea for it," the duke said, handing the sketchbook back to James.

James' mouth dropped open for a moment. "That's very kind of you, but…"

"No, really, Warwick, a guinea is much too little. I think it's worth at least five pounds, perhaps ten," the duchess said, giving Jamie a smile.

If she thought to soften him up with that, she was going to be sadly mistaken. He returned her smile but shook his head.

"Fifteen but it's my final offer," the duke said. "Honestly, it's just a pencil sketch."

"I do beg your pardon, Your Grace, but I wouldn't sell for a hundred pounds," James said, pocketing his sketchbook.

"What?" Lady Margaret breathed.

He turned to her. "Not for a thousand," he added.

CHAPTER EIGHT

"**B**ut..." she started, now looking adorably confused.

"That's rather odd. It's just a sketch," the duke started.

"You could do another for yourself," the duchess said, agreeing with her husband.

Jamie shook his head. "It wouldn't be the same. I would never be able to capture that exact expression."

"Have you ever seen me with that expression?" Lady Margaret asked curiously.

Jamie could only smile. "I honestly don't know, but that's how you look in my imagination."

"Well, you clearly are very creative," she said with a little laugh.

"If you won't sell her the sketch, would you be willing to paint a portrait of her? I'm assuming you paint as well as you sketch?" the duke asked.

"I do. I can show you some of my paintings, if you'd like," Jamie said, becoming rather excited at the prospect of finally doing what he'd come to London to do. If he could paint a portrait of Lady Margaret, perhaps others would see it and commission more paintings from him. Slowly but surely, his business would grow as his reputation did so.

"I would like to see your work," the duke said with a nod. "If I like them, I'll commission a portrait of Margaret, and if I like that, I'd like one of my lovely wife as well."

Jamie had to hold his breath for a moment to keep a stupid grin from covering his face.

"However, the duchess and I have a previous engagement we must get to at the moment. I'll send round a note as to when you can call on me—I assume you have them here?"

"Yes, Your Grace. I have a number paintings I've done with me, and I'll do my best to be available to you at your convenience," James said, bowing.

"Very good." The man nodded and then escorted his wife toward the door, which Jamie jumped to open for them.

When he'd closed it again, he found Lady Margaret still standing in the foyer, staring toward the door.

"Is there anything else you need, my lady?" Jamie asked.

She started, as if she'd been thinking very deeply. "What? Oh, no. I just..." She stopped and then gave a little laugh and shook her head. "Nothing. It's nothing. Thank you, James."

She turned and started to walk toward the stairs. She paused before mounting them, however. "When you go to show Warwick your work, I'd like to see it as well. Would that be all right?"

"Of course, my lady. You may see it anytime you'd like. It's here in my room."

She gave a little nod. "I'll wait until you show my brother, so you don't have to take it out twice." She then turned and floated up the stairs. She had a way of moving that just seemed to defy gravity.

James just stood and watched her, wishing for all the world that he could somehow capture that in a painting.

~April 7~

Jamie slept on the idea, waiting for the duke to call for him to show his work, and realized that if he really wanted this commission, he was going to have to take the initiative. The duke was probably a very busy man.

Jamie wouldn't have been at all surprised if the idea had disappeared from his mind the moment he'd left the house. Oh, Jamie didn't think for one moment that the duke *wasn't* serious about commissioning a portrait of his sister, it just wouldn't be a top priority. Whereas for Jamie, it was of the utmost importance.

When he'd first arrived in London six months ago, he'd waited for commissions to come to him. Clearly that hadn't worked out so well. No, he wasn't going to simply sit back and wait for the duke. He was going to go to him.

The following day was Jamie's half-day, and he was going to use it to get himself hired to paint a portrait. He gathered together a few of the paintings he had—three small canvases and two miniatures—and started toward the door. He stopped halfway there, however, remembering that Lady Margaret had said she'd like to be there when he showed his work to her brother. He turned around and instead went to the library where Lady Margaret was frequently to be found working.

"Come in!" she called in answer to his knock.

"I beg your pardon, my lady," he said, coming into the room.

"Oh, James," she said, looking up. She stopped and frowned. "You're not in your livery."

"No, my lady. It's my half-day. I have the morning off," he explained with a little smile as she looked over his clothing. He wasn't dressed in his best clothes, but he didn't think what he was wearing was too out of fashion. He *had* taken some time to shine his boots—not that he'd be riding, but it was acceptable for gentlemen to wear boots regardless.

"Oh, of course!" she said. He caught a glimpse of her reddening cheeks as she turned away.

"I decided to take my work to His Grace, the Duke of Warwick, rather than wait for him to call for me. Do you think he will mind?" he asked, sure that she would know better than anyone whether he was doing the right thing.

She looked up at him again, her beautiful blue eyes wide. "No. I think it's a wonderful idea. I'm sure he'll appreciate it. Do you... Do you have your work with you now?"

"I do," he said, holding up the paper-covered roll of canvases in his hand.

"Oh, of course. They're not framed," she said with an embarrassed little smile.

"No. I've got three canvases and two miniatures for him to see," Jamie explained.

"Would you mind if I came along? I'd like to see them as well," she said, standing.

"Not at all!"

She smiled shyly at him. "And with me there,

you're much more likely to actually get in to see him."

Jamie laughed. "Yes, you're right. Actually, I hadn't thought of that. In that case, your presence will be even more greatly appreciated."

"Just give me a moment to get my pelisse," she said, heading out the door.

Within fifteen minutes, she was sitting in her little open carriage, with Jamie up on the bench next to the driver, on their way to the home of the Duke of Warwick. Shockingly, after they had walked into his grand London home, Lady Margaret simply walked straight to the duke's office, announcing herself after only a very brief knock on the door. Jamie could only shake his head at his good luck in thinking to ask Lady Margaret about approaching her brother. He probably wouldn't have gotten past the front door alone.

"Margaret! What a lovely surprise," the duke said, standing.

Another gentleman sitting at a smaller desk in the corner of the room also stood as Lady Margaret entered.

She gave a brief curtsy and then moved farther into the room. She smiled warmly at the other man. "Martin, how wonderful to see you. It's been so long."

"It has," he agreed. "We all miss you terribly, you know. It's just not the same without you here."

She shook her head. "But it's also a good thing. You have the duchess now. I would have just gotten in the way."

"Never!" he said quickly.

She gave a laugh and turned back to her

brother. "James had the most wonderful idea to bring his paintings to you right away rather than wait for you to call for him."

"I see. Yes, that was very clever." He raised an eyebrow at James, but there was a twitching of his lips, which told him that he wasn't actually annoyed.

"Your Grace," Jamie bowed low. He gave the other gentleman a slight bow as well, just for good measure, but Jamie got the feeling he was the duke's secretary or man of business. "If I may?" Jamie asked, moving to the table in between a sofa and some comfortable-looking leather chairs by the fireplace. He needed some space to open his canvases, and that seemed to be the one spot where there weren't papers strewn about.

"Of course." Both men came forward to take a look at what Jamie had, as did Lady Margaret.

Jamie unrolled a canvas and turned it around so that everyone could see the portrait. It was of his mother—one that he'd done just months before she'd died.

"Oh, how lovely," Lady Margaret said softly.

"Who is she? Obviously, a noblewoman," the duke said.

"Er, she is someone I knew before coming to London," Jamie said.

"She looks both kind and stern," Margaret said, tilting her head a little as she studied the painting. "She knows her place in the world."

Jamie smiled and looked down at his mother. "Yes, that she did, and she never let anyone forget it."

"Is she gone?" Lady Margaret asked, surprise

lacing her question.

"Yes, sadly, I painted this just a few months before she passed," Jamie said. There was a tightness in his chest, but he took in a deep breath and set aside his emotions. There was no place for that here or now.

Jamie rolled up the canvas and unrolled another he'd brought. This was of an older man from the village near his home.

"What a fascinating face," Margaret said, standing back from it a little.

"Very expressive," her brother agreed.

"That is most definitely *not* a nobleman," the other gentleman commented.

"No. He's a farmer," Jamie agreed.

"So I see from his implements and the background," the duke said, pointing to the objects in the painting.

Jamie allowed the canvas to roll up on itself and then pulled out the miniatures he'd painted, handing one each to Lady Margaret and the duke. They were very small ovals painted on a slip of wood meant to be inserted into a locket.

They each looked at the ones they'd been given then traded to see the other.

"You have quite a knack for capturing your subject's personality," the duke said. "It's odd, but you can see exactly what sort of person this is simply from their expression, their clothing, their hair. It's quite fascinating. Few painters have that sort of ability."

"Thank you, Your Grace," James said with a slight bow.

"I wonder how he would portray me," Margaret

said with a little laugh.

Her brother turned and smiled at her. "Very much the same way he did in the sketch, I imagine."

"I will most certainly do my best to capture her accurately," Jamie said.

The duke studied him for a moment and then nodded his head. "I believe you would. All right, then. I'd like a portrait of approximately that size," he said, turning toward the painting hanging above the fireplace. It was a large canvas with a man and a woman portrayed—the woman seated in a chair, the man standing behind her. Aside from the rich clothing, the couple both wore rather bland expressions as if the artist were proclaiming that he didn't know these people at all. Either that or they were just very dull people.

"Are they your parents?" Jamie guessed.

"Yes," the duke answered.

Jamie kept his opinion of the work to himself and just nodded. "I can certainly paint a portrait of that size. I would, however, need an advance to purchase the materials I would require."

"Of course. How much would you charge for the completed work? I could give you half now and the other half after you're done," the duke said, handing the miniature back to James and returning to his desk.

They negotiated the price in no time—it was so easy to work for wealthy people. Either the duke had very little regard for money, or he valued his sister a great deal and was eager to have her portrait painted, because they came to an understanding quickly and easily. James was rather shocked that his first price was immediately accepted—he'd started high, planning on lowering the price as the duke bargained with him. Instead, Warwick simply accepted the price and turned to his man to deal with the particulars.

"Be sure to give him at least part in coin, Martin," Lady Margaret said from the sofa where she was still studying the two miniatures.

"My lady?" the gentleman asked.

"We should probably go to a shop to purchase what James will need today," she answered. "It's his half-day, and I'd like him to get started as soon as possible." She looked up at Jamie as he stood in front of the duke's desk. "Would you mind if I went with you to purchase your items? I've never purchased art materials before. I believe I'd find it quite fascinating."

Jamie did his best not show his surprise but instead nodded. "Of course, my lady, I'd be honored with your company."

"Excellent. In coin, Martin, if you please."

Chapter Nine

"You really don't need to come with me to buy the supplies," James said, as he assisted Margaret into her coach.

"But I want to." She sat back on the well-padded seat and adjusted her skirts. It was such a shame James couldn't sit with her in the carriage instead of up on the bench. It looked so uncomfortable, and they wouldn't be able to talk with him there.

It was also another sharp reminder to them both that he was a servant, which made things just a touch odd actually. She put that thought from her mind, though. He wasn't a servant just now, he was an artist who would be painting her portrait. Why did that sound so enticing? "Besides if I don't, how will you get that enormous canvas back to the duchess's home?"

"I'd hire a hack," he said, still waiting to climb up onto the bench with the driver.

"You know, just at the moment you're not the duchess's footman. You're an artist. I'm sure you could sit here with me—"

"No. I beg your pardon, but I am the duchess's footman no matter where I am or what I'm doing. So long as I am in her employ, I'll sit up on the bench." He paused and then added more gently, "But thank you." With that he put up the steps, closed the door, and climbed up next to the coachman.

Class was such a funny thing, Margaret thought. She'd always thought so. Despite the fact she was the daughter of a duke, she'd always been so much closer to the servants in her parents' household, who treated her with kindness and respect. Her mother, by contrast, would only frown and criticize her day and night and remind her that, despite her inadequacies, she was still the daughter of the duke and should keep the servants at arm's length.

She didn't know how she was going to do it, but in her own household—when she finally married—she was going to create a more balanced and equal system. For now, all she could do was sit and stare and James's back and feel awkward.

Margaret had been to Ackerman's before. They sold a wonderful variety of goods. She had never ventured into the area where the art supplies were sold, however. James escorted her to the correct area and then said, "I need to speak with a clerk to get all that I'll require. Do you want to join me or would you prefer to look around?"

There were stacks of prints and all sorts of pieces of art which looked enticing, so Margaret said, "I'll just look around while you get what you need."

James gave her a nod and went off to conduct his business.

"Lady Margaret, what a surprise. I didn't know you painted," an older woman said, causing Margaret to spin around.

"Oh, Mrs. Aldridge, how do you do? No, I don't actually, I'm here with someone," Margaret said. "Do you paint, ma'am?"

"It's just a silly little hobby of mine," the lady said. Oddly, she seemed embarrassed by the fact the she did so. Margaret couldn't imagine why, when it was a common enough thing for a lady to do.

"Who are you here with?" Mrs. Aldridge asked, glancing around.

"That gentleman over there," Margaret said, nodding toward James as he stood at the counter conversing with one of the clerks.

"Oh, I don't believe I know him," the lady said.

James happened to turn around just at that moment. He sought out Margaret with his eyes and smiled when he saw her. How strange that such a little gesture should make her feel warm and comforted.

"Oh, he is a handsome one, isn't he?" the older lady said with a little titter.

Margaret laughed, but everything within her perked up and agreed most whole-heartedly.

"He's an artist who's going to be painting a portrait of me. Warwick just hired him," Margaret said. She had no idea why she didn't mention that he was also footman to the Duchess of Kendell, but it just didn't seem to be appropriate. No, she told herself, it was much more relevant that he was an artist.

"Really? How lovely! And he's here buying the materials he'll need. Isn't it unusual for him to bring you along for this?"

"It is, but actually I asked if I could join him.

I've never shopped for artists' materials before," Margaret said with a little shrug.

"Well, it was very sweet of him to agree to bring you. I do hope you don't find it too tiresome to sit for him. Although, if I had to sit and stare at *him* for a few hours a day, I don't think I'd mind," she said, giggling again.

"Mrs. Aldridge!" Margaret said, a little shocked even as she gave a little giggle.

"Oh, I'm just teasing you," Mrs. Aldridge laughed.

"Good afternoon," James said, joining them. "It will be just another few minutes while they gather the things I need, my lady."

"No worries. As you see, I've met a friend. Mrs. Aldridge, may I present James..." Margaret paused. Had he ever told her his last name? She couldn't remember.

"Douglass," he supplied quickly.

"Yes, I'm sorry, Mr. James Douglass," Margaret finished. She could feel her face heat with embarrassment. "Er, Mr. Douglass, this is Mrs. Aldridge. She's a member of the Ladies' Wagering Whist Society, which I'm sure you've heard of."

"How could he have heard of us?" Mrs. Aldridge giggled.

"The Duchess of Kendell is a member," James started.

"And he knows the duchess," Margaret finished for him, jumping in before he blurted out that he worked for her.

He gave her a quick side glance.

"Oh, of course! Have you painted her portrait as well, Mr. Douglass?" Mrs. Aldridge asked.

"Not yet. I've been deciding how to convince her to allow me to do so," he said with a sly smile as if it were a wonderful joke.

The lady laughed. "I'm sure you won't have any problems. She is rather, well…" Mrs. Aldridge suddenly turned bright pink. "Anyway, I wish you the best of luck with your portrait. It was lovely meeting you both." She turned around and walked away.

"I wonder what she meant by that," Margaret said.

James gave a little laugh. "I think she might have meant that the duchess was the sort who would *want* to have her portrait painted."

"You mean she meant that the duchess is conceited?"

"Or that she's aware of her station, and it's something that such people like to have," he said with a little shrug.

Margaret thought about that with a little frown. "Well, she most certainly is aware of her station, but, well, she's a duchess!"

"Yes, she is. And I'm a footman, which I noticed you didn't mention to Mrs. Aldridge," he said with a teasing smile.

Margaret felt her own face heat a little. She gave a shrug. "It wasn't appropriate to the conversation. And in this context, you aren't a footman, you're an artist, which is why I told her that."

"Umm-hmm." He gave a little laugh but then spun around when his name was called by the clerk. "I believe my things are set. Are you ready to go?"

"I am," Margaret said.

~*~

Their game of whist was cut short on Wednesday by Lady Blakemore's revelation that her niece's twin sister had been in town and living in her home without the lady ever having been aware of it.

Alys was preparing to leave when Mrs. Aldridge's presence by her side was anticipated by that of her dog. Its dirty little black nose sniffed around the hem of Alys' dress forcing her to stop to avoid the creature. "I met Lady Margaret yesterday," Mrs. Aldridge said. "She and that handsome Mr. Douglass were at Ackerman's buying supplies."

Alys looked up from the dog. "I have no idea what you are talking about, Mrs. Aldridge," she said, frowning at the woman.

"Lady Margaret? Your ward for the season?" the woman said slowly as if Alys were an idiot.

"I know who Lady Margaret is, and she is not my ward. I'm merely acting as her chaperone."

"Whatever," the lady said dismissively. "I met her at Ackerman's yesterday."

"Yes, I heard that, but I have no idea who this handsome Mr. Douglass is to whom you referred, nor why she would be at Ackerman's with him. She never mentioned the outing to me." Which was nearly as disturbing as the fact that Margaret was out with a gentleman. She must speak with the girl immediately about going out without telling her. She'd never done anything like this before.

"Oh, that's odd. He said he knew you. Said that he was trying to convince you to allow him to paint your portrait," Mrs. Aldridge said. She was looking like a cat with a cream pot.

Alys did her best to rein in her temper. "I do

not know any gentleman by the name of Douglass. Clearly the man was lying to you—perhaps to puff up his own credibility."

Mrs. Aldridge's eyes went wide. "I don't know why he would need to do that. He's just been hired by the Duke of Warwick to paint Lady Margaret's portrait. I would think that alone would give him excellent credibility, unless Lady Margaret was lying too."

"Lady Margaret never lies," the duchess said immediately. On the other hand, she also had not mentioned a word of this to Alys, which was very suspicious.

"Well, then, I think you might want to look into it. It sounds like you don't know what's going on with your"—Mrs. Aldridge floundered for a moment—"chaperonee."

"Ladies, ladies, may I have your attention a moment before you all go," Lady Norman called out. Alys was grateful for the interruption. "Just a reminder that next week we'll be meeting at my new home," the lady said with a huge grin on her face.

"And we'll be seeing you on Sunday at the wedding," Lady Colburne said happily.

"And on Monday evening at the wedding ball," Lady Welles said with a giggle.

"Yes. So, don't forget! Next week at Lord Ayres' home," Lady Norman said. Her cheeks were slightly flushed. She was clearly thrilled with all the changes about to come into her life.

Alys was very happy for her—almost happy enough to momentarily forget about the fact that Mrs. Aldridge was better informed with what was happening under her own roof than she was!

CHAPTER TEN

~April 8~

James knocked on the library door, hoping he would find Lady Margaret there. He knew the duchess was out at her Whist Society meeting, and he was all set to start her painting; he just needed his subject.

There was no answer, however. He slowly opened the door and, indeed, found the room empty. He worried for a moment that she had gone out, in which case, he would have to wait another week before he could get started. He only had Tuesday mornings and Wednesday afternoons free.

He found Michael, another other footman, just taking up his post at the front door. "Michael, have you seen Lady Margaret? Has she gone out?"

"She's upstairs in the drawing room," he answered. "Isn't it your day off?"

"Yes, it is. Thank you," Jamie said, giving the fellow a nod. Michael was a bit of a gossip. Jamie wasn't about to tell him what he was up to. Jamie wondered if he dared go up the main stair. It would be the fastest route to the drawing room, but use of the stairs by the staff was frowned upon unless you were in a hurry carrying out an order. A side glance told him that Michael was still watching him, so he went down to the kitchens and then up the servant's stair.

Lady Margaret responded right away to his knock.

"I beg your pardon, my lady, but would you have some time to spare, so I can get started on your portrait?" he asked after he'd come into the room and bowed to her.

"Oh, yes! I'm actually at loose ends right now. Is this a good time for you?" Lady Margaret said, her face lighting up.

"It is. If you wouldn't mind coming with me," Jamie said, bowing to her again.

She got up and followed him out of the room. With her, he took the main stairs up to the third floor and the servants' quarters. It was one very nice thing about working for a duchess. Even a footman could have his very own room. At the Coningsby's, he'd had to share with another man.

He hesitated for a moment just outside his room. This was awkward. Jamie had tried to think of another option but there simply didn't seem to be one. With a deep breath in, he opened the door and held it open for Lady Margaret, but she stopped just outside and peered into the room. "Is there something wrong?" he asked.

"Is that...? That's your, er, your private room," she said hesitantly.

"Yes, I'm afraid so."

"But I can't go into a bedchamber alone with a gentleman," she said turning her wide blue eyes on him.

Jamie cringed. "I was worried it might be an issue. I just... I don't know where else to work. I can't very well set up my easel in the drawing room or one of the public rooms downstairs."

"Oh, no," Lady Margaret said, resting her chin on her fist as she thought.

Mentally, Jamie went through every room in the house. There just didn't seem to be one where he had permission to be and where he could leave his work undisturbed. His gaze roamed the hallway as he thought. Suddenly, the narrow stair at the end of the hall caught his attention. "Of course!" he exclaimed.

Lady Margaret turned and looked at him hopefully.

"The attic! Would that work for you?"

"The attic?" She turned and followed his line of sight to the narrow stair leading up. "I don't know. I suppose it would, I mean, what would be up there? Old trunks and furniture?"

"Shall we find out?" he asked, giving her a mischievous grin.

She laughed. "All right."

She was about to start up, when Jamie stopped her with two thoughts in mind. One he voiced, and the other he kept to himself. "You'd better let me go first. There might be cobwebs or rodents there that you wouldn't want to encounter," he said. And if he followed her up, there was a good chance that he'd get to see even more than her pretty little ankles. The stair was very steep and a gentleman always preceded a lady up the stairs for just that reason.

"Oh!" She stood back to allow him to pass her. "I didn't think of that. Yes, you go first."

He climbed the stairs quickly and checked inside the room at the top. It wasn't as bad as he'd expected. There were some cobwebs but not too many, and there wasn't any sign of mice. He turned around and motioned for Lady Margaret to join him.

The room was large, extending the entirety of the house. Trunks and old furniture were scattered throughout, but the light was excellent, streaming in through windows at either end. His eyes immediately landed on a throne-like chair covered in red velvet material. He pulled it forward, so it sat facing the windows where the sun was streaming in.

"If you would just give me one minute, I'll get my things," he said after brushing the chair off as best as he could. "You can sit here."

He ran back down to his room, grabbed the pile of new paper, a couple of pencils, his pen knife, and the tall three-legged stool he'd purchased soon after he'd arrived in London. It was perfect for perching on while he sketched or painted. He could bring up his easel, paints, and canvas later.

Lady Margaret was investigating some of the other furniture in the room when he returned. She returned to the chair he'd pulled forward for her. With a little laugh, she said, "It looks rather like a throne, doesn't it?"

"It does. I think it will do very well for the portrait, don't you?" he asked, smiling back at her as he settled himself on his stool.

"Only if you plan on painting me like a queen," she said with a giggle as she sat down.

He tilted his head as he began to sketch her. "How would you like to be painted?"

"Oh, I don't know. I haven't even given it much thought," she said.

"Well, then, why not as a queen? You are the

sister to a duke, after all."

"Yes, but, while that may seem awfully lofty to you, I can assure you it is far from being queen."

He just smiled and continued sketching, drawing the shape of her face and the outline of her figure. He would fill in the details as he went. "How is it being the sister of a duke and the daughter of one, then?" he asked.

She laughed. "Not as grand as it sounds, I can assure you."

"But grand, nonetheless. You had a nanny, a governess? Dozens of servants at your beck and call?" he asked, just to make conversation.

She gave a little shrug and turned her head to stare unseeingly at a stack of trunks. "I did have a governess and servants, yes. They were the kindest people in my life. They were my friends, my family—more so than my actual family, I can assure you. Well, except for Warwick. He was always wonderful."

"You cared for your servants?" Jamie asked, lifting his pencil. Most nobles he knew didn't even notice their staff. But then, Lady Margaret *did*. He'd noticed that about her and had always thought it odd.

"Of course!" she said, as if the answer to the question was obvious.

"I have to say you are unusual in that regard. I *have* noticed, though, that you treat the staff with a great deal more respect than most." He chuckled. "You asked me my name the first time we met."

"Of course I did!" she said, surprised.

"I don't believe the duchess knows it even now. She calls me Michael," he commented.

Lady Margaret shook her head sadly. "I know the names of everyone on the staff."

Jamie scoffed. He couldn't help it.

"Do you doubt me?" she asked in surprise.

"I'm sorry, my lady, but there is a rather large staff here in this household. You couldn't possibly know everyone."

"We had a much larger staff at Warwick, and I knew the name of every single person who worked there," she said with a little lift of her chin that Jamie found adorable.

"Really? Then what is the name of the scullery maid who cleans the ashes out of the fireplaces?" he asked, daring her.

She gave him a little smile. "The girl who does it in my bedchamber is Mary. She's a sweet thing. She came in with you. She says that the two of you are friends."

Jamie started, nearly jumping from his stool. "What?"

"Oh yes. She told me all about your heroic save of her when Lord Coningsby tried to touch her inappropriately. She quite worships you, you know." Lady Margaret laughed.

Jamie settled back down on his stool and went back to his sketching. "You shouldn't believe everything she tells you. She's got quite the imagination."

"I quite like her," Lady Margaret said.

Jamie worked silently for a few minutes, thinking about this strange, beautiful young woman. He didn't know very many young ladies of the nobility, but he had a strong suspicion that they weren't all like her. No, Lady Margaret was a very unique person, he was certain.

Something nagged at him, though. Something she'd said. It suddenly hit him. "You said that the staff was more like a family to you than your own," Jamie said.

"Well, my brother has always been—"

"Wonderful," he supplied.

"Yes."

"But not your parents? Not even your mother?" Jamie asked.

Lady Margaret grew very quiet and, oddly, seemed to shrink into herself slightly. "My mother wasn't happy with me."

"How do you mean?"

"I was supposed to have been a boy," she explained. When Jamie stayed quiet, she continued, "She wasn't even supposed to have a second child after Warwick. Apparently, his birth was a difficult one, but she took the risk and had another. The duke wanted a second son just in case anything should happen to the first."

"A spare," Jamie said, nodding. It was a common enough practice.

"Yes. But instead they had me. Both my parents blamed me for being female, and my mother could never have any more children."

"But *you* didn't decide your gender," Jamie said, laughing at such stupidity.

"No. But my mother was never happy with me, regardless," Lady Margaret said, shrinking a little more.

Jamie caught on that Lady Margaret had had a difficult childhood, despite being the daughter of a duke. "In what way?" he asked gently.

"Oh, in all ways, really." She gave an awkward little giggle. "I could never do anything right. I was told I was stupid and ugly. That I would never find a husband or really be fit to do anything more than be an aunt for Warwick's children if he allowed me to continue to live in his household. In short, I was told that I was a burden and always would be."

Jamie realized he'd stopped sketching. How could anyone tell their child such horrid lies? He started drawing again, now with a much greater understanding of why Lady Margaret was so sweet, gentle, and shy. She'd probably hid from her mother her entire life, trying to make sure she hadn't been noticed, so she could escape her harsh criticisms. "Where is your mother now? You father, I assume, has passed since your brother is the duke."

"Both my parents died of influenza three years ago," Lady Margaret said.

"I beg your pardon, but I'm rather glad to hear that. I imagine you are well rid of them."

Lady Margaret laughed. "I would never say so." She might not, but Jamie could see it in her body and how her expression had lightened considerably.

He continued to sketch her for another twenty minutes in silence. He was pleased with his preliminary work. He could finish it on his own and then begin painting the next time they met.

Lady Margaret followed Jamie down the stairs, but his mind was still on the sketch in his hand.

"Lady Margaret! James, what...?" It was Michael. Jamie cursed himself for not looking out to see if anyone was in the hall before descending.

Chapter Eleven

"We were just, um…" Jamie started.

"Alone in the attic," Michael said. "I don't imagine the duchess or Mr. Holton knows about this, do they?"

"There was nothing untoward," Lady Margaret started with a lift of her chin.

"Of course not, my lady," Michael said, bowing to her slightly. The look in his eyes, however, said otherwise. Jamie was tempted to blacken one of those eyes, but he was certain it would shock Lady Margaret, and it would certainly do nothing for their cause.

He bit his tongue but remembered the sketch still in his hand. "It truly was nothing. I was sketching." He showed the drawing to the other footman.

He glanced at it and then said with a sly grin, "I'm sure you won't show me the other sketches you made."

"How dare you!" Lady Margaret said, her eyes flashing as she looked down her nose at him. Jamie was shocked and impressed by the hauteur the girl could pull up when needed. He would have laughed if he weren't seeing red at the moment.

"There aren't any!" Jamie said, his voice low

and dangerous. How dare Michael imply that he had not only done something inappropriate with such a sweet young lady, but that he would have sketched it as well.

Michael gave them both a slight disbelieving smile before he bowed went into his room. Jamie knew there was nothing he could do to change the fellow's mind or take it from the cesspit in which it dwelled. The more he argued with him, the more Michael would think them guilty of something that hadn't happened.

What made things even worse was that the idea of doing such things with Lady Margaret made Jamie wish he could have, that he actually had. He was nearly as disgusting as Michael!

But no, he wasn't. Being attracted to someone and acting on that attraction were two very, very different things. He would never do anything inappropriate with someone so sweet and gentle as Lady Margaret—or anyone else, for that matter.

"I should... I should go." Lady Margaret's voice cut into Jamie' thoughts.

"Of course. Thank you for your time, my lady." Jamie bowed as he watched her retreating back.

~*~

Margaret slowly descended the stairs, wondering what in the world had gotten into her. She'd never in her life told anyone about her mother and the way she'd been treated. What had induced her to tell James?

What he must think of her!

It must have been the intimacy of the setting. That's all she could possibly think of. She'd felt as if they were the only people in the world up there in that attic.

He'd sat there perched on his stool, one foot on the cross-bar, the other on the floor, looking so incredibly handsome and kind. He'd smiled at her not only with his lips but with his eyes and his cheeks. He'd been leaning forward, sketching, looking back and forth between her and his work. He'd look...interested!

Perhaps that was it. He had seemed interested in what she was saying, and before she knew it, she had told him everything. How horribly embarrassing!

"Margaret!" the duchess's voice broke through Margaret's thoughts.

"I beg your pardon, Your Grace," Margaret said, suddenly flustered. She hadn't even been watching where she was going. She was in the drawing room, standing just inside the door. How and when had she gotten there? And how long had the duchess been trying to get her attention? The lady must have returned from the Ladies' Wagering Whist Society meeting while she was upstairs with James.

Margaret felt her face heat. She came forward and curtsied.

"Where have you been? I sent for you nearly half an hour ago as soon as I returned home," the duchess said. She was sitting in a chair by the fireplace. There was no tea tray in front of her, not a book nor sewing in her lap. Oh, dear. It looked as if she was simply sitting there—waiting.

"I... I didn't know. I was upstairs." Margaret stammered.

The duchess waved away her excuses. "It doesn't matter. You are here now, and I want to know what is going on. I just had the most embarrassing conversation with Mrs. Aldridge, who seemed to know a great deal more of your whereabouts and activities than I do. Can you please explain to me how this could be so?" The lady's hard eyes bore into Margaret's own.

"I... I don't know," Margaret said, wringing her hands together. "Mrs. Aldridge? Oh, yes, I met her yesterday at Ackerman's."

The duchess continued to stare silently, waiting for more information.

"I... I, er, was there with James, Your Grace. He needed to buy some art materials, so I accompanied him. It was his morning off."

"James? Who is *James*?"

"The new footman."

"You were out with the footman while he ran his own personal errands?" The woman sat forward, nearly starting from her chair in her shock.

"It... It wasn't exactly a personal errand," Margaret quickly explained. "We'd gone together to Warwick's to show my brother James's work. Did you know that James is an artist?"

"He's a footman. What do you mean, he's an artist?"

"I believe he was an artist before he became a footman," Margaret said. She wasn't sure. She'd meant to ask him while he'd been working on her portrait but had forgotten. "Anyway, he drew the most beautiful sketch of me. When he wouldn't give it to me, Warwick offered to buy it from him. He wouldn't sell it. But then Warwick said he might commission James to paint a picture of me if he liked his work. So, James and I went to Warwick's to show him the work, and after getting the commission—because his work is really incredible—we went to Ackerman's to buy the materials he'd need to paint the portrait." Margaret stopped for a breath.

The duchess was silent for a moment. "That is the most convoluted story I think I've ever heard from you. You're usually such a clear-thinking, steady young lady." She paused, but continued again before Margaret could say anything. "Do you know how disconcerting it is to have someone inform me about what you are doing? Do you realize just how disturbing it is when *Mrs. Aldridge* tells me that she saw you out with a gentleman, and *I* didn't know about it? It has been a very long time since I was put into such an embarrassing situation and I never—I repeat, *never*—want to be in such a position again. Is that clear?"

Margaret blinked to clear the burning from her eyes as she nodded. She swallowed but was determined not to let her emotions get the better of her. "I am sorry, Your Grace," she whispered. Her voice getting caught in the lump in her throat. "It's been a rather eventful two days, but I should have kept you informed—"

"That would have been the very least you could have done!" the duchess interrupted.

Margaret nodded, keeping her eyes lowered. "I do beg your pardon."

"So, what that woman said is, in fact, true. You were out with the footman?"

"Yes, Your Grace, I was with James at Ackerman's and met Mrs. Aldridge there. I assure you, if I had known we would be going, I would have informed you. I should have mentioned we were going to Warwick's as well, but you were busy, and I didn't want to disturb you. James is—"

A knock on the door interrupted her. She turned as the butler came into the room.

~*~

Threes. Things always came in threes, Alys thought to herself as Holton came into the room.

The first was Mrs. Aldridge, her tittering revelations, and the glee at knowing something that Alys hadn't.

Then it was Margaret and her convoluted story of sketchings and portraits and something having to do with the new footman and Warwick. Alys truly hadn't been able to follow what the girl had been saying.

And now it was the butler. She was going to need a very strong drink after this.

"What is it, Holton?" she asked, not letting her anger and frustration show through the veneer of her face.

"Er... if I may, Your Grace, have a moment of your time," he said looking Alys but stealing side glances at Margaret.

"You have it. Speak," Alys commanded him.

He opened his mouth and closed it again like a fish. "Alone, if you don't mind."

"Whatever it is, you may discuss it in front of Lady Margaret. She is a member of this household."

"Er, yes, Your Grace, but this, this concerns..."

"Her?" Alys guessed. It seemed that Margaret was the center of all this shady business.

"Er, yes, Your Grace," the man said, looking distinctly uncomfortable. It did make Alys feel a little better watching him squirm.

She sighed. "What is it?"

"It's just... Michael, one of the footmen, just told me that he saw Lady Margaret coming from the attic with James, the new footman. I know I should not say this, but he said it looked distinctly fishy." He turned to Margaret. "I do beg your pardon, my lady."

"It was nothing of the sort," Margaret said, straightening herself so that she could look down her nose at the little man. The daughter of a duke stood before them, and Alys applauded her. It was one of the things the duchess did so admire about Margaret. She might be a little mouse of a girl most of the time, but when the situation called for it, she could be as condescending as the best of them.

"Then would you care to explain what you were doing alone in the attic with him?" the butler asked clearly not as cowed by Margaret's stance as he should have been.

"I do not answer to you, Mr. Holton. What I do and with whom is none of your business," Margaret answered.

"No, it is not his business, but the footman is. Just as you are *my* business. Now, do explain yourself to me, if you please," Alys said, matching Margaret's condescension with her own.

Margaret shrank down just a touch. "As I was just telling you, Your Grace, James has been commissioned by Warwick to paint a portrait of me. We were in the attic while he sketched an initial picture to use for his painting. We were *there* because there was no other place for him to do his work."

"James is painting a portrait? He's a *footman*," the butler said, looking very confused.

"Apparently, he's also a painter," Alys said, repeating back what Margaret had told her earlier. "Although, I would like to see proof of this. Holton, send someone to fetch James and tell him to bring his work. I would like to see it."

The butler bowed, turned on his heel, and left the room.

"He truly is very good," Margaret said, losing all her previous bravado.

"I shall determine that for myself," Alys said with a sniff. She honestly had no idea *what* to think anymore. This day had been much too trying for a woman not used to dealing with younger people. She wasn't used to such excitement.

"Sit down, Margaret, you're making me nervous standing there. No, wait, pour me a drink first. I most definitely need a drink."

Margaret gave her a little smile before going over to the side table and pouring a small glass of sherry. "I'm so sorry to cause you so much trouble," she said sweetly as she handed Alys the glass.

The sip Alys took set her on the road to relaxation. The fact that Margaret was sitting looking very contrite also helped.

After a brief knock on the door, Holton came back in followed by the new footman—James, apparently. Alys was rather embarrassed to admit she'd never really paid very much attention to the fellow's name despite the fact that it had been told to her several times.

He came forward, bowed, and proceeded to unroll a canvas in front of her. "My work, Your Grace."

Alys was confronted with the ghost of a woman she'd known as a girl. She was much older, but then so was Alys. "I know her!" she gasped.

The footman nearly dropped the painting. "You do?"

"Yes, that's Victoria Brighton. She was presented to society about the same time as I was. She married..." Alys searched her memory. "She married a few years after me. That Scottish fellow, what was his name?"

"Rossburke," the footman supplied.

"Yes, that's it!" Alys turned a smile to him as she remembered the girl from her youth. "She was very sweet. Very gentle. I always wondered how she fared in Scotland."

James smiled as if he, too, were remembering something pleasant. "She did very well. Rossburke isn't very far north. It's close to Glasgow. She loved it there."

There was something in his voice...as if he knew her well. Alys frowned at him. "How did you know Lady Rossburke?"

The footman's eyes grew wide and then wary before shuttering completely. "I painted her portrait, as you see. It was done just before she passed."

"She's gone?" Alys said, shocked to hear it. "But she wasn't any older than I am!"

"Tuberculosis," he explained briefly.

"Oh, I am sorry to hear that." There was a slight heaviness in her heart for the poor woman. She then refocused on the painting itself, which was the actual reason it was being shown to her. It was very good. "And *you* painted this?"

"Yes, Your Grace." He rolled it up and unrolled another, this one of an elderly man, clearly a farmer. "And this."

Alys nodded. His work was excellent. "Then what are you doing working as a footman?"

He smiled sadly. "I'm afraid I couldn't find much work as a painter. I tried for about six months before my stomach demanded I find another occupation."

Alys gave a little snort of laughter. "I see. But now you've been hired to paint a portrait of Lady Margaret?"

"Yes, Your Grace. His Grace, the Duke of Warwick, was kind enough to ask me to do so. I assure you, I won't allow it to interfere with my duties within your household, however."

"Just when do you plan on working on this, then?" she asked, skeptical that it wouldn't.

"On my free time. I have some evenings, Tuesday mornings, and Wednesday afternoons off," he explained.

Alys nodded. It sounded as if he would be devoting every spare minute he had to this. She liked that sort of dedication. She also hadn't missed the fact that Margaret seemed to be hanging on every word the man said. This could be very bad... Margaret was an impressionable young woman who needed to find an appropriate, *eligible* gentleman to marry. Hopefully, this was nothing, and Alys was creating castles out of clouds. She dismissed her thoughts as nonsense and turned back to the waiting footman-artist. "Very well. You may continue this activity, but not... Where was it?"

"In the attic, Your Grace," the butler supplied.

"Yes. Not in the attic. You may use the second drawing room downstairs." It used to be the music room, but since no one played music, it had become a spare drawing room used only when Alys gave parties.

"Thank you, Your Grace, that is very generous of you," James bowed and then rolled up his canvases.

"Warwick will be so pleased," Margaret said quietly even as she gave the footman a smile, looking more like she was the one who would be pleased.

Chapter Twelve

~April 9~

"James!" Mr. Holton's sharp voice pulled Jamie from his daydreaming the following afternoon. He'd just finished a mid-day repast and had allowed his mind to wander where it would go—most recently that had been inevitably to Lady Margaret.

"Yes, sir?" Jamie asked, looking up at the man glowering at him from across the table. He had not been happy with the duchess's acceptance of Jamie's extra activities.

"I want you on the front door, now! The duchess is at-home to callers this afternoon and will be receiving guests in the formal drawing room on the ground floor, is that clear? My leg is paining me," he added so softly James almost missed it. James had heard the man had had a bad break of his leg, which had never healed properly. It was why he didn't tend to the front door himself as was customary.

"Yes, sir." *The same as every Thursday afternoon*, but Jamie kept his thoughts to himself.

"We are expecting more visitors than usual due to the fact that Lady Norman's wedding is on Sunday," the butler explained as if he were speaking to a child. "As you know—"

"Yes, sir," Jamie interrupted. "Lady Margaret has been one of the main organizers of the event. I imagine there are a number of people who will be here this afternoon looking for details about what has been planned."

One would have expected the butler to be happy that his footman had a thorough understanding of the situation, but sadly Mr. Holton clearly was not. He glared angrily at Jamie for a moment and then spat, "Get up there."

He was probably never going to get along with the man. He'd tried at first. Now, he was simply ready to give up the effort. Jamie got up, cleared away his place, even though there were other servants to do that for him, and went off to take up his post.

There were indeed a good number of callers from the moment the duchess started accepting them. Jamie found himself very busy for the first half hour or more. The majority of the first callers were ladies, but there were almost an equal number of gentlemen who eventually joined them. Jamie found it fascinating there were so many eager for advanced information. He gathered from the snippets of conversation he overheard that the wedding itself was going to be a small, private affair while the ball to celebrate it would be one of the events of the season with hundreds of guests in attendance. The Duchess of Warwick would be hosting both with Lady Margaret.

He finally thought the rush was over, and had just leaned back against the wall to take a breath, when once again there was a decisive knock on the door. It was either a lady's footman or a gentleman caller. It was definitely the knock of man. Jamie could only shake his head at the fact that he knew that.

He opened the door and then had to physically stop himself from gasping out loud. He nearly ended up coughing but resisted the urge to cover his face. He desperately wanted to, both to stop his cough and to hide from the man staring at him with widening eyes.

"Rossburke?" Jamie's best friend from school stood staring at him.

"Shhh!" Jamie whispered furiously. Then in a normal tone of voice, just in case there was anyone within earshot, he said, "Please, my lord, do come in."

"What the hell are you doing answering the door? And...wait... Why are you in livery? Don't tell me your estate...?"

"For God's sake, Powell, lower your voice!" Jamie whispered, looking behind him to make sure no one was nearby.

"You *are* going to explain this to me," his friend said threateningly, despite the whisper.

"Yes, I will, but not here. Not now," Jamie said, keeping one eye on the drawing room door.

"I own a gentleman's club, Powell's. It's on Pall Mall. I expect to see you there this evening—unless you're *working*," he added, looking Jamie up and down with disapproving eyes.

"No. I'll be there. Your father?" Jamie asked, just needing to know how to announce him.

Powell shook his head. "I'm Wickford now."

"I am sorry about that." He reached out and put his hand on his friend's arm.

Wickford patted it, saying, "Not as sorry as I

am to see you here, like this."

"I'll explain it all this evening, I promise." He then opened the drawing room door and resumed his footman's mantle. "Viscount Wickford," he announced.

~*~

Margaret was doing her best to look interested. Miss Pensley went on and on about how unfair it was that Miss Kendrick had the attention of both Lord Conway *and* Lord St. Vincent.

"Really, she needs to make up her mind. She can't keep them both in her pocket for the entire season. It just isn't fair to the rest of us. I'm sure you agree, Lady Margaret," the blonde young woman said. The poor thing really needed someone like Tina in her life, Margaret thought. The white dress she was wearing completely washed out her already fair features. Her hair was almost white-blonde, her eyes a pale shade of green. If she wore a slightly creamier white, Margaret imagined she would look much rosier.

"Viscount Wickford," James announced from the door before bowing out again. The poor man was constantly popping in and out with guests. Never before had they had so many visitors when the duchess had been at home. Everyone wanted the inside scoop on Tina's ball and exactly who had been invited to Lady Norman and Lord Ayres' wedding.

"If you will excuse me, Miss Pensley, I need to greet our newest guest," Margaret said, grateful for the opportunity to leave the young woman's side.

She curtsied to Lord Wickford as he bowed in return. "Lord Wickford, how wonderful to see you. It's been some time."

His bright, white smile shone from his darker complexion—he wasn't as dark as some people of African descent Margaret had met, but it was clear where his origins were. His father, she believed, was English and clearly a titled nobleman, but his mother must have been African. It was his eyes, however, that were quite stunning—they were almost a gold color—and at the moment smiling warmly at Margaret. "How did I not see you at Lady Darby's ball?" he asked with a sly but charming look.

"I don't know. I was most certainly there," Margaret said, widening her eyes at him innocently. Of course, he might have easily missed her because she'd managed to spend a portion of the evening standing half-behind a potted plant whenever the duchess hadn't been noticing.

"And I suppose you've been too busy planning the wedding of the season to go out driving in the park or to other daytime amusements?"

Margaret sighed dramatically. "I'm afraid so."

Lord Wickford laughed. "Well, I imagine you and your sister-in-law are going to be very relieved when this whole thing is done."

"Indeed!" Margaret said, thinking just the opposite. Once the wedding and ball were finished, she didn't know what she was going to do with herself... Or more accurately, how she was going to convince the duchess that she *couldn't* go to various parties or driving in the park. Being out and about was trying enough in the evening; she didn't want to add afternoons to her social schedule.

"I imagine that you, like most others, are here to find out who will be attending the wedding?" Margaret asked, smiling sweetly at him.

"Well, I do have a reputation to maintain, my lady," he said.

"And a gentleman's club where all your guests will expect you to have the latest news, I suppose."

He burst out laughing, throwing his head back in amusement. "I have been found out."

"It wasn't hard to deduce, my lord."

He leaned a little closer. "So, what can you tell me that you haven't told everyone else here?"

She gave a little shrug. "Nothing really, I'm afraid. It's all quite open. There will be fifty of Lady Norman and Lord Ayres' closest friends and family at the wedding and then the rest of society at the ball."

"Any surprises in the guest list for the wedding?" he asked, quirking an eyebrow.

Margaret went over the list in her head. "I don't think so. Lady Norman's sons will be there. A couple of Lord Ayres' cousins have come from Ireland."

"And among the friends?"

"The ladies of the Wagering Whist Society, some closer friends of Lord Ayres, or their sons if the gentlemen themselves are unable to come for any reason."

"Can you name any?" he probed.

Margaret rattled off a couple of names. She didn't believe any of the information was secret.

"Wait, Lord St. Vincent is going to be there?" Wickford asked, picking up on one name.

"Yes. His father and Lord Ayres went to school together. They were apparently quite close."

Lord Wickford nodded. "I don't suppose Miss

Kendrick will be in attendance?"

"Yes, as a matter of fact she will. She's the niece of Lady Blakemore, who is a member of the Whist Society. Miss Kendrick is staying with the countess for the season. We couldn't very well invite Lady Blakemore and not her niece."

"Hmmm, yes, of course."

"You're thinking of the fact that Lord St. Vincent has been seen in Miss Kendrick's company quite frequently, aren't you?" Margaret asked. She didn't deliberately keep up with gossip, but she couldn't help but know about a friend.

"I am. There are bets on whether Lord St. Vincent or Lord Conway will win the good lady's hand, you know."

Margaret shook her head. "Gentlemen will bet on anything!"

"Well, yes, as a matter of fact they will. Still, it's an interesting uncertainty to keep an eye on."

"I am more interested in the bride and groom, personally. I think it's a beautiful love story that has blossomed into reality."

Lord Wickford smiled. "That is what makes it the wedding of the season, of course. Everyone adores a good love story with a happy ending."

~April 10~

Jamie wondered for a moment whether he should find the servant's entrance to his friend's club or just go in the front door. He shook his head ruefully at himself. He'd only been a footman for about six months, and already he was beginning to think like one.

His knock on the door brought a footman who looked at him in askance.

"I'm James Douglass, here to see Lord Wickford. He's a friend," Jamie told him.

The man nodded and allowed Jamie in. "If you would wait here just a moment, I'll find his lordship."

The foyer was surprisingly quiet for a club. Jamie looked around, but there wasn't very much to see, just a closed door on the left and one on the right. A long hallway leading to the back was decorated with mediocre landscapes.

Wickford came from the room on the right, laughing as if someone had just told him a joke. Jamie was surprised at the sound level coming from the room, which exploded into the hall when his friend opened the door, then nearly disappeared when the door had closed again.

"Rossburke! Great to see you," Wickford said coming forward, his hand outstretched.

Jamie took it in a warm grip. "The sound containment here is amazing."

Wickford smiled broadly. "Specially designed walls and doors. Come, let me show you around." He opened the door he'd just come from.

Jamie followed him in to a long room filled with gaming tables. Footmen roamed, delivering drinks and picking up empty glasses. The sound level was considerably louder than Jamie had imagined with men laughing and talking, exclaiming over hands lost or won.

"The gaming room," Wickford said. "We've got just about every card game you could want."

"Impressive," Jamie said with a little laugh.

They went back out the door and into the room across the hall. It was nearly as quiet as the gaming room had been loud. Groups of three, four, or five wing-back chairs were scattered about the room filled with men either chatting quietly or reading. Everyone had a drink by his side, frequently accompanied by a decanter of a rich golden liquid.

"The reading room," Wickford said quietly. "There's a dining room as well, but come, let's have a drink." He led the way to the back of the room where there were two chairs situated closely together, a small table between them.

He made eye contact with a footman as he sat down and gave the fellow a nod.

"In just a moment, you are going to be served the best rum you've ever—"

"Not as good as what you gave us at school, surely?" Jamie asked, interrupting his friend.

"Better! That was three-year-old rum, this is *eighteen*. I assure you, this is going to be the *best* you've ever had."

Jamie nodded and then accepted the glass that was soon handed to him by a footman. He took a sip. The sweet liquor slipped over his tongue and burned deliciously down his throat. "Oh, that is smooth!"

"Good, isn't it?" Wickford said, taking a sip of his own.

"Yes. You are right. It is," Jamie couldn't disagree. He took another sip. It had been too long since he'd had a drink. He should probably take it slow, he realized.

"Now, you are going to tell me what you've been up to and what the hell a *marquess* is doing working as a footman!" Wickford glared angrily at him.

Jamie could only laugh. He gave a little shrug. "You know that my father's estate was never profitable," he started.

Wickford nodded but stayed quiet, waiting for his answers.

"Well, after I returned from school, I had no idea how to run the place and no interest in learning. I decided I was going to become an artist."

His friend frowned. "You were always very good at sketching."

"Painting too. It was all I did for years after we graduated. I leased some of the surrounding land to local people and the rest of it to a man from Glasgow, and my mother and I continued to live in the manor as it slowly fell apart around us."

Wickford shook his head in wonder.

"After Mother passed, I decided to leave and try my luck here in London."

"So, you just abandoned your estate?" Wickford asked, shocked.

Chapter Thirteen

"I didn't abandon my estate. It's tended to much better than my father ever did. Some of the land is being farmed, some of it is open fields for sheep, and I don't have to think about any of it because it's not my problem any longer."

At Wickford's look of wonder, he added, "I've got no aptitude for farming, Powell, never have." Sadly, he took after his father in that way. His grandfather too, although he'd been clever enough to have an estate manager. His father had gotten rid of the man because of the expense, and then watched as his income fell, all the while preaching to Jamie the importance of family, continuity, and heritage. Now as an adult, it simply made no sense. He wondered how much of it was the liquor his father had imbibed in great quantities and how much was just wishful thinking.

"Surely, you could hire someone to manage things?"

Jamie shrugged again. "I could, but that would take money I don't have."

"I hear it's pretty common for young noblemen to marry for that," Wickford said dryly.

Jamie could only smile. "I couldn't do that to a young lady. Marry her and then drag her up to

Scotland to live in a ramshackle manor house that's been falling down for generations." He shook his head. "I actually thought I might earn some money with my paintings and then take that back home—use it to set things right."

"But…"

"But it seems you have to know people to get commissions. You have to be an established artist to become an established artist. I know no one, have never worked professionally, and don't know where to begin. Could you see the advertisement in the paper—'Marquess of Rossburke seeks artistic commissions for portrait painting endeavor.' That would go over brilliantly, don't you think?" He studied the nails of his right hand.

Wickford frowned at him before exclaiming, "You know me!"

"But I didn't know you were here, now, did I?" Jamie said.

Wickford sighed. "No. I'm afraid I haven't been very good at keeping in touch. I think I received your last letter, what, a year ago? I think your mother had just taken a turn for the worse," he said quietly.

Jamie nodded. "She passed not long after I wrote that. I think I was still holding out hope at that point. Ridiculous, I see now, but…well."

"Of course. I imagine we all hope for the best even when the reality is staring right at you." He was silent for a moment as he finished his rum. "So, you came to London, tried to be an artist…"

Jamie nodded. "Failed and ran out of money. The easiest thing to do was get a job as a footman. I wrote myself a letter of recommendation, claiming I'd worked for the Marquess of Rossburke for the past five years. Gave my name simply as James Douglass. No one knew the difference. Douglasses are everywhere. James Douglass could be anyone from a marquess to a street sweeper in Glasgow."

Wickford laughed. "I think that's a bit of an exaggeration but all right. So now you're working for the Duchess of Kendell."

"Yes. And shockingly, I just got my first real commission—to paint a portrait of Lady Margaret. If that goes well and her brother, the Duke of Warwick, who commissioned the painting, is happy, I'm hoping it might lead to other work."

"And then you can go back to being an artist, earn money, and return home to save your estate," Wickford finished.

"That's the plan," Jamie nodded.

"Do you have any finished pieces?" Wickford asked.

"I've got a few." He pulled out his watch into which he'd painted a miniature of his mother as she'd been as a younger woman. He had the larger canvas of her just before she'd died, but this was the way he preferred to remember her. He showed it to Wickford.

"Beautiful. What about something I can put on the wall?"

"I've got a few portraits I've been using as examples of my work and a couple of landscapes— better than what you've got, I can assure you," Jamie said with a laugh.

"Excellent. Give them to me—"

"They're not framed," Jamie said, interrupting.

"Give them to me," Wickford said again. "I'll get them framed and put them up. Maybe they'll sell. If so, you can paint some more."

Jamie was quiet for a moment, staring at his friend, letting his memories of their time together at school flow gently through his mind. "I'd appreciate that a great deal," he said.

"It would be my pleasure."

~April 11~

Margaret was surprised to find that the chair from the attic had been properly dusted and brought down to the second drawing room. She had been requested to meet James there the following evening if she wasn't otherwise occupied. Margaret was more than happy to claim that commitment as an excuse for not attending Lady Pinkerton's party.

"I'll allow it this time," the duchess had said during dinner, "but don't expect it to happen a second time."

Margaret made a note in her mind not to use the excuse again within the week. Surely, the duchess wouldn't remember if she tried it again after that—at least, Margaret hoped not.

"Lady Margaret," James greeted her from behind a large easel. "Good afternoon, my lady. Have you given a thought to what you would like to be wearing for the portrait?"

Margaret stopped. "No, I haven't!"

"You should probably do so. I will start with your face and sketching in the general outline, but probably the next time we meet, you could wear whatever it is you would like me to paint."

"Yes, of course," Margaret said, sitting down in the deep red chair.

"Could you sit facing the other way?"

Margaret shifted so her knees pointed to the left.

"Yes, that's right. That's the position you were in last time," James explained with a smile.

He angled his easel a little more sharply, so he could both see her and sketch onto the large canvas at the same time.

"The last time we met, I told you all about my upbringing. Perhaps this time you can tell me about yours," Margaret said. She'd been practicing the line all day and was pleased with how casually it came out.

James, however, frowned. He then gave a little shrug. "My upbringing wasn't very interesting, I can assure you. I was raised in Scotland."

"Really? But then how is it that you don't speak with a Scottish accent?"

"My mother was English and made sure I knew the 'proper' way to speak," he said with a little laugh. "My father, proud Scot that he was, grudgingly agreed that being able to speak like a Sassenach would stand me in good stead through my life."

Lady Margaret laughed. "I've heard the term Sassenach before. It's not a very polite way to refer to the English, though, is it?"

James' cheeks turned slightly pink. "No, it isn't. I do beg your pardon."

She lifted a negligent shoulder. "It's all right. I don't mind. I think you speak very well. You have only the slightest twinge of a Scotts accent. One might even think that you were from Yorkshire or thereabouts."

James tried not to laugh but failed. "You aren't very familiar with accents are you?"

"Oh dear, am I wrong? I have to admit I spent

most of my life in Warwick, which is in the west, closer to Wales. So, no, I'm not very familiar with different accents. But I do know a Scots accent when I hear one, and you most certainly don't have one."

"No. No, I don't," he agreed. "At least not when I'm speaking with you." He gave her a sly grin. "Now, put me in a room filled with Scots, and my brogue will rival the best of 'em," he said in a strong Scottish accent complete with rolling Rs and those fascinating round vowels.

Margaret laughed.

"I have to admit I don't quite understand why you don't have suitors banging down your door. You're a very easy-going, charming woman," James said from behind his easel.

Margaret could feel her happiness seep away as her mind turned to her social life, to the way she was at a party with gentlemen of her own class and status. She gave a little shrug as she turned her gaze downward. "It's easy to be open and honest with you. You make me comfortable so I can carry on a conversation, laugh and joke. But put me at a party filled with gentlemen in their finery, bowing and scraping, or looking me up and down like I'm some prized filly they're considering purchasing, and I...I freeze. I want to run away and hide. I...I know I'll never be good enough, pretty enough, clever enough. My mind stops cold and I don't know what to say. It's horribly embarrassing."

"Lady Margaret, if you'll forgive me, but you are clever and beautiful. I can't imagine why anyone would think anything less of you," he said, coming out from behind the canvas to look directly at her.

She shook her head as an odd mix of heat and

ice ran over the surface of her skin. She so wanted to believe him. But then again, what did he know? He was a footman with no experience with proper society. "It is very sweet of you to say, but—"

"You simply need to prove to yourself—and others—that you are a confident, beautiful woman."

"Like the one you sketched," she whispered, thinking of the drawing he'd made of her. She supposed that was how he saw her. Sadly, she didn't see herself the same way.

"Yes! Just like that," James agreed, ducking behind the easel again.

"I don't know how to do that. How to be that person," Margaret admitted.

He came out again and cocked his head at her. "You said you find it easy to be so with me."

"Yes."

"I believe I'm going to be at the next social event you attend—it's going to be Lady Norman's wedding, isn't it? Or do you have another party between now and then?"

"No. No, I don't," Margaret said, thinking about it.

"Well, then, I've been asked if I would work both the breakfast and the ball. They need all the help they can get. If I'm there, within easy sight of you, would you feel more comfortable? You can pretend you're speaking with me rather than some gentleman who is taking your measure for a saddle."

Margaret burst out laughing at the image he'd created in her mind, but when she thought about it, she wondered if that would actually work. If James's presence *would* make her feel easier. "I don't know. It might. It very well might!"

Chapter Fourteen

"What do you think? Isn't it perfect?" Tina asked, pulling a gown from its paper wrapping and holding it up for Margaret and the duchess to see. It was Margaret's gown for the wedding ball that Tina had designed and had made for her. It only needed the last fitting, which Tina would do herself because she was very particular about the finishing of a dress. The three women were in the duchess's bedchamber making their final preparations for the ball—what they each would wear.

"It is lovely," the duchess said.

"I can't wait to try it on," Margaret agreed.

Their dresses for the wedding itself were already completed. They would all be wearing shades of blue to match Lady Norman's own wedding dress, which was a beautiful deep blue silk and white lace gown, perfect for her age and status.

Margaret's maid stepped forward to assist her mistress in removing her morning gown. Both she and Tina then helped Margaret to slip on the ball gown, without getting pricked by one of the many pins holding the dress together. Once the dress was in place, Tina went to work, making adjustments here and there, repinning pieces, and making sure the dress fit like a glove.

Margaret couldn't help but stare at herself in the cheval mirror. The gown, with all of Tina's tucks and maneuvering as well as the feather-light fabric, clung to Margaret's few curves, accentuating them. If she were built like an ordinary woman, she thought, Tina would have had to make the gown with a heavier material to hide her curves. But no, she was like a bean pole, as her mother had told her on numerous occasions, with almost no bosom and no hips. She was long and lithe, straight and flat. Creating curves where there were none was a special talent of Tina's that Margaret was exceedingly grateful for. It was why she'd engaged Tina as her modiste to begin with after she'd done wonders with the dress for her coming-out ball the previous season. And despite the fact Tina was now her sister-in-law and a duchess, she still relied on her to create dresses that complimented and enhanced her figure.

"You are going to look beautiful," the Duchess of Kendell said with an approval so rare for Margaret, she could feel herself blushing.

"All the gentlemen who see you are going to be begging for your attention," Tina said with a broad smile. "That's the goal anyway."

"And Margaret, you are not going to do anything to discourage them," the duchess informed her.

"Yes, Margaret," Tina echoed.

"I know, I know!" Margaret said, suddenly feeling overwhelmed and angry. "You are always reminding me! Can't you two just leave me alone? Do you not believe me intelligent enough to remember from moment to moment what I'm supposed to do? I *know* I'm supposed to put myself forward. I *know* I'm supposed to smile and be gracious, make interesting, clever conversation, giggle, and smile, and nod. I know *all* of this, I assure you."

Never in her life had she been so bold. Never had she become angry in someone else's presence—at least not the person against whom her anger was directed. She'd railed at Warwick when their mother would criticize her, but never to their mother. She cried to her governess about how stern and demanding her father was, but never to her father. For a moment, Margaret was as shocked as Tina and the duchess at her outburst.

"I...I'm sorry," she stammered. "I didn't mean... I know you mean well."

"No, you are right," Tina said, going back to her pinning of Margaret's gown. "I suppose we *are* constantly harping on you, repeating ourselves too often.

"We just want to help you," the duchess the said with some contrition.

"I know that," Margaret said. "But I assure you, I know what I'm supposed to do."

"We understand that," Tina said.

"And I know what's at stake," Margaret added, catching the duchess's gaze in the mirror.

The woman nodded. "I'm certain that you do."

"But telling me to be bolder, more assertive, doesn't really help," Margaret finished.

"What would help?" Tina asked gently.

Margaret thought about it for a moment, but she didn't need to think long. James came to mind immediately. He had said exactly the right thing.

He'd said that he would be there. That was all. He would be there. Somehow just knowing that made all the difference. He had faith that she would be able to do this. He knew that all she needed was his quiet presence; his gentle, unspoken support.

"Just be there," Margaret said. "You don't need to do anything, or say anything. Have confidence in me and be there." Margaret had no idea why her eyes were burning with tears. She blinked a few times and lowered her gaze. She couldn't look Tina or the duchess in the eye after baring herself to them. "You did that at my coming out ball, Tina. Remember when I came to you panicked because the prince was there?"

"Yes, of course!" Tina responded.

"You were there for me. You calmed me down and then you just stood in the background. I couldn't even see you, but I knew that you were there, supporting me. That's all I needed."

"And you were wonderful with the prince. You completely charmed him," Tina said around a mouthful of pins, putting her hand on Margaret's arm.

"That's all I need," Margaret told her sister-in-law.

There was silence for a moment.

Tina nodded decisively. "I can do that."

"As can I," the duchess echoed.

Margaret took in a deep breath and let it out slowly. Maybe this was going to work out after all.

~April 12~

"The wedding couldn't have been more perfect," Margaret commented to the duchess with a happy sigh as they made their way from the church to

Tina's home for the wedding breakfast.

"It truly was a special ceremony. I especially liked the way the vicar commented on the strength of the bond they've maintained for so many years when they couldn't be together," the duchess said. She, too, looked content.

"Yes! That was wonderful—and so true! It is a testament to their love, to their devotion that they've stayed together and have finally been able to marry. Do you think, though, that Lord Norman and his brother were hurt hearing this about their mother?"

The duchess frowned for a moment as she thought about it. "I don't believe so. Granted, I didn't see their expressions when the vicar was speaking, but they knew their father, and I'm sure they were aware of the difficult relationship he had with Lady Ayres. I can't imagine they would begrudge her the feelings she kept for Lord Ayres."

"No. They are very nice gentlemen," Margaret agreed.

Tina and Warwick had somehow managed to arrive before the rest of the party to their home for the wedding breakfast and were there, ready to greet the guests.

Margaret immediately went to work, however. She wasn't a guest, but one of the hostesses. "Have you checked on everything?" she asked her sister-in-law the moment she walked in the door.

"No, I haven't had a chance. We wanted to be here at the door to greet everyone," Tina said with widening eyes.

"I'll pop down to the kitchen, then," Margaret said, giving Tina's hand a squeeze, trying to tell her that everything would be fine. "You're right. It's much better that you're here."

"Margaret Louise Eleanor Bronley, if you use being a hostess as an excuse to avoid meeting and speaking with the guests I will be—" her brother started, his voice deep and stern.

"Oh, my goodness! You sound just like Father!" Margaret said, cutting him off.

That shocked him into silence. He pursed his lips together.

"Don't worry, brother dearest, I promise I will not hide in the kitchen, if that's what you're worried about. I'll just pop down, check on things and then be back up to greet people and play the good hostess," Margaret said, poking her brother in the ribs. With a laugh at his frown, she headed downstairs.

All of the footmen were standing in a row like soldiers when she stepped off the bottom stair into the hall leading toward the kitchen. The butler seemed to be inspecting them prior to letting them loose to pick up their trays of champagne glasses or heading to whatever task they'd been assigned.

"All in order, Mitchell?" Margaret asked the butler.

He stopped fixing one man's neckcloth and turned to bow to her. "Yes, my lady. Just some last-minute details, that's all."

Margaret nodded and turned to smile at the men. She noticed James standing third in the line but resisted the urge to give him an extra special smile. "You all look very nice. Please do remember that while this is going to be a smaller affair, you should consider it a dry run for the ball tomorrow night. Today we're only having about fifty guests. Tomorrow it's going to be closer the three hundred.

There will be more staff tomorrow, but you are the core, the backbone if you will. You will set an example for all the others who will be coming to help. I have faith that you will all set an excellent example for the temporary workers. Thank you all, in advance, for your hard work. It's going to be a wonderful day for Lord and Lady Ayres. One which they will remember for the rest of their lives." With a nod, she walked down the line and into the kitchen where organized chaos ruled.

There were at least four cooks manning the stoves and ovens. Another six people were at the central table and side counters, preparing platters, arranging food and decorations. Their artistry always amazed Margaret. Today she peered over shoulders as she walked by, giving positive comments as she did so. The head chef heard her and turned around to bow.

"We have everything ready, my lady," he said, looking as calm as if he were preparing a family dinner for three rather than an elaborate banquet for fifty.

"It all looks wonderful, Pierre. Thank you so much for your hard work."

His face relaxed into a smile. "It is absolutely my pleasure, my lady."

"Our guests are arriving. Just as we discussed earlier, we'll sit down in about forty minutes. Everything looks just about ready to go," Margaret commented as she glanced around the busy kitchen.

"Yes, my lady, everything is prepared and will be ready to be sent to the dining room, you should have no worries."

"With you in charge, I most certainly do not. I

just wanted to come and thank you personally."

He bowed and she let him return to work.

The footmen had dispersed when Margaret went through the hallway again on her way back upstairs. They would be handing out glasses of champagne by now and seeing to their guests' comfort. She had worked hard on seeing to the details, and now she had to let it all go and have confidence that everything would be fine. If it wasn't, she or Tina would be there to handle it.

~*~

Jamie watched as Lady Margaret came out of the door to the kitchens. She was so beautiful this morning in her pale blue dress. He did like her in that color—it brought out the blue of her eyes and the gentle flush in her cheeks.

There were quite a number of guests now in their wedding-best. It would probably take nearly a hundred people to actually make a room of this size feel crowded. It was, he thought, a drawing room fit for a duke: crystal chandeliers, gold, silk-covered walls, and art that made his own work look ordinary. He paused to wonder if the portrait he was painting of Lady Margaret would ever adorn these hallowed walls. His wandering mind redirected his gaze to the subject of most of his thoughts recently.

She looked much calmer than he'd expected. He'd taken a look in the kitchen. There'd been about twenty people running around like chickens, the chef had been barking out orders, trays of food were being carried this way and that—in short, it had been chaos. Perhaps it had calmed down since he'd seen it. In any case, James was certain that he had exactly what Lady Margaret needed.

He by-passed two newcomers and approached her with a small bow. "Lady Margaret, would you care for a glass of champagne?"

She'd been surveying the room but now turned and gave Jamie a warm smile. "Thank you, James, that is very considerate of you, but I really need to keep my wits about me today."

"Indeed, my lady, however one glass of champagne won't hurt and may help in calming your nerves so that you can relax, talk to people, and enjoy the party," he suggested gently.

She looked up at him, her eyes seaming to search for something in his own. He gave her an encouraging smile, mentally trying to communicate confidence to her. Finally, she gave a little nod. "Thank you. I suppose one glass couldn't hurt." She reached out and took one from his tray.

He gave her a little nod and then moved on to offer wine to the other guests.

He turned and nearly dropped his tray.

Chapter Fifteen

Standing not ten feet away from Jamie was a fellow he'd gone to university with—Jacob Ayres was an out and out cad. A ladies' man who would boast to anyone and everyone about his conquests. No detail was too small or too private to tell, not to Ayres.

But what terrified Jamie more than anything was being recognized. He was certain Ayres wouldn't be nearly as understanding as Wickford. No, in fact, he was certain the man would have the greatest laugh and be entirely too smug if he found Jamie in his current position. It would take all of Jamie's self-control not to punch the idiot in the face if it came to that, and then his cover would gone as would his position with the duchess. No, he couldn't risk being—

Just then Ayres turned, his gaze flitting past Jamie as he answered the summons of another gentleman. He hadn't even seen Jamie. But of course, Jamie nearly shook his head at his own stupidity. A man like Ayres *wouldn't* see him. He was a footman in livery. He might as well be a chair for all Ayres would notice him. Jamie nearly laughed.

He wondered if he should test out his theory and offer the fellow a glass of wine. No, that would be stupid. There was no need to test fate. On the other hand, the man who'd called Ayres over was now introducing him Lady Margaret. Jamie didn't like that at all.

A cold sensation came over Jamie, as if someone were staring at him. He looked past Ayres and noticed the butler glaring at him from across the room. Jamie had been standing there, not passing out wine as he should have been, and he'd been caught. He swallowed and turned to walk in the other direction searching out people without a glass in their hand or with an empty one that he could exchange for a full one. He'd warn Lady Margaret about Ayres later.

~*~

"Margaret, this is lovely, just lovely!" Lord Ayres said, coming up to her soon after he and his new wife had arrived.

"Thank you, my lord, I'm so happy that you're pleased with it. Wait till you see what we have for lunch," she said, giving him a big smile. "I assume all went well at the church after the ceremony?"

"Oh, yes. Just the last few formalities, you know," he said with a smile.

"It was a beautiful ceremony," Margaret said.

"Was it? You know it was all a blur to me. All I could see was my beautiful wife, hear those incredible words come from her lips, and well…" He laughed.

"I wish you both happy."

"Thank you, thank you. And now we've got to see about getting you into this same delightful position, eh? Ah, there!" He raised his hand and motioned for a gentleman to join them.

The man was the same height as Lord Ayres

and had similar features. It was obvious they were related although clearly not of the same generation since the other man was much younger, most likely closer to Margaret's age than his lordship's. "Lady Margaret allow me to introduce my second cousin, Jacob, the Viscount Ranelagh. Ranelagh, this vision before you is Warwick's sister, Lady Margaret."

Margaret curtsied as Lord Ranelagh bowed. "It's a pleasure," Margaret mumbled, suddenly feeling a little overwhelmed.

No, she couldn't become nervous now. She'd promised herself, Tina, the duchess, and James that she would put herself forward, that she could do this. She was tempted to find James just to have a glance of support from him. She gave a quick scan of the area just to see if he was nearby. She caught sight of his retreating back as he went off to distribute more wine to the guests.

All right. This was going to be up to her. She could do this. She could make polite conversation with this gentleman. She took a deep breath and pulled her lips up into a smile. Now what? Now what did she say?

"Lady Margaret has worked tirelessly with the Duchess of Warwick to put this gathering together for us," Lord Ayres said, giving her a smile.

"Really? That's quite impressive!" Lord Ranelagh said. "I'm sure a party of this size must take a lot of work."

"Oh no," Margaret said. "This is small. Wait till you see the ball tomorrow night," she laughed.

"Ah, yes, I've heard it's going to be the event of the season."

After the required fifteen minutes of small talk, Margaret excused herself to see to other guests. In fact, she'd simply run out of polite things to say.

She was grateful to find Bel Kendrick not far away. She was talking with Mr. Norman, Lady Ayres' younger son. When she caught sight of Margaret, however, she quickly excused herself.

"Margaret, how are you doing? Is everything going smoothly?" Bel asked.

"Yes, thank you. Everything is just fine. How about with you? I saw you were speaking with Mr. Norman just now," Margaret said.

"Attempting to anyway," she said with a giggle. "Some people are just more difficult to speak with. Have you found this to be true as well?"

Margaret laughed. "I think *I'm* one that others have a difficult time speaking with. I just never know what to say to a gentleman."

"Oh, I'm actually quite good at talking about nothing at all. My sister always tells me it's is a particular talent of mine," she said with a laugh.

"I need to learn how, I think. I just get so bored with the ordinary pleasantries," Margaret lamented.

"I didn't say I find such conversations fascinating, but I manage to keep my mind occupied with other things while conversing."

Margaret was intrigued. "Really? How do you do that? Don't you lose track of the conversation?"

"Not really. It's all pretty rote by now. The weather, the latest parties—or for today how wonderful it is that Lady Norman and Lord Ayres are finally married," Bel said.

"And what do you do to keep yourself entertained?" Margaret asked.

Bel gave a little shrug. "I think about what my

sister would say about such dull conversations, try to determine what makes the gentleman I'm speaking with more interesting or special compared with other men I've met. Silly things like that. Or if I've just met him, I try to associate his name with something he's wearing that he'd be likely to have the next time I see him—a pin or a watch—so I'll be able to remember his name again."

"That's *very* clever!"

"I'm just terrible with names," Bel admitted with a little giggle.

"I understand completely! There are so many people to keep track of," Margaret said. She now knew how she was going manage. She could think of other things while making polite conversation. It was such a simple idea and yet so clever.

She gave Bel's hand a squeeze. "Thank you, Bel, that is really the most useful thing anyone has ever told me. I'm definitely going to use this trick of yours."

Bel squeezed Margaret's hand back. "I'm so happy I could help," she laughed.

~April 13~

The following morning Margaret found James and two other footmen polishing silverware in the dining room.

"James, your assistance please," she said from just inside the doorway.

All three men jumped to their feet and bowed.

"Yes, my lady, what can I do for you?" James said, setting down the spoon he'd been wiping.

"Come with me," she said, turning around and walking out the door. She led him into the extra drawing room. His easel and her chair were unmoved from the other day when he'd spent some time working on her portrait.

She went directly to the chair and arranged herself into the same position she'd taken the other day. She then smiled at him. "If you don't mind, I'd like you to continue working on the portrait."

His mouth dropped open a touch. "I... I would love to, my lady, but I've got work I have to do."

"No, you don't. I spoke with Holton, and he's agreed to release you from your duties for the next hour. I'm afraid that was all he would give us."

"That was very good of you but didn't the duchess specifically say I could do this only if it didn't impact on my work?" he argued.

"Yes, but I don't think one hour is going to make a difference." She tilted her head a touch and looked at him. "Do you not want to work on the painting?"

"I would love to but—"

"You have an hour, James. Please don't waste it arguing with me," Margaret said, trying not to sound as if she were begging. She was still feeling awkward about the whole thing. It was she who'd wanted him to work on it. He was keeping to the agreement he'd made with the duchess.

"Very well, my lady. In that case, would you mind a great deal if I took off my coat? I know it's not appropriate, but I don't want to risk getting paint on it."

"Oh, no, I don't mind at all. That's true," she said, thinking about it. "You do usually wear your own clothes when you paint, don't you?"

"Yes. It's safer that way."

"Go right ahead, then." She nodded and then

watched with much more fascination than she should have while he did so. He was still wearing a waistcoat and his neckcloth but seeing him in just his shirt-sleeves was… Well, it made her stomach feel rather odd, actually. She wasn't quite sure why. Perhaps it was the intimacy of it, she thought.

She quickly looked away when he looked up after hanging his coat on the back of a nearby chair. He then went to the table next to his easel and scooped some paints out onto the piece of wood he held in his hand. He spent a moment blending them together to get the right color.

"There wouldn't be a particular reason why you wanted us to work on this today, would there?" he asked without looking up.

"No, of course not." Absolutely there was, and Margaret was well aware of it. She'd debated for nearly half an hour on the stupidity of doing this, then decided she was going to do so anyway. She wanted to speak with him. She wanted to spend time with him.

He made her feel good.

"I find this very relaxing, actually," she admitted out loud.

He gave a little nod, a smile playing on his lips even though he still paid more attention to his paints than to her. "And this evening is going to be very stressful for you."

"It is," she sighed.

"I'll be there, you know," he said, finally looking up.

"Will you? Oh, of course you will. You'll be serving," she said, quickly realizing what he meant. He wasn't going to be a guest. That was silly. He was a footman. He would be working.

"Yes. I'll try to stay in the ballroom if you'd like."

Margaret didn't even need to think twice about that. She nodded. "Just knowing that a friend was nearby would be a great help, actually."

He disappeared behind his easel before she could see his response to her calling him her friend. It wasn't too strange, was it?

Oh, who was she kidding, it was *very* unusual. Sisters of dukes were not "friends" with footmen. It just wasn't done! And yet, here she was depending on him as if he were in fact a friend—just as she'd done her entire childhood with her governess, her maid, and others who worked for her parents. When you don't have actual friends, you find them where you can.

But Margaret did have actual friends now. She should probably be relying on them instead. None of them made her feel as comforted and secure as James did, though.

"There is one word of warning I'd like to drop in your ear if I may be so bold," James said from behind his easel.

Margaret perked up. "What's that?"

"Lord Ranelagh. I've, er... I've heard some rumors about him," he said, showing half his face as he resumed his painting.

"Oh? He's a cousin to Lord Ayres," Margaret said, remembering the very charming gentleman she'd met the day before. "Lord Ayres himself introduced us."

"Yes, I'm aware of who he is. It's just that he's got a bit of a reputation for one with the ladies. He turns them up sweet, talks about her with his friends, and then gives her the cut direct when she no longer amuses him."

"That's horrid!"

James gave a brief jerk of his head to agree. "I would stay away from him if possible."

"I just… I can't believe a gentleman would behave in such a manner. Where did you hear this?"

"Er…overheard some gentlemen talking yesterday at the breakfast," James said.

"They must have been speaking about someone else," Margaret said, shaking her head. "I just can't believe a cousin of Lord Ayres' would do such dreadful things. Lord Ayres is such a kind and thoughtful man, I can't believe his cousin would be so very different."

"Sadly, kindness doesn't always run in families," James said. "Do, please, be wary."

Chapter Sixteen

Jamie was lucky, he'd originally been assigned to work the front door, taking the ladies' shawls and gentlemen's hats, but he'd managed to switch with another fellow who'd been hired just for this party.

The man had laughed when Jamie asked to switch. "Why'd you want to be in that 'ot, stuffy ballroom? Oi'd much rather be by the door," he'd said when James asked.

"I need to keep my eye on a couple of someones," James had replied.

"Oh, yeah?" the man asked, raising his eyebrows.

"Yeah," Jamie said, without elaborating. He slapped the guy on the back. "I appreciate it."

"So is it a fella or a girl yer keepin' yer peepers on?"

"Both. Just need to make sure a fellow keeps his hands where they belong, and a girl doesn't get stupid and disappear into the garden with him."

"Gotcha!" the other footman nodded sagely.

Jamie happily took his tray of champagne into the ballroom. He hadn't yet seen Lady Margaret and the duchess, although he knew they had already arrived. There'd been a dinner before the ball for fifty of the newlywed's closest friends, but Jamie, not being a member of the Warwick staff, hadn't been called upon to work then.

There were only a small handful of people in attendance as yet, which gave Jamie the opportunity to roam about offering champagne—and then he caught sight of Lady Margaret.

She was a vision. Never had he seen her look so beautiful. The dress she was wearing slid sensuously along her slender curves. The material was a creamy diaphanous stuff that floated around a sleek pale-blue silk underdress. He was glad for the overdress because it was the silk gown that clung to her form, making his mouth go dry. Her hair was intricately arranged, so a single coil hung over one shoulder, teasing the swell of her breasts. His fingers itched to touch her skin just along the lace edge of the dress's neckline. He could imagine it was as velvety soft as it looked—

"Young man, are you just going to stand there or are you going to offer me one of those glasses of champagne on your tray?" the sharp voice cut into Jamie's thoughts.

He hadn't even realized that he had stopped, frozen, just out of reach of a lady guest.

"I do beg your pardon, my lady," Jamie said, bowing his head and holding the tray, so she could easily take a glass.

"Harrumph. It is not your place to ogle. You probably shouldn't even be noticing the guests," the woman said sternly.

"No, my lady. Thank you, my lady," Jamie said, nodding to her again and moving on to offer the wine to more guests. He desperately wanted to reach Lady Margaret. It was almost a need; he felt it so strongly.

He mentally shook himself. He should *not* approach her. That would be the height of folly. Why tease himself with something he absolutely could not have. On the other hand, he did so nearly every single day, and even more often now that he was painting her portrait.

He sighed heavily and turned in the other direction. Lady Margaret didn't need him hovering around her. At least at the moment, she seemed to be doing quite well. She was smiling and laughing at something one of the young ladies she was speaking with said, and the duchess was by her side. No, he was not required.

About an hour later, the ballroom was considerably more crowded. Jamie made his way around the perimeter, offering wine and looking for Lady Margaret. He'd lost track of her for a while, and now he wanted to find her again just to make sure she was all right.

Sadly, he found her hovering near the wall, watching but not participating.

"A glass of champagne may help," he said, offering his tray.

She turned suddenly, startled by his voice. "Oh, James!" Her smile gave him a warm feeling, but it was the lowering of her shoulders that really made him feel good. She was relaxing just with his presence.

"Are you all right?" he asked.

"Yes, I'm just taking a little break. It's quite... It can be a little overwhelming, that's all," she said with a little laugh.

"I'm sure it can. But you look absolutely incredible this evening, and I'm certain there are quite a few gentleman here who have felt a little nervous asking you to dance. If you stand back, they may be too scared to approach you," he said with an encouraging smile.

She laughed. "You do say the sweetest things. All right, I'll put myself forward. You'll be nearby?"

"I'll stay right here. I won't move except to go and refill my tray every so often—if I don't, I may get reprimanded." He gave a little shrug.

"All right. But try to come back here so I'll know where to look to find you. Please?" She asked so sweetly, there was no way he could say no.

He nodded. "As you wish, my lady. I will be here."

She took in a deep breath before turning and stepping forward. It wasn't even five minutes before a gentleman approached and started speaking with her. Very soon after that, she was giggling behind her fan and looked to be having a wonderful time. The man held out a hand, which she took, and he led her out onto the floor for the dance that was just forming.

Jamie watched fondly as she smiled and conversed with her partner and the lady next to her. Only then could he return his attention to his own job. He offered wine but made sure not to stray too far.

~*~

Alys had been having a most interesting conversation with Lady Sorrell on the topic of Shakespearean plays and keeping half an eye on Margaret. At first, the girl had retreated toward the wall as she usually did, but since she'd asked her and Tina not to hover, she turned back to her conversation and hoped that Margaret was only taking a short break from socializing. She *did* also note when Margaret passed her on Sir Reggie's arm and took to the dance floor, silently applauding the girl for stepping forward again on her own.

She and Lady Sorrell moved closer to the French doors to catch what little movement of air there was and continued with their conversation. Alys couldn't help but notice, however, that Margaret's eyes were continually turning toward the wall where she'd been standing.

"If you'll excuse me, Your Grace, Lord Sorrell is motioning for me," Lady Sorrell said, breaking off what she'd been saying. It was a good thing, since Alys had completely lost track of the conversation.

"Yes, of course," Alys said. As she watched the lady go, her gaze returned once more to Margaret. She was laughing at something Sir Reggie had said, then turned once again toward the wall. It was the strangest thing.

Miss Kendrick and Lady Blakemore were standing nearby, probably also desperate for some air.

"Then?" Lady Blakemore asked as Alys approached them.

She hated to interrupt, but she needed another's opinion. "Have you noticed that Lady Margaret keeps looking over toward the wall by the door?" Alys asked as she joined them. "Oh, good evening, gentlemen," she added, belatedly noticing Lord Roseberry and Mr. Hershawn.

"I had noticed that, actually," Lady Blakemore said.

They all turned to watch Margaret, who was laughing at something her dancing partner had said. Her eyes, however, once again strayed toward the wall.

"That is very odd," Miss Kendrick said. "Who is standing there? I see Lady Blackglass and Lord Bertram standing in the vicinity. There are two young ladies who look like they're trying to blend into the wall and a footman."

Lord Roseberry and Mr. Hershawn both laughed. "The young ladies do look that way, don't they?" Mr. Hershawn said.

Alys couldn't help but *tsk* her tongue. She was completely at a loss as to what Margaret was up to. "There is no one there for her to be looking at."

"It *is* rather odd," Lady Blakemore agreed.

"Well, if you will excuse us," Lord Roseberry said.

"But you haven't told us what you were doing when you should have been soliciting young ladies' hands for the dance," Miss Kendrick protested.

"Oh, er, speaking with some other ladies," Mr. Hershawn said in an overly nonchalant way that immediately aroused Alys' suspicion. She shared a look with Lady Blakemore, who was clearly thinking the same thing she was.

"Yes. Lady St. Vincent and then Lady Shipton, but neither were interested in, er, dancing," Lord Roseberry said.

Alys gasped, glaring at the men. This was not at all an appropriate conversation for Miss Kendrick to be party to. Luckily the girl had no idea of the reputations of the two women named or what the gentlemen were not so discreetly referring to.

"And what has this reprobate said now to make two beautiful women frown so?" asked a startlingly handsome older gentleman, coming up to join them.

Alys was just as shocked—although happily so—by the new gentleman. She didn't know him. How extremely unusual. It quite made her wonder how it was that she had never met him before. He was dressed in the fashionably, but with a quiet elegance as befitted his age. His dark hair was generously salted with gray, and there were deep smile lines curving toward the edges of his mouth and crinkling from the corners of his eyes. His smile was oddly infectious, and Alys was surprised to find herself quite fascinated by him without even having spoken a word to the man.

"Ah, er, nothing, nothing at all," Mr. Hershawn said. He'd clearly been caught and he knew it. "Ladies, have you had the opportunity to meet my father?"

His *father*? Alys wracked her memory for who Mr. Hershawn's father was and why she couldn't recall ever meeting him.

Before she could come up with anything, Miss Kendrick giggled and said, "La, sir, you never told us your father was in attendance!"

"No, we have not had the pleasure," Alys said, turning toward the gentleman. She was *most* interested in making his acquaintance.

"Her Grace, the Duchess of Kendell, my Lady Blakemore, and Miss Kendrick, may I introduce my father, the Earl of Gorling," Mr. Hershawn said.

Lord Gorling bowed deeply over a delicately extended leg, but Alys was certain he was looking directly at her. Her face heated with his marked attention. "My, my, Henry, you not only keep grand company, but I am also happy to see you've learned something from your old pater and are friends with the most beautiful ladies in attendance."

Alys gave a little laugh. My goodness, but she felt warm. She hadn't felt this way since… Oh my! Not since her dearest Kendell had been alive three years ago.

"But naturally, Father. Would you expect anything less of me?" Mr. Hershawn asked. His eyes were shifting back and forth between his father and Alys.

But Alys was still confused and indecently curious as to how she could never have met this man. She started to reprimand herself for having such thoughts but then realized she was a single woman. There was no reason to feel guilty for being interested in a gentleman. She was certain her beloved husband would not have wanted her to end her days alone. She quickly pulled herself and her thoughts together and asked, "Lord Gorling, how is it that we've not had the pleasure of your company before?"

"Been away, Your Grace, exploring wild, untamed lands," the man said, widening his deep blue eyes.

"Where?" Lady Blakemore asked.

"America, my lady," the gentleman answered, turning away from Alys.

"Oh my, that sounds fascinating," Alys said. It came out much quieter than she had intended.

"I would be more than happy to tell you about it if you would be so kind as to dance the next set with me," he said.

Alys could feel her face heat once again. She unfurled her fan and plied it in a vain attempt to cool herself. She hadn't danced in years. "I would be delighted, my lord."

"Well then, we'll be off," Mr. Hershawn said.

"Enjoy your dance." He and Lord Roseberry turned and strode off toward the refreshment room while Lord Gorling offered his arm to Alys.

She happily took it and allowed him to lead her in the opposite direction.

Chapter Seventeen

"Children are a damned nuisance. Have any?" Lord Gorling asked conversationally as they strolled away.

"No, I never did." It wasn't for lack of trying, certainly, Alys added silently to herself.

"Didn't miss anything, I can assure you."

"How many children do you have?" Alys asked.

"Oh, er, five? Yes, five."

Alys gave a little laugh. "You don't sound very certain of that."

"It's just been a while since I gave any thought to them, you know," he said with a laugh. "Let's see now, there's George, he's the eldest and my heir naturally. Then there were three girls, Mary, Charlotte, and Ann—my wife named them all. And then there was Henry. He was rather an afterthought but good to have. A spare, you know."

"And they are all married, I presume?" Alys asked.

"Oh, yes, yes. There's a bevy of grandchildren running about here and there. Henry's the only one who hasn't gotten caught yet. I don't know if he will ever marry. Doesn't seem to be the sort. It's fine, though. Chatworth—er, that's George—he's got a handful of offspring so all's right and tight with the title."

"You're very lucky," Alys commented. "And Lady Gorling? Is she here tonight?"

"What? Here? No, no. She's passed. Er, six years ago now."

"Oh, I'm so sorry," Alys said, actually not sorry at all, although she did feel a twinge of regret.

"Yes. I made it back for the funeral but left again just afterward. The children had everything well in hand. Didn't need me hanging about mucking things up," he said jovially.

"I'm certain they wouldn't have thought anything of the sort," Alys protested.

Lord Gorling laughed. "You don't know my children. Never happier than when I'm not around. Lady Gorling was the same way, as was I. I'm what I suppose one might call an adventurer. I was never one to be happy staying home and looking after things."

"Ah, like Lord Rivers," Alys said, nodding and understanding immediately.

"Rivers? Don't know him."

"No, I don't suppose you would. He's the father of a friend of mine. He races horses and has traveled around the continent doing so."

"Sounds interesting!"

"Yes, the catch was that he brought his daughter with him and taught her to race as well."

"Don't see a catch there so long as she was amenable," Lord Gorling said, with a broad smile.

"She was. She's an excellent horsewoman and nearly always wins the races in which she rides. It's just that it meant she grew up without a mother.

Lady Rivers stayed home and looked after their estate and younger son."

"I see. Yes, yes. Lady Gorling and I had a similar arrangement except she refused to let me go until Chatworth had settled down. Once she was certain he was well married and ready to produce heirs, she nearly shoved me onto the next ship leaving at the dock." He gave a little laugh, as if remembering the occasion fondly.

"I can't imagine why she would do such a thing," Alys said, surprised.

"I was a bit of a nuisance—or so she said. And to be truthful, I believe she may have been right. I needed to get out, see the world, make a bother of myself elsewhere." He gave her a bright smile.

Alys returned the smile. "And did you do so? Did you make a nuisance of yourself in America?"

"Oh, yes! Not right away, though. I was in India for five years where I was a pest to the leaders of the East India Company. Then I shifted over to America and meddled there. You know, same sorts of things we Brits have been doing for centuries. I imagine it's in our blood."

Alys could only shake her head and laugh.

"Now that's all about me. Tell me about you," Lord Gorling said, giving her hand, which was still resting on the crook of his arm, a pat.

"I have nothing nearly so interesting to tell. I married the Duke of Kendell during my second season, and we lived a pleasant, quiet life for twenty years. He passed three years ago when his heart gave out on him. End of story," she said with a small lift of her shoulders.

"Sounds awfully normal and dull," Lord Gorling said with absolutely no malice at all.

"It was, but it was happy."

"What you need, then, is a little excitement in your life."

"Do I?" she asked with a giggle.

"Absolutely!"

"Are you certain it isn't a little quiet and calm that you need in yours?" Alys asked with a tilt of her head.

He pursed his lips as he considered that. "You know, I don't quite know. I'm absolutely certain it's one or the other, though. Now, I do believe we have talked through the entirety of the last dance and another is now forming. You did promise me a dance, Your Grace."

Alys laughed and nodded her head. "Lead on, my lord. I shall follow—but I warn you, it's been a number of years since I last danced."

"Same here. We'll bumble through together. Shall we?"

~*~

Margaret was couldn't locate her chaperone around the edge of the ballroom. Sir Reggie had escorted her to the edge of the dance floor and seemed to be at a loss as to where to leave her. He couldn't very well just abandon her, but her chaperone was about to dance.

"It's all right, Sir Reggie," Margaret said with a little laugh. "I'll be just fine on my own."

"Oh, no, I wouldn't do that," the man protested.

"You may not have to," Margaret said as she noticed Lord Ranelagh approaching her. She felt a momentary twinge of worry but could feel Sir Reggie was eager to move on, so she shooed him away and welcomed Lord Ranelagh with a welcoming smile.

"My dear Lady Margaret," Lord Ranelagh said after giving Sir Reggie a nod of dismissal. "You look absolutely stunning this evening. That gown—well, I'm certain you've received a great many compliments on it as well as glares of jealousy from the other young ladies present."

She laughed. "No glares, as far as I know, but a few compliments. They all rightfully go to my sister-in-law, however, who designed the dress."

"Your sister-in-law, the duchess?" he asked, as if to make sure he knew who she was referring to.

"Yes. She has an incredible talent for fashion," Margaret said.

"How very lucky you are!"

"I know. And Warwick is incredibly fortunate to have her too because she is also a very sweet, wonderful girl," Margaret said. She did love her sister-in-law. She truly considered herself the lucky one in their relationship.

"Ah, then she is similar to you," he said with a nod and twinkle in his eye. "But surely no one can compare to how lovely you are."

Margaret giggled, her cheeks heating with embarrassment at his compliment. She shook it off and lifted her gaze to his again. "Are you enjoying yourself this evening?"

"Most definitely! It is an excellent affair and a wonderful way to celebrate my cousin's nuptials."

"I'm so glad. Lord and Lady Ayres most definitely deserve to have such a grand celebration after waiting so very long to realize their dream of being together," Margaret said. She just loved the story of how her friends had waited until the time was right and they could be together. It was so romantic.

"Indeed. We all might wish for such devotion and love, but Ayres and his lady are actually living it, aren't they?"

"Yes."

"And what about you, my lady? Have you given your heart to some lucky gentleman?"

"Me? Oh, no!"

"Ah, still looking for just the right man to whom you might entrust that delicate organ of yours?" he asked with a little smile and a glance down at her chest where her heart was beginning to beat a little more rapidly.

"Er, yes, I suppose so."

He waved a hand in front of his face. "My goodness but it's warm in here. Are you warm, my lady?"

"I..." Margaret started. She knew immediately where this was leading—with him escorting her out into the garden, and she knew for a fact she didn't want that. It was precisely what James had warned her about, and she didn't want to get caught in this snare. She looked past Lord Ranelagh for James. He'd been standing against the wall for the longest time...

"I beg your pardon, Lady Margaret?" a different footman, one who she didn't know, approached her from her other side.

"Yes?"

"Please excuse the interruption, but the Duke of Warwick is looking for you. He's just over by the door." The man nodded toward the door where her brother was standing, talking with Tina and Lady Ayres.

"Oh, thank you," Margaret said, trying not to let her relief enter her voice. She turned back to Lord Ranelagh. "I am so sorry, my lord, but you must excuse me." She didn't even wait for him to do so before turning and walking away.

As she made her way through the crowd of people, James joined her. "He's not actually looking for you," he said quietly.

She stopped and turned toward him. "He's not?"

"No. I sent the other footman over to tell you that, so you wouldn't have to try to make up an excuse not to go out into the garden with Lord Ranelagh. Will you forgive me?"

"Of course!" She blinked up at him. "Is there a reason why you didn't come and rescue me yourself?" she asked, tilting her head in curiosity.

"I... Well, to be honest, I didn't trust myself to be polite in his presence. Men who take advantage of others infuriate me," he said. His eyes flashed with a restrained anger that sent chills down Margaret's arms.

"Oh. I see."

"I can't discuss it here or now, you understand. Already, we're getting odd looks just speaking this long. You'll please excuse me and return to your guests?" he asked, bowing.

Margaret wanted to hug him; he was so sweet and thoughtful. She held herself back, however, as well as the broad smile that was trying to form on her lips. Instead, she nodded coolly and continued on toward her brother.

"Lady Margaret," a woman's voice interrupted her progress toward her brother.

"Yes," she turned and found Lady Findlater, the most notorious gossip of the *ton* bearing down on her. "Good evening, my lady. I do hope you are enjoying the evening?"

"I am. Are you?" the woman asked, raising a suspicious eyebrow.

"Why, yes." There was clearly something the lady was eager to get out, and the sooner she did, the sooner Margaret could continue on to her brother. She just prayed it wasn't anything unpleasant, like a piece of gossip she would have to deal with.

"I was wondering because that is the second time I've seen you speaking with that footman," the woman said.

Margaret's heart stuttered. She'd been noticed speaking with James? What in the world was she to do? What could she say? Even more importantly, what would this woman say to others? Margaret channeled her own mother and lifted her chin to look down her nose at this horrid woman. "That footman is a member of the Duchess of Kendell's household and a trusted servant. He is keeping an eye on things for me, ensuring I am appraised of anything that could possibly need my attention. It is simply impossible for the Duchess of Warwick and I to keep an eye on everything. Do you have a problem with the way I am hosting this party?"

"Oh, er, no, my lady. So, he is informing you of things you need to be aware of?" the woman asked.

"Yes. Now if you will excuse me, he just informed me of something which I must discuss with my sister-in-law. Have a pleasant evening,"

Margaret said turning her nose toward the door and moving away, not evening turning to see if the woman had anything else to say.

"Is everything all right?" Tina asked when she joined her and Warwick.

"Aside from Lady Findlater being, well, Lady Findlater, yes, why?"

Tina gave a little laugh at that, but then said, "No reason. I just saw you speaking with a footman, and I wondered if there was anything I needed to be aware of."

Margaret gave a quick shake of her head and determined not to say another word to James for the rest of the evening—it was simply too dangerous. Too many people were noticing. "No. Everything's just fine. I think this is definitely going be the talk of *beau monde* for a few days at least."

Tina laughed. "If not longer."

"Oh, no, I don't think longer. Society's memory isn't that long unless something *really* scandalous happens—and I hope it doesn't."

Tina nodded her agreement but did stand back with Margaret to survey the guests as they talked, danced, and enjoyed themselves.

~*~

Jamie stood back and watched Ranelagh approach some other innocent. Within a few minutes, they were on their way out the French doors and all Jamie could do was stand there clenching his jaw. He didn't know the girl and couldn't risk his old acquaintance recognizing him here in his livery.

He hadn't been lying to Lady Margaret when he'd told her men like Ranelagh infuriated him. That poor girl would find her reputation ruined before long, possibly even tomorrow. Thank goodness, he'd been able to save one person from such a fate. He wished desperately he could save them all, but as a footman... Well, it wasn't forever.

He turned back to find Lady Margaret in the crowd. She'd gone toward her brother, so at least he knew she would be watched well. He didn't know what had happened to the duchess.

This entire evening had been a study in frustration and—dare Jamie admit it—jealousy.

Seeing Lady Margaret laughing, dancing, and gracing other men with her smile and charm hadn't been easy. It was wrong in every way, but he wanted to keep her for himself.

"Is that Ranelagh you're staring at?" a voice said, making Jamie jump. Wickford was standing there, looking in the same direction Jamie had just been looking.

"Yes."

"He was always a horrid excuse for a man," his friend said.

"Yes. Well, he hasn't changed a whit. I had to send another footman over to rescue Lady Margaret from being pulled out into the garden with him."

Wickford nodded. "Didn't want to risk him recognizing you. Smart. Come by the club tomorrow," he said, turning toward Jamie.

"I've got the morning off. Are you free?"

Wickford winced. "Morning, eh?"

"Don't tell me you're like these swells who don't get up until afternoon?" Jamie asked with a laugh.

His friend sighed heavily. "I don't normally get to sleep until morning. But all right, for you, James Douglass, and for no one else will I awake before noon. Come to my private apartments, in that case. They're just above the club. The entrance is on the side of the building."

"Is there something in particular you'd like to discuss?" Jamie asked, curious.

"Yes. I was thinking about your predicament, and I think I might have a solution for you—other than being a footman."

"Oh? Considering how much my feet hurt just now, I might seriously consider anything you propose," Jamie said, shifting his weight from one foot to the other. It was generally better when he balanced on both feet, but then the pain would just move up to his calves. He couldn't win and he couldn't sit down.

Wickford gave a little laugh. "I'm thinking your estate might just be the investment I've been looking for."

Jamie didn't find this amusing at all. "No."

"What? You haven't even heard my proposition," Wickford said.

"And I don't need to. My land is already leased to others—"

"But surely you could get it back," Wickford argued.

"Even if I did, I'm not a farmer. I know nothing of agriculture."

"And you wouldn't learn if you had the opportunity? Oh come, now, even your father made an effort to learn," Wickford said.

Anger was growing in the pit of Jamie's stomach, and this wasn't the time or place to have this conversation. "And he failed. I am an artist, or at least, I want to be an artist. I have no interest in following in my father and grandfather's footsteps. You can keep your money right where it is." He started to turn away to get back to work, but Wickford stepped in front of him, cutting him off.

"Jamie—"

"You need to either yell at me or take a glass of champagne. I'm getting odd looks from the butler. I would go with the former since you're obviously stopping me from doing my job."

CHAPTER EIGHTEEN

"Why can't I commend you for the excellent job you're doing?" Wickford asked. "Honestly, you should come work for me." The last bit he added in a slightly louder voice, so he could be overheard by anyone standing nearby.

James was grateful as the butler chose that moment to approach them. "My lord, is there a problem with this footman?"

"Yes, there is. I want to have a word with his employer, and he is refusing to tell me if he's employed by the Duke or Warwick or someone else," Lord Wickford told the butler.

"I beg your pardon, my lord, but I have no interest in seeking employment elsewhere," Jamie said, working hard to keep his face completely bland as befitted a proper footman. He was pretty sure some of the anger he was feeling at Wickford's ridiculous proposition was evident.

"I told you, I'll double your salary," Wickford argued, giving Jamie a meaningful look as if to say *'I'm offering you a way out of this position. I'm offering you a loan.'*

"I appreciate that, my lord, but I have no interest in taking your—" Jamie started. He had nearly said straight out that he didn't want his money. He didn't want a loan.

"My lord, I do beg your pardon, but this is not the place for such negotiations," the butler said, interrupting. He turned toward Jamie. "You're one of the Duchess of Kendell's people, aren't you?"

"Yes, sir," Jamie said, looking over the man's shoulder, trying his best to calm himself down.

He nodded. "There, you may speak with the duchess at another time. For this evening, however, may I suggest you simply enjoy yourself, my lord?"

Wickford sighed heavily, gave Jamie a disappointed shake of his head, then turned on his heel and walked away without a word.

Jamie sighed in relief but remembered the butler standing by his side. "I'm very sorry about that, sir. I didn't solicit his attention in any way—"

"No, no, I believe you. He's done this before, trying to poach my men. He runs a well-respected gentlemen's club, and he's always on the lookout for staff. From what I hear, it's growing quite popular."

"I have heard of it, sir, but I'm very happily situated where I am," Jamie said. He honestly didn't want to leave his job with the duchess. If he did, he wouldn't be able to see Lady Margaret and that... Well, he didn't like the thought of that at all. Not even to work for a friend. And he most certainly didn't want Wickford's money. He had no interest in becoming indebted to him or anyone. He would rather deal with aching feet.

"I understand, and it speaks very well of you to be so loyal to your current employer. Don't worry about it. If the duchess values you as she should, you will certainly have nothing to worry about."

"Thank you, sir."

The man nodded. "Carry on, then."

~*~

"Have you seen the Duchess?" Margaret asked Lady Ayres a short time later.

"Which duchess?"

"The Duchess of Kendell," Margaret answered with a little laugh.

"Ah, you mean the one who's supposed to be your chaperone?" Lady Ayres replied, also giving a little laugh.

"Yes, that's the one. I haven't seen her for a while, which is unusual. She usually stays nearby."

"Isn't that her dancing with the handsome older gentleman?" Lady Ayres asked, nodding toward the line of dancers.

"What? I'm certain the duchess…" she started to say as she turned toward the dance floor. Margaret's words trailed off as she saw it actually *was* the duchess dancing, and laughing, and looking about five years younger.

"You shouldn't let your mouth hang open like that, Margaret. It's not ladylike at all," Lydia said, joining them.

"But have you seen? The duchess is *dancing*!" Margaret protested.

Lydia turned toward the dance floor. "Well, look at that! Good for her. Who's the gentleman?"

"I don't know," Margaret said. She turned to Lady Ayres. "Do you know him?"

"Yes. We met when he came in. He's Mr. Hershawn's father, Lord Gorling," Lady Ayres said.

"Really? Well, that's very interesting. I assume he's a widower?" Lydia asked.

"Yes, I do believe he is," their friend answered.

"I can't believe it. The duchess has an admirer," Margaret said.

"Well, why shouldn't she? She's a handsome woman, very kind and clearly entertaining," Lady Ayres said as they watched Lord Gorling guffaw loudly after the duchess said something to him.

"But isn't she supposed to be chaperoning Margaret and not off finding a beau of her own?" Lydia asked.

"Oh, that's all right. I can look after myself," Margaret said quickly.

"But are you? Are you meeting gentlemen as you should be? Why aren't you dancing?" Lady Ayres asked, pointedly.

"I had been speaking with Lord Ranelagh but then my brother requested my presence for a moment, so..." She looked at her friends, who were looking back at her skeptically. She sighed. "Very well, I will dance the next dance, I promise!"

Lydia laughed. "Excellent, there's Lord Conway." She gave a little flutter of her fan in the gentleman's direction. He changed the direction in which he'd been heading and joined them.

"Good evening, ladies," he said with a little bow.

"My lord, absolutely horrendous news!" Lydia said dramatically.

He widened his eyes. "My goodness, I am so sorry to hear this! What is it, my lady? Can I be of any assistance?"

"As a matter of fact, you can," Lydia said.

Lady Ayres took up the thread. "Lady Margaret's chaperone is off enjoying herself, but she hasn't been asked for the next dance," she said woefully.

"We don't want to ruin the duchess's evening by having poor Lady Margaret standing by the wall all by herself," Lydia said with equal misery.

The gentleman's eyes turned toward Margaret, who could feel her face heat under his scrutiny.

"I can't believe the gentlemen of the *ton* could be so remiss! My lady, you must allow me to remedy this situation immediately." His warm smile soothed Margaret's embarrassment.

"You are too good, my lord," Margaret whispered.

"Not at all, my lady. It will be my pleasure, I assure you. But you must promise to tell me all about whoever it is the duchess is spending her time with rather than being by your side," he said with a little wiggle of his eyebrows.

She couldn't help but giggle. "I wish I could, but I know nothing of Lord Gorling. Do you?"

He shook his head. "Never heard of him before in my life."

"Well, then, we are all at a loss over this gentleman's history," Lady Ayres said.

"I'm sure we'll find out soon enough," Lydia said. "And if we don't, I think I might be able to do some reconnaissance."

"Yes, you do have incredible talents in that direction," Margaret agreed with a little laugh. Margaret looked forward to finding out more about this man and was certain Lydia was exactly the person to discover it.

~April 14~

"My God, Rossburke, it's nine o'clock in the

morning," Wickford said, dropping down onto the fashionable but masculine-looking sofa in his drawing room and rubbing a hand over his stubbly face. "How could you do this to me? I thought we were *friends*!"

The room was very comfortable in deep tones of maroon and beige. It was evident that Jamie's friend was doing very well for himself with his club. He could not only afford the latest style of furniture, but he had some very nice paintings on his walls too, including some that looked to be of his home in Jamaica.

"You told me to come 'round in the morning. It's morning," Jamie said with a laugh.

Wickford looked like he'd just rolled out of bed. Jamie supposed he should be grateful his friend had put on a banyan.

"Yes, but I didn't think you'd show up *this* early! Honestly, it is inhuman."

His manservant came into the room, bearing a tray with a coffee service on it.

"Oh, thank God," Wickford sighed. He sat up and waited impatiently for the man to pour out a cup of the rich, bitter liquid.

"Oh, is your name God?" Jamie asked the manservant with a smirk.

The fellow started, nearly missing the cup he was pouring into. He worked really hard to keep a straight face. "It is Henley, my lord."

"Ah! There you are Wickford. I know it's early, but you should say 'thank Henley,' or more properly, 'thank *you*, Henley.'"

"You're very amusing," Wickford said, not even cracking a smile. "I'd forgotten what a comedian you are."

Jamie laughed. He held up his hand as Henley tried to pass him the cup he'd just poured. "No, no, you'd better give that to your employer."

"Yes, give it to me. Rossburke and I don't stand on ceremony, and I need it a great deal more than he does," Wickford said, holding out his hand for the cup.

Within moments, he was sighing happily. Jamie accepted his cup soon enough. "Thank you, Henley."

"You are most welcome, my lord," Henley said with a bow before leaving them.

"Now, do be quiet for a few minutes while I imbibe. You may talk to me while I have my second cup," Wickford informed him. He sat quietly taking deep breaths with his cup under his nose as if merely the aroma of the coffee would help wake him.

James laughed but valued their friendship enough that he kept quiet until Wickford had finished both smelling and drinking the ambrosia that was a good cup of coffee.

"All right, now," Wickford said, after taking a sip of his second cup.

"Feeling more the thing?" Jamie asked with a smirk.

"Beginning to. You didn't get into trouble last night, did you?"

"No, thanks to your quick thinking. Apparently, you're well known for trying to poach other people's footmen?" Jamie asked.

"Yes. Well, it's hard to find good men. I go after them when I find them. And it is true, by the way, should you ever wish to work for me—"

"Thank you, no. I like where I am very much. If I have to work, it's going to be for the duchess," Jamie said quickly. "And please, whatever you do, do not bring up that crazy idea of lending me money. It's not going to happen—ever—is that understood?"

"My God, Jamie, you'd think I was offering... I don't know what!" Wickford complained.

"Well, you don't need to. I am an artist, Joshua. That's what I want to be. That's what I'm *trying* to be. I have absolutely no interest in investing either your money or my time in a failing estate. All right?"

"Well, if you're going to address me by my given name... I suppose you're serious about this," Wickford said before taking another sip of his coffee. "So...you like your current position. Or is it just that you like being wherever Lady Margaret is?" Wickford asked, looking at Jamie over the rim of his coffee cup.

Jamie didn't answer but just took another sip of his own coffee.

"Ha! You can't possibly imagine I wouldn't notice." He paused and then added, "You *are* going to tell me about her, you know, so hiding behind your cup isn't going to do anything."

"Why do I need to tell you about her? You know perfectly well who she is," Jamie said as innocently as he could.

Wickford frowned at him. "That's not what I meant and you know it."

Jamie sat back in his chair. He both hated and loved the fact that Wickford knew him so very well. And he should have known his good friend had noticed everything that had happened last night—

and possibly the significance of what *hadn't* happened. Most likely he had already formed firm opinions of his own but wanted Jamie's confirmation of what he'd already figured out. Was there any point in denying anything? Jamie didn't know, but since he hadn't fully figured everything out himself, he supposed he should start there.

"Just stop it," Wickford said, interrupting his musings.

Jamie looked up. "Stop what?"

"Trying to decide how much you're going to tell me. You used to try to do that all the time when we were at school, and you always ended up telling me everything, so just cut to the chase, will you?"

"My word, but you have a good memory!" Jamie complained.

"Like an elephant, now spill."

Jamie could only laugh. Yes, there was no point in trying to keep anything back from Wickford. How silly of him to even think of doing so. "Very well. Lady Margaret is... Well, I don't need to tell you that she's sweet, and gentle, and beautiful. Anyone can see that."

"Indeed," Wickford said with a slight nod. "It is telling that *you've* noticed."

"Her brother commissioned me to do a portrait of her, did I tell you that?"

Wickford nodded. "I think you'd just gotten it when we last spoke."

"Right. Yes, so we're, er, spending a good amount of time together," Jamie said with a shrug.

"Alone," Wickford supplied.

"Yes, but I assure you it's all very proper. I'm painting, and she's, well, she's talking. She had a horrendous childhood. Terrible parents."

"Just about all noble parents are horrible. I think the higher the rank, the worse they are. I learned that at school," Wickford said.

"Yes, but hers were truly awful. It's why she's so shy and has trouble putting herself forward. I'm trying to help her," Jamie said with a shrug.

Wickford looked at Jamie skeptically. "You're trying to help the sister of a duke put herself forward in order to find a husband."

"Yes."

"When it is practically clear as day that you, yourself, would like to become said husband?"

"What?" Jamie jumped from his chair and started to pace the room. Jamie felt as if he'd been shot with one of those arrows Wickford had excelled at firing off with great accuracy in archery class.

"Thank you for confirming my idea," Wickford said with a laugh.

Jamie stopped pacing and ran a hand through his hand. "I don't know that I want to *marry* her."

"Oh? You'd rather have some sort of illicit affair, then—with the sister of a duke?"

"No! Don't be daft!"

"Then? You aren't going to tell me that you're 'just friends' because I wouldn't believe that for a second."

"She thinks we are," Jamie said, pausing to stare out the window.

"What she thinks isn't the point here. What do *you* think?"

"I'm trying not to," Jamie admitted.

"Wise man," Wickford nodded.

"I just… Hell, I don't know what to think." Jamie dropped back down onto the chair he'd been sitting on.

"Well, let's examine the situation, shall we?" Wickford said in the same way he used when he helped Jamie with his mathematics homework.

"I don't think there's much to examine. I'm a footman. She's the sister of a duke who has to marry by the end of the season. By that time, I will either still be a footman, I will have become an artist—if I can get more actual commissions for my work—or I will have given up on all this and gone back to Scotland, which is probably what I *should* do."

"If you were intelligent? Probably. However, let's work with what we've got," Wickford said, nodding.

Jamie frowned at his friend.

Wickford laughed. "Sorry, I didn't mean to imply you were stupid. But let's do be practical about this because…well…"

"There's no point in *not* being practical," Jamie supplied for him.

"Yes, precisely."

"All right. In all practicality and honesty, I don't stand a chance with Lady Margaret, and I should just forget she exists and go on with my life."

"That's one way to look at it."

"Is there another?" Jamie asked, with a lift of his eyebrows. He poured himself a second cup of coffee, more for something to do than because he actually wanted one.

"Yes. You're here. You're living in the same

house as her and, for God's sake, painting her portrait. There's no way you can just ignore her."

Jamie nodded miserably.

"That being the case, I say you should have fun."

He looked up at Wickford. "Fun?"

"Yes. While it's true you don't stand a chance with the girl in your present circumstance, there's no reason why you can't enjoy being with her—discreetly, of course."

Jamie jumped to his feet again. "Just what the hell are you suggesting?"

"Oh, get off your high horse, Jamie. I mean you should dance with her. Talk with her. Enjoy her company. Nothing more, I assure you."

Jamie sat back down. "What are you getting at?"

Wickford sat up, smiling at Jamie. "What I'm getting at is that in approximately five minutes I'm going to get up and get dressed. Once I am properly attired, we, my friend, are going to my tailor's where we're going to get you a costume for my Venetian Ball, which you are going attend."

"Now who's being daft? May I remind you that I'm a footman?"

"Rossburke, would you please listen to me? I said *Venetian Ball*—it's a masquerade."

"Oh! As in everyone comes masked and in costume," Jamie said, beginning to understand where his friend was going with this.

"Precisely," Wickford smiled.

"I can go—assuming I can get the night off—dance and talk with Margaret and she'll never know it's me," Jamie said, thinking this through.

"At least you'll have the one night with her," Wickford said quietly.

"It will last me a lifetime."

Chapter Nineteen

As Wickford predicted, half an hour later they were on their way to Saville Row to get a costume for Jamie.

"Do you have a decent pair of breeches? A coat?" Wickford asked as they climbed into his carriage.

"No. I, er, I don't," Jamie was embarrassed to admit. What he didn't say was that his nicest clothes had been sold to pay for food before he'd come up with the idea to become a footman.

"Right, then. That's first. Secondly, you'll need some sort of costume," Wickford said.

"I'm thinking something simple. Perhaps just a cape and a mask. I don't want to be too memorable to Lady Margaret."

Wickford nodded. "Yes, good thought. Very well, a cape it will be."

After being a footman for the past four months, Jamie had to remember how to be a nobleman. It felt odd at first, but then it was as if he'd never been anything else—like putting on an old, comfortable pair of boots.

"Meyers, my good friend Rossburke, here, needs a new suit of clothing—breeches, coat, waistcoat—" he turned and looked at Jamie, "a shirt or two?"

"Er, no, just the suit and a cape for the masquerade," Jamie said, mentally wondering how in the hell he was going to pay for this. Ah! The portrait. He'd just have to finish Lady Margaret's portrait, then he'd be flush in the pocket.

"Right," Wickford said, rubbing his hands together. "Show us what you've got and the latest styles. My friend must be dressed at the height of fashion. Nothing showy, but nothing dull either."

"Quietly elegant," Jamie put in, as he went over to a table displaying a number of fabrics.

"Of course, my lord, of course," Mr. Meyers said, hopping right to work. He pulled out some fashion plates as Jamie and Wickford chose fabrics.

"Black," Jamie said, pulling forward a nice piece of wool.

"Green," Wickford contradicted him.

"Black," Jamie said again. "I don't want to stand out—and it would be nice if I could wear it again."

"What's wrong with green? Your eyes are green."

"Yes, and your eyes are gold. I don't see you wearing that color."

Wickford nodded. "Touché. On the other hand, with your blond hair and fair coloring, wouldn't black stand out even more?"

Jamie thought about it for a moment but then shook his head. "Enough men wear black that I'll blend into the crowd."

Wickford just shrugged, clearly aware he wasn't going to win this one.

They spent some time looking over designs and arguing over silly details like button size, and whether his waistcoat should be embroidered with gold or silver. Jamie, of course, wanted neither but Wickford insisted. It was a ball, after all. Jamie conceded that point and quickly decided he had damned well better get another commission quickly or else he'd have no money whatsoever after paying for his finery.

It was nearly time for him to be back at work just as they completed the finishing touches.

"And what name shall I put this under, my lord?" Mr. Meyers asked, looking at Jamie.

"James, Marquess of Rossburke," Wickford said before Jamie could say a word.

It was odd, but hearing the name and title together still brought his father to mind. Jamie had been a child when his father had died, but he still missed him. He shook his head to dispel his morose thoughts. "I'll pick it up myself," Jamie told the tailor.

"But have the bill sent round to me," Wickford added.

"What? No!" Jamie objected immediately. He pulled his friend aside out of the hearing of the proprietor.

"It's not a problem," Wickford said lowering the volume of his voice.

"Yes, it damn-well is. *My* clothes, *my* bill. *I* will pay for them" Jamie whispered furiously.

"But this was my idea and you—"

"Can pay for my own clothes, thank you." Jamie would not accept charity. Not in the form of a loan for his estate or as clothing. Just because he was having a difficult time of it at the moment... No! He had the money—or would as soon as he'd finished Lady Margaret's portrait—and he would use it for this one night with the lady. It would be worth every penny.

Jamie moved back to the proprietor. "Prepare the bill and hold on to it. I will pay it when I pick up the clothes."

Mr. Meyers raised his eyebrows. A proper gentleman never paid his bills right away, and Jamie knew it, he just didn't care. He wouldn't be indebted to anyone. "Very good, my lord. I will see you next week, in that case."

Jamie nodded to the man and then led the way out of the shop.

~*~

It had been a wonderful evening, celebrating the success of the wedding ball. Having the Duke and Duchess of Warwick and Lord and Lady Ayres over for dinner had been an inspired idea of Margaret's. After seeing their guests off, Alys went up the stairs with Margaret following behind her. She stopped at the door to her room with one hand on the knob.

"Margaret, who were you looking at during the ball?" Alys had a feeling she knew the answer, but she had to ask. She'd been going over it again and again in her mind, picturing the room and who was where.

"I beg your pardon?" Margaret asked, stopping on her way to her own room.

"During your dance with Sir Reggie and then again a number of times afterward, you kept looking toward one spot in the ballroom." With a sigh, she added more softly, "It was that footman, wasn't it? What's his name?"

"James," Margaret answered quietly.

"Yes. He was the only one in that area who didn't change. At various times there were other young ladies trying to escape notice, but it was James who was always there."

Margaret had the grace to blanch slightly. "Yes. He—"

Alys held up her hand for the girl to stop talking. "It's all right. I understand, at least I think I do."

"No, Your Grace. I mean, we're friends, that's all."

"Well, I should *hope* there's nothing more than that," Alys said. "It's more than enough that you should befriend a footman."

The girl clasped her hands in front of her body. "I was always friends with the staff at my parent's home. Sometimes... Sometimes they were my only friends. I hope you don't mind."

Alys wasn't in any position to mind, but Margaret didn't know that. "No, I do not mind. Just...please be discreet. You are not to give him any special treatment nor allow him to take advantage of your friendship, do you understand?"

"Yes, Your Grace. I'm sure he wouldn't—" she started, but Alys held up her hand to stop her.

"Hopefully, no one else noticed who you were looking at." She remembered herself remarking on Margaret's gaze toward the footman to Lady Blakemore and added, "Luckily, most people don't even see footmen."

"It is sad, but true," Margaret agreed.

Alys nodded. "Just please be more careful in the future." With that she went into her own room, taking her worries with her.

~April 15~

The following afternoon was the Ladies' Wagering Whist Society meeting. Alys was, along with all of the other ladies, quite relieved a solution to Lady Blakemore's problem with her nieces would soon be resolved. After they learned her niece Beatrice was actually supposed to be visiting Lady Sorrell's sister, it was a simple matter of Lady Sorrell "disappearing" for a few days and then "reappearing" with Miss Beatrice for all to see.

Alys did wish the discussion hadn't been carried out by the ladies calling across the room to each other in a very un-genteel manner. At least Lord Ayres' card room was a good deal smaller than Lord Norman's had been, so the tables were actually much closer together.

They had completed their game and were just preparing to leave when Mrs. Aldridge came over, her nasty little dog in her arms. "You seemed to have had a very enjoyable evening the other night at Lady Ayres' wedding ball," she said suggestively.

Alys straightened her back and looked down her nose at the animal in the woman's arms. "Yes, I did. Did you not?"

"Oh, yes, I did, most definitely. But I was rather surprised to see you dancing. I don't believe I've ever seen you dance before."

"I admit, it's been quite a long time since anyone has asked me," Alys said, softening her stance a little.

"Who was that clever gentleman who asked you?" Lady Ayres asked, joining them.

Alys gave her a little smile. "Lord Gorling. He is Mr. Hershawn's father, just returned from five years in America and an equivalent amount of time in India."

"My goodness, he's been away for the past ten years? No wonder no one knows him," Lady Colburne said.

"Indeed," Alys agreed. "I must have met him some time, but I certainly didn't remember him. Do you Lady Blakemore?"

"I'm sorry?" the lady asked, turning around. She had been speaking with Lady Sorrell, perhaps finalizing their plans for bringing Miss Beatrice into London.

"Do you remember Lord Gorling?" Alys repeated.

"Lord Gorling? Oh, you mean Mr. Hershawn's father who we met at the ball." The lady frowned as she thought for a moment. "I do remember him, now that you mention it, from a very long time ago. Perhaps when I was first brought out?"

"He's recently returned to England," Mrs. Aldridge supplied. "And he was dancing last night with the duchess," she added unnecessarily.

"Yes, I was there when he asked her," Lady Blakemore said, giving Alys a happy smile.

"It's of no consequence, I can assure you," Alys said. She most certainly did not want her own private affairs to be discussed among the ladies. It was bad enough to admit to them that she needed help with Margaret, but for her own life to be talked about was simply too embarrassing. "Lady Margaret did very well at the ball. She was quite out-going for such a quiet girl," she said, deftly changing the topic.

"She was. I noticed that," Lady Welles said, joining in the conversation.

"This is a very good sign. I do hope she continues to do so well. Did she have any callers yesterday?" Lady Blakemore asked.

"We were not 'at-home,' but she did receive a few bouquets of flowers which were very lovely." She deliberately didn't mention the token she herself received from Lord Gorling.

"That's excellent. I'm sure she'll find herself a husband by the end of the season at this rate," Lady Ayres said. She was always the optimist.

"Well, she must, so yes, I certainly hope so," Alys agreed.

"And perhaps you will too," Mrs. Aldridge added with a teasing little laugh that seemed to crawl under the duchess's skin.

~April 16~

Margaret was certain she would be waiting at least ten minutes for James when she went into the small drawing room for their painting session on Thursday.

"Oh!" She stopped just inside the door. James was already there, working away.

He looked up and smiled at her. "You're early. I thought I'd get a bit of a head start before you came in, but I'm very pleased to see you."

Margaret laughed and started toward him. "I didn't realize you'd be here so early," she admitted.

He held up a hand to stop her forward progress. "So, you thought you'd just sneak a peek at what I've got so far, did you?" His voice was teasing even as he accused her.

"Oh, no, I would never!" she said, putting a hand to her chest in mock surprise. She hadn't planned on doing that, but it wasn't such a bad idea. It was a shame she couldn't do so now.

"Uh-huh." He looked at her sideways as he turned back to his painting. "You may sit right down, my lady, in your chair."

Margaret laughed but did as she was told. "You're no fun, you do know that."

"Yes, as a matter of fact, I've been told as much on numerous occasions," he said.

She just laughed and shook her head.

They were quiet for a little bit as he worked, but Margaret couldn't help but speak what was at the forefront of her mind. "How is it that even though we're in the same house, I feel as if I haven't seen you in days?"

"I blend into the background," he answered with a little smile playing his lips. He continued to focus on the painting. "You're not meant to see me. I'm a footman."

"But I *do* see you," Margaret protested.

"Oh, well, then perhaps you just haven't been in the same place as I have. It is a rather large house," he said, looking up briefly.

"Yes, perhaps. I think the last time I saw you was on Tuesday at dinner," she said thinking about it. It was only two days ago, and yet it felt like a lifetime.

James nodded. "I served for the Duke and Duchess of Warwick."

"Yes. I noticed that you were very good at keeping my brother's wine glass full."

James gave a shrug. "It's my job."

"You do it well," Margaret commented. She didn't say how good it had felt knowing he was in the room during that dinner. How his presence gave her confidence and made her, well, feel good. She still couldn't quite figure out why that was, but she guessed it was because he was a friend, and she hadn't had very many of those in her life.

"Thank you. I do take pride in my work," he said in an off-handed way. He seemed to be concentrating rather hard on his painting. He stopped, stood back, and examined it for a moment. He then shook his head and pulled out a rag and began rubbing at the painting.

Chapter Twenty

"Did you make a mistake?" Margaret asked as she tried to peer around the large canvas where James was working. It shook as he dabbed at it with his cloth.

"I'm not happy with your face," he answered her distractedly.

She just laughed. "I'm not always very happy with it either, but I don't think there's a lot I can do about it."

He burst out laughing, finally looking up. "That's not what I meant. You have a very beautiful face. I didn't represent it here as well as I would like to."

"I knew what you meant. I'm just teasing you." She giggled.

"Yes! It's that expression that I wish to capture," he said, staring at her for a moment before ducking back behind his canvas.

Margaret tilted her head a little. "What expression is that?"

He looked back up at her. "Joy. Happiness. Confidence."

"Oh." She could feel her face heat. She was quiet for a moment, not saying that all those emotions were entirely because of him. Instead, she said, "Speaking of confidence, I wanted to thank you for being there for me at Lady Ayres' ball the other night."

He gave a little shrug. "I didn't do anything. I was just passing out champagne and lemonade."

"You know very well you were doing a lot more than that. You were helping me. You gave me the courage I needed to put myself forward. I appreciate that."

He shook his head. "It was you. I tell you, I was just standing there."

"And you saved me from Lord Ranelagh," she added.

"That I *did* do," he admitted giving her a smile. He lost it again too quickly. "It infuriates me when men like him try to take advantage of women."

"And I hate being taken advantage of, but there didn't seem to be a polite way of saying no."

"You could have simply said no," he suggested gently.

"I... I not always comfortable doing so," Margaret admitted. It was too awkward. Too uncomfortable to outright tell a gentleman you're not interested in doing what he wants. "And he was very insistent," she added.

"That I can believe. He's quite charming and persuasive."

"Yes, he is."

"And he has absolutely no honorable intentions whatsoever," James added with a frown.

"Well, I appreciate that you gave me a way out of such an awful situation," she said, so wanting to see his smile again. His eyes lit up when he smiled at her. It made her feel good.

"I wish you could be there at every party I go to," Margaret said a little wistfully. "It would make them so much easier."

He did smile at that. "Sadly, I cannot."

"Why not?"

He looked up. "What parties are you going to next?"

Margaret thought about for a moment. "I've got Lady Farham's soirée on Tuesday and then Lord Wickford's Venetian ball on Saturday. Perhaps you can work at the ball?"

He seemed to freeze for a moment, just staring at her. He shook his head. "No, I'm sorry. I don't know Lady Farham and people rarely hire extra help for a soiree, and I'm not able to work on Saturday."

"Why not?"

He opened and closed his mouth. "I, er, actually, I was going to ask to have that evening off. I need to visit a friend of mine…who's sick. Yes, he's not doing well at all. I told him I'd try to come and spend some time with him next Saturday. Since you and the duchess will be at the ball that evening, I was hoping to get the night off to see my friend."

"Oh, I'm so sorry," Margaret said, feeling bad that James would have to wait over a week to see his friend. "Hopefully he'll be better by then."

"Yes, hopefully, but, er, unlikely. He's got, um, he's got tuberculosis," James said, keeping his eyes on his canvas.

"Oh dear! I am so sorry to hear that." Poor James! Margaret's heart went out to him. "I'll make sure you get the evening off in that case. Is it very bad? He will still… I mean he won't have…" She didn't know how to say this gently.

"Died?" James supplied.

"Yes."

"No. I mean, I shouldn't think so. I don't think it's that advanced. I, er, I won't know for certain until I see him, of course."

"Yes, of course. Well, you *shall* see him, and I'll manage."

"You'll do very well. You know how to put yourself forward, Lady Margaret, you just need to put yourself into the right frame of mind to do so," James said with gentle encouragement.

"I suppose." The right frame of mind. She thought about that and wondered if it was possible to talk herself out of being so shy. She would have to try it when she went to Lady Farham's soirée.

~*~

Jamie got a good amount of work done on the portrait that afternoon and, as Lady Margaret had said before she left, it *had* been very nice to spend time together again. He was a complete idiot for feeling anything for her—but he did, and he was going to enjoy what time they had together while he could.

But in order to spend a real evening together at Wickford's ball, he needed the money this portrait would get him. If it wasn't for that, he would drag the painting of this portrait out for as long as he possibly could just to have the excuse to be alone with Lady Margaret.

Lying in bed, as he was, wasn't going to get that portrait finished, however. He was exhausted from working all day, but he just didn't have the time to sleep. He pulled himself up, threw on his breeches, and took his bed candle downstairs.

The house was silent as he snuck down the corridor where the duchess and Lady Margaret's bedrooms were. It was the middle of the night; no one was going to object to him using the main stair.

He lit another candelabra in the small drawing room and put it on the table he was using to hold his materials. It was just enough light to see by. It was going to be a bit tricky mixing colors in this light, but he had a good idea what he needed. If the colors were a little off, it would be all right. He simply needed to get more of the background finished. Lady Margaret, herself, was all but done.

He stopped to look critically at his work. He was finally satisfied with her expression. Her eyes weren't quite as bright as they were in real life, but he'd done his best. It was hard to capture the liveliness in her eyes when she smiled and laughed.

James caught himself just staring into the painted Margaret's eyes. He needed to get to work and so he did.

Only when he could no longer keep his eyes open did he finally give up and stop for the night. He would be back at it the following day, if he had any time, and most certainly the following night. If he could, he wanted to have this finished by Tuesday when he would have the morning off to deliver it to the duke.

~April 18~

Alys scolded herself. She was behaving like a silly, young girl. She was a grown woman, for goodness sake! A widow! She was forty-five years old and giggling like she was twenty-five. She gave herself a good shake, mentally.

"What's so amusing, Your Grace?" Margaret

asked from the sofa behind where Alys was sitting at her escritoire.

"Oh, nothing," Alys said quickly. "We've been invited to go out driving this afternoon with Mr. Hershawn and his father, Lord Gorling. I thought I would accept for both of us."

"With Mr. Hershawn?" Margaret said curiously. Alys turned around to see Margaret's gaze float up the ceiling as she considered the gentleman.

"He's a younger son but well connected," Alys said. She couldn't lie to her protégé just because she wanted to see the gentleman's father.

"Yes," Margaret said, considering. "And he *is* quite pleasant."

"I should expect he's one of the gentlemen you would be more comfortable with, seeing as how you've known him since your debut last year."

Margaret nodded. "Yes, you're right. I am quite comfortable with him, and he's a very nice man." She gave a little giggle. "I don't know that I've ever seen him not in Lord Roseberry's company. This will be a new experience for me."

Alys smiled. It was strangely true that the two men were constantly together. She supposed they were simply close friends. "So, I'll respond to this saying that we'd be delighted?" she confirmed.

"Yes, of course. Thank you."

Alys gave a nod and dashed off the note. She rang for the footman to take the note 'round to Lord Gorling's home.

~*~

The ladies were called for at precisely three o'clock that afternoon. Alys happened to be watching out the window when Lord Gorling and Mr. Hershawn pulled up to the house in a smart barouche pulled by a pair of matching grays.

"Oh, Mr. Hershawn, how lovely," Margaret said as they came out of the house. She was attired in a pretty pale pink carriage dress with a fetching hat and two bobbing feathers.

"Thank you, my lady. I have to admit, the equipage is my father's," Mr. Hershawn said as he handed her up into the carriage.

"Just purchased it," Lord Gorling said as he took Alys's hand in preparation to hand her into the vehicle after Margaret.

"Really? Well, it is very handsome," Alys said, quite impressed.

"Been away so long, I needed a new carriage. The pair came with, happily," the gentleman said, following her up and sitting next to her on the facing seat. The younger couple sat across from them.

"Is that common?" Margaret asked. "For the horses to come with a carriage?"

"Oh, er, well, no, but I knew a fellow who needed the blunt and was happy to sell them to me at a good price," Lord Gorling said.

His son looked at him skeptically. "That wasn't Egerton was it?"

"As a matter of fact, it was, why?" his father asked.

Mr. Hershawn just shook his head. "Wondered why he was looking so glum last night at Powell's."

"Ah, yes, well, he had an off night. I was happy to help him out, however," Lord Gorling said. He then turned to Alys and said, "This is horrendously boring for you, isn't it? We shan't say another word on the subject, I promise."

Alys laughed. "No, no, it's fine. I know how you gentlemen love to talk about your carriages and horses and what-not."

"I don't usually, but this was a special situation," Lord Gorling said.

They pulled into the line of carriages, making their way around the park.

"Now, let's see who we've got here today," his lordship said with a gleam in his eye and a mischievous smile.

Chapter Twenty-One

Alys could only laugh at Lord Gorling's enthusiasm. She then remembered something, so she turned to him. "How would you know who is who? I thought you'd just returned from America, my lord?"

He looked shocked for a moment and then burst out laughing, throwing his head back. When he could finally speak, he said, "Yes, yes, you are quite astute, Your Grace, absolutely. I don't know hardly anyone, *but*... I have met quite a number of people in these past few weeks and have already insinuated myself into society well enough that I am quite interested in seeing who is with whom. You see, madam, gossip, I have found, is the greatest way to not only understand a society, but also to discover who truly holds the power."

"Really?" Alys was thoroughly intrigued.

"Yes, of course. For instance, while a duke may own a great deal of land and have a lot of money, he may not be a very strong voice in Parliament. On the other hand, Lady Sorrell, not even a patroness of the famed Almack's or a holder of, well, any position at all, nonetheless has a great deal of power in Parliament. Purely by the fact that her husband *does* have a very strong voice and quite likely the ear of the Prime Minister. Therefore, I would sooner become fast friends with Lady Sorrell than, say, the Duke of Warwick." He turned to Margaret and added, "My apologies, my lady, I do not mean to disparage your brother, but you do understand my point, I'm sure."

Margaret laughed. "No offense taken. I know for a fact that my brother has no political aspirations or interest, and I also know that Lord Sorrell does. Happily, both the duchess and I are close with both my brother *and* Lady Sorrell."

"Ahhh, see, you are good people to know," Lord Gorling said, putting a finger to the side of his nose.

Mr. Hershawn laughed. "They are good people to know, Father, but I enjoy doing so not only for their excellent connections but for their wit and charm as well."

"And beauty, my boy, do not forget their beauty," Lord Gorling added with a nod of agreement.

"Yes, I do beg your pardon, and beauty," Mr. Hershawn added, looking at Margaret.

"There are a great deal more beautiful people all around us," Margaret said, coloring slightly.

"Oh, look, there's Lord and Lady Colburne," Alys said, spying her friends.

"Now see there, I don't know these people, please tell me about them," Lord Gorling said even as Alys waved.

"Lord Colburne is an excellent person to know," Margaret offered. "He is one of the finest physicians in London."

"He quite cured Lady Colburne's father after he had an apoplexy or some such thing while riding in a horse race," Alys added.

"Really? That *is* a good man to know," Lord Gorling said as the Colburnes pulled their horses to a stop next to the barouche.

"Lord Colburne, you are looking magnificent on your new horse," Margaret said.

"Why, thank you, Lady Margaret. I'm beginning to feel a little more confident riding her. How are you all doing today?" Lord Colburne said, smiling around to everyone.

"Very well, my lord," Alys answered. "Have you met Lord Gorling?"

"No," Lord Colburne said immediately before Alys could make the introductions. "Colburne. Pleased to meet you."

"A pleasure," Lord Gorling said, nodding to him.

"And this is my lovely wife," Lord Colburne said, indicating Lady Colburne.

Lord Gorling nodded to her as well. "My lady."

"You are not on your thoroughbred today, Lady Colburne," Mr. Hershawn commented.

The lady laughed. "No. She intimidated my husband's new mount too much. The poor thing shies away when Nike is near and is difficult to manage." She turned to Lord Gorling and explained, "Lord Colburne hasn't ridden since he was a child."

"Ah, but once you learn, I imagine you learn for life, no? You did not forget how to ride, did you my lord?" Lord Gorling asked.

"No, I'm just not very comfortable with horses. My wife, however, is an amateur racer so she insists I ride every so often."

"Really? How fascinating!" his lordship said,

turning to look at the lady a little more closely.

"We should move on," Lord Colburne said, noticing that they were causing some difficulties for others who were trying to get around them.

"Lovely to see you again," Margaret called out with a wave.

"I'll see you on Wednesday," Lady Colburne said to Alys with a little laugh.

As they rode away, Lord Gorling turned to her and asked, "Wednesday?"

"The duchess and Lady Colburne are both members of a very elite group of women called the Ladies' Wagering Whist Society," Margaret said with a broad smile. "They gather every Wednesday to play whist and decide on some lucky person's marital fate."

Alys burst out laughing. "That's putting it a little strongly." She turned to her very interested companion. "We have helped a few young people to marry, that's all."

"Including Lord and Lady Colburne and my brother and Tina," Margaret added.

"They also raise funds for the poor of the Rookeries with a highly regarded whist party every year," Mr. Hershawn added. "You will want an invitation to that, I assure you."

"Yes, it sounds as if I will! Thank you," Lord Gorling said. He then turned and smiled at Alys in a way that made her heart flutter a little. "Do you think...?"

"Of course, I'll add you to our invitation list, my lord," Alys said, giggling. My word, she did feel just like a silly girl. How ridiculous and absolutely the most fun she'd had in a very long time!

~April 21~

Jamie was exhausted. All he wanted to do was sleep. He'd been up every night—sometimes just about the entire night—finishing this painting.

But as the morning sunlight began to creep into the drawing room from behind the curtains, he stood back and examined the finished portrait. He couldn't tell if it was any good or not. At this point, he could barely keep his eyelids open to look at it. He needed sleep. He wondered if Holton would fire him if he showed up at his post a little late.

He stumbled up the stairs to his room for a quick nap.

He woke up to the sound of the clocks chiming. He stopped to listen and then bolted from his bed when he counted past nine. He was going to be fired. He was certain of it. He was about to lose his job.

He'd never dressed so fast.

He was downstairs in ten minutes flat. Holton himself was on the front door, an occasion so rare that he was certain he was in deep trouble.

"Mr. Holton, I'm so sorry. I overslept. Please, accept my most sincere apologies. It won't ever—"

"Mr. Douglass, what are you going on about? It's Tuesday, your morning off," Mr. Holton said, frowning at Jamie.

"Tuesday?" Jamie said stupidly. He blinked and then finally breathed. "It's Tuesday. I... I'd lost track of the days. Thank you, sir. Thank you." Jamie gave him a quick bow and then ran back up to his room to change out of his livery.

If it was Tuesday and his painting was finished, that meant he had to get it over the Duke of Warwick as quickly as he could. My God, where did the days go? Jamie could only shake his head.

It didn't take him long to change. He grabbed the painting off the easel, not even taking another look at. He just covered it with its cloth and went out to hail a hackney.

"Your Grace, Mr. Douglass, the artist, is here to see you," the footman announced after knocking briefly on the duke's study door. He stood back to let Jamie enter the room.

"Thank you," Jamie said, giving the man a nod. He paused just inside the room and bowed to the duke, who was sitting behind his enormous desk. "Good morning, Your Grace."

"Good morning," the man said. A little smile lit his eyes. "You seem to have something for me. That was very fast." He stood and came forward. Rubbing his hands together a little, he said, "Let's have a look."

Jamie nodded and propped the painting up on the mantel piece, leaning it up against the painting that was already hung there. He pulled away the cloth with a touch of dramatic flair.

"Oooh," the duke whispered. It was almost a sigh. He took a step back for a better view of the whole piece.

Jamie joined him, finally looking at it in its entirety. It wasn't half-bad, he thought.

"That's magnificent," the duke's secretary said, coming forward.

"It is quite good," the duke agreed.

"He captured her expression..."

"It's a look I always longed to see on my sister's face," His Grace said a little wistfully.

"Confidence," the secretary agreed.

"She looks remarkably like my mother, only without the arrogance," the duke commented.

"Much more beautiful, if you ask me," the secretary said boldly.

"Yes, yes, I believe you're right. She is prettier," His Grace agreed. He turned to Jamie and put out his hand. "Excellent work, Mr. Douglass. I am very happy with it."

Jamie shook the offered hand. "Thank you, Your Grace. I'm... Well, I have to admit, I'm relieved you're happy. I am pleased with the way it turned out."

"You should be. You've created an excellent likeness and given her a look and demeanor of confidence that we all want to see in Margaret. You've highlighted her beauty and given me something I can proudly display and will enjoy admiring for years to come," the duke said, looking back at the painting.

The clock on the mantel next to the painting struck noon.

"Thank you, Your Grace. If it would be all right, I'll come by tomorrow for my payment?"

"Of course! Martin will have it ready for you," His Grace said, giving a nod to his secretary. "Oh, has Margaret seen it?"

"No. No, she hasn't. I only finished it in the wee hours this morning and then hurried it over before I needed to get to work, which I must do just now. I do beg your pardon," Jamie said, bowing to the men.

"Ah, then I'll have the pleasure of showing it to her later. Very good. We'll see you tomorrow, then." The duke very kindly walked Jamie to the door and saw him out.

As Jamie walked back to the duchess's house, he felt as if he'd forgotten something. His hands were empty and it felt as if there was a growing pit at the bottom of his stomach. He had no reason to be alone with Lady Margaret any more. It felt like a first step away from her.

At that thought, his stomach positively cramped, and he had to stop walking for a moment. It almost made him sick to think of a life without her.

He shook his head. What fancies he had! Ridiculous, really. She was just a girl. And besides, he would spend the entire evening with her on Saturday. She wouldn't know it was him, of course, but still, he would know. And he would have the memory of the night to keep him warm on his cold and lonely Scottish nights.

Chapter Twenty-Two

*S*he *could do this. She could do this.*

Maybe if Margaret said this enough times to herself, it would come true. Surely, she *could* do this. She had been able to put herself forward when James was doing nothing more than standing by the wall, surely she could do so again without him.

"Lady Farham, how lovely to see you, thank you so much for inviting us this evening," the duchess said, greeting their hostess.

"Of course, Your Grace. Thank you for coming. Lady Margaret, I do hope you will have fun tonight," Lady Farham said, giving Margaret a calculated smile. It was because Miss Farham was also trying to find a husband, Margaret knew, but it still unnerved her.

She pulled up a smile. "Thank you so much, my lady. I will do my best."

They moved on, entering the Farham's drawing room where some space had been made for a few couples to dance. Everyone else crammed together around the edges of the room.

"Have no fear, Your Grace, I won't let the lady or her daughter push me back this evening," Margaret said, as she noticed the worried look on the duchess's face.

"I'm certain you won't," the duchess said. She gave Margaret's arm a little squeeze. "You will do very well tonight."

"Thank you for your confidence."

"Oh, look, there's Lord Gorling and Mr. Hershawn," the lady said, brightening immediately.

Margaret could only laugh. She'd had the hardest time not allowing her jaw to drop every time the duchess had giggled when they'd been out driving with the two gentlemen the other day. Never had she seen the esteemed lady behave so, well, like she'd dropped ten years or more from her life.

"Margaret, how wonderful to see you," Diana said, catching hold of Margaret's attention before they reached the men the duchess was making a straight line toward.

The duchess stopped too, looking a little dismayed at the interruption.

"You go on ahead, Your Grace," Margaret said quickly. "I'll join you shortly."

Margaret was a little surprised that the lady gave a nod and then went off without her. Rarely had she left Margaret on her own—except when Lord Gorling was around.

"You have *got* to tell me who this gentleman is the duchess was with the other day in the park," Diana said in hurried whisper.

Margaret could only laugh. "It's the same one she's on her way to greet right now," Margaret said, nodding toward the man her chaperone was heading toward.

Diana's mouth dropped open for a second.

"Who is he?"

"He's Mr. Hershawn's father. He's just come back from five years in America," Margaret said. "And he has the duchess eating out of the palm of his hand."

The man was greeting the duchess warmly even as they watched the encounter from across the room.

"Or is it the other way around?" Diana asked.

Margaret laughed. "I don't know, but it certainly is amusing to watch. I swear, I'd never heard the lady giggle, but she could hardly stop every time Lord Gorling said anything on our drive."

"Giggle?" Diana said incredulously. "She was *giggling*?"

Margaret could only laugh and nod her head, which made Diana burst out laughing as well.

"Well, I can't wait to see where this goes!" Diana finally getting a hold of herself.

"I know!"

"Oh, here's Lord Bertram," Diana said, turning and noticing the gentleman coming toward them. "Good evening, my lord."

"Good evening, ladies," his lordship said, bowing to them. "Lady Margaret, might I have the honor of the next dance?"

"Is Lady Blackwell here this evening, my lord?" Diana asked.

His smile slipped a little as he answered, "No, I'm afraid she's not."

"I shall be honored to take her place," Margaret said, forcing her back straight. She wanted more than anything to hunch her shoulders forward and slip away toward the wall, but she'd promised herself, the duchess, and James she would put herself forward this evening, and that meant accepting every invitation to dance.

"I would never presume to ask you to take her place, my lady. It will be my very great pleasure to spend time with you," he said politely.

It made it a bit easier knowing the gentleman didn't actually have any intentions toward her, so Margaret smiled and accepted his hand when he offered to lead her out on to the floor.

Margaret was surprised when she couldn't find the duchess after her dance. She thanked Lord Bertram and went off with a confidence she didn't feel in the direction she'd seen the duchess last.

She eyed the wall where a few other young ladies were standing—or hiding. It would be so easy to join them, but in her mind's eye, she could see James standing by the wall in Tina's ballroom. The look on his face stopped her. He expected better of her. *She* expected better of her.

She paused and looked around the room. Mr. Hershawn and Lord Roseberry weren't far. They were talking with each other without any women nearby.

Taking in a deep breath and plastering a smile onto her lips, she walked straight over to them. "Gentlemen, what's this? I can hardly believe you aren't charming some young lady with your wit. Is everything all right?"

The men jumped guiltily.

"Lady Margaret, you are just the person..." Mr. Hershawn started.

"The *only* person," Lord Roseberry added.

Margaret tilted her head curiously. "You weren't speaking of your father and the duchess, were you?" she asked slyly.

Both men smiled. "Yes!" they said in unison.

"While I haven't seen my father in a good long time, I have to say I don't believe I've ever seen him so thoroughly…" Mr. Hershawn floundered for a word.

"Enthralled?" Lord Roseberry suggest.

"Enamored?" Margaret offered.

"Yes to both!" the gentleman said with a laugh.

"Mr. Hershawn, *she giggled*," Margaret said, with a giggle of her own.

"Wait, the duchess? The Duchess of Kendell *giggled*?" Lord Roseberry asked. He turned to his friend. "You didn't mention that."

"It was quite…"

"Incredible!" Margaret supplied for him.

Mr. Hershawn threw his hands up in the air. "I'm at a loss for words this evening!"

Margaret laughed. "It's completely understandable, sir. You are experiencing something quite remarkable, I'm certain."

"You would not believe! My father… He *doesn't* behave this way. At least, I've never seen him do so."

"Ah, and there is the couple in question," Lord Roseberry said, looking toward the door.

"Oh, quick, Lord Roseberry, ask me to dance," Margaret said, as the duchess began looking around the room for her.

The gentleman obediently bowed and offered her his hand.

Margaret curtsied and allowed him to lead her onto the floor. "I do apologize. That was exceedingly rude and bold of me," she admitted as they began to turn about.

"It wasn't precisely rude but most definitely bold. I have to say, I kind of liked it," he said with a little laugh. "Now, mind you, if it had been anyone else, I would have been offended beyond anything, but coming from you, my lady, it was charming."

Margaret felt her cheeks heat slightly and was grateful the dance took them apart for a minute. By the time they came back together again, she had thought of how to change the subject. Not only that, but she managed to hold a completely innocuous conversation throughout nearly the entire dance. It was almost...comfortable.

~April 22~

The following afternoon Jamie headed back to the home of the Duke of Warwick. The gentleman himself was not at home, but his secretary, Martin, had a purse with his payment all ready for him.

Jamie hadn't had this much money in hand for a very long while. He thanked the man and headed out to Bond Street to pick up his clothes.

"Ah, my lord! How very precise you are," Mr. Meyer, the tailor, said with some surprise. It was so strange to go from his employer's home where he was a footman to the Duke of Warwick's where he was an artist, only slightly higher in status, to the tailor's where he was a marquess to be fawned over. It was enough to put a man's neck out of joint, Jamie thought with a laugh.

Instead, he lifted an eyebrow at the tailor. "Do gentlemen not come when they say they will?"

"Not usually, my lord, sadly, not usually.

However, I have your order all ready for you. If you would just come this way, so you may try it on." He led the way to the back where there was a large dressing room.

The clothes fit better than anything Jamie had ever owned. "I am impressed, Mr. Meyer," he said, admiring himself in the mirror. His fair complexion and blond hair provided an interesting contrast to the black suit, but he rather thought he like it.

"Fits like a glove," the man said with satisfaction.

"Indeed. And the costume?" Jamie asked.

"Ah, yes!" The man gave a clap of his hands and his assistant came forward with Jamie's cape draped across his arms. Mr. Meyer picked it up with a flourish and put it around Jamie's shoulders.

It was perfect. All black with just a small white lace embellishment along the edges. The tailor showed him how to pin it back so that it wouldn't get in his way as he danced. He then produced a stark-white full Venetian mask with black lips and eye holes rimmed in black that dripped down the cheeks. A black tricorn specially made with a cloth that draped down the sides and connected to the cape completed the costume.

Jamie tried it all on to make sure he would be able to breath and see properly. The affect was incredible.

"Stunning, my lord," the proprietor said.

Jamie turned his head this way and that to both look at himself and make sure he could see. It was a little restricting but not too bad. "At least I can breathe. Not well, but it's possible."

"Do we need to make the holes a little larger?" the man asked, coming forward.

"No, I believe it's all right."

"Ah, and I have the gloves Lord Wickford ordered for you here as well." The man produced a pair of soft, black kid gloves.

Jamie took them and put them on with a little laugh. "I was sure we would forget something."

"Yes, luckily, his lordship remembered and came back," Mr. Meyer said.

With his full costume on, not one inch of Jamie's skin could be seen. No one, not even his own mother, would recognize him.

He gave a nod of approval. "Excellent. Excellent work, Mr. Meyer." He pulled off the mask and hat, feeling the cool air with relief. It would be trying, wearing this costume all night at a stifling hot party, but it would be worth it. Lady Margaret was definitely worth it.

"How much do I owe you?"

"Let me just see to having this all wrapped up for you, my lord," the man said, busily helping Jamie remove clothing and handing items off to his assistant.

After Jamie had resumed his own slightly shabby clothes, the man *tsked* at the ill-fitting coat.

"I've, er, lost a little weight since I had this made," Jamie said a little self-consciously.

"I understand, my lord."

The tailor led the way to the other side of the shop where he presented the bill. Jamie had to bite the inside of his cheek not to gasp at the price. Needless to say, his purse would be returning with him much, much lighter.

The assistant came forward with the clothes all neatly folded on a large piece of brown paper.

"Ah, yes, and as a small token of our appreciation for your business, my lord, we've added a few handkerchiefs," Mr. Meyer said with an embarrassed little laugh.

Jamie picked up one of the white squares sitting on top of the pile of his clothes. It was fine linen and had the initials JR prettily embroidered in black on the corner. He laughed at the mistake. If they had asked, he would have told them that he'd always fashioned his initials as JD with the R for Rossburke overlaid on top. It didn't matter. He tossed it back onto the pile.

Chapter Twenty-Three

~April 24~

Margaret was sitting in the duchess's private drawing room reading. James knocked and came into the room, carrying a brown paper package.

"This just arrived for you, my lady," he said.

Margaret jumped up and nearly clapped she was so excited. "Oh! That's my costume for the Venetian ball."

James's face broke into a bright smile. "That is exciting." He handed over the package.

Margaret took it, pulling off the string holding the paper together. A pale pink velvet gown spilled out, followed by her mask and a matching pink tricorn. She couldn't help but laugh as she held up the dress. It was absolutely covered in white lace. There were rows of it going down the skirt and a wide boarder of lace at the neck and drooping from the three-quarter length sleeves.

"That is certainly..." James paused. "Lacy," he finished with a laugh.

"It is," Margaret said, turning a bright smile on to him. "And so *pink*!"

"Indeed. Very pink."

She set it aside and picked up the full-face mask. It was a beautiful creamy face with pouting red lips and pink swirls decorating the cheeks and around the eyes. Margaret held it up to her face and peered through the eye holes. She started when she felt hands tug at the pink ribbons. James pulled them around to the back of her head and tied it for her so she wouldn't have to hold the mask to her face.

"What do you think?" she asked, turning around to face him.

He tilted his head one way and then the other. "I'm afraid I like your real face better. This is interesting and certainly quite mysterious, but you are much more beautiful."

Margaret's breath caught her throat. That was the sweetest thing anyone had ever said to her. She turned her face away automatically when she felt it heat with embarrassment, then realized he couldn't see her burning cheeks. She gave a little laugh. "Well, I'm sure it's very different."

"That it is," he agreed.

"I'm quite excited to be going to the party, I just hope..." She paused as she untied the mask and placed it back in the paper packaging with her hat.

"You hope what?" James prompted.

She turned to face him. "I hope I don't ruin the evening by hovering against a wall. I mean, I'll try my best not to but..." She shrugged. "Sometimes it's just easier, safer. It's a shame you won't be there."

"But there's no need for you to stay by the wall or be shy at all." His eyes crinkled a little and glittered as he smiled at her. "This is a masquerade, Lady Margaret. No one is going to know who's who. No one is going to know you are you, so you can be anyone you want to be."

Margaret thought about that for a second, her gaze straying around the room as she considered his words. "Oh, my goodness! You're right!" She thought about it a moment longer and then added, "My brother and Tina will know. Tina designed my gown, and the duchess will know, she'll be my chaperone, but…"

"No one else will," he finished for her.

"No, they won't."

"You can do whatever you like, and no one will think any less or more of you for it."

Margaret suddenly realized her mouth was hanging open, and she snapped it closed and smiled. "Yes, I can. I can dance and talk with anyone, and no one will know it's me."

"No one but those who love you most," he said with a slight grin.

Margaret jumped forward and put her arms around James and gave him a squeeze. "Thank you! Oh, my word, thank you so much, James!" She stepped back again and was shocked to see his face had turned bright red. He was pink all the way from his narrow cheeks to the tips of his ears, the bright color standing out against his deep green eyes.

He coughed and cleared his throat awkwardly. "I, er, I should get back to work. No one, um, I don't think anyone is watching the door."

He left the room so quickly Margaret was giggling. Or maybe it was the knowledge that he was right, and she had absolutely nothing to worry about at the Venetian ball. It was such a feeling! Freedom with a touch of terror mixed in with her excitement.

She could do *anything*.

~April 25~

The duchess looked stunning. She was in a deep red gown with her hair powdered white. Her half-mask was the same red as her dress and rimmed in white lace. Red feathers bobbed above her white head, and she toyed with a matching red and white lace fan.

"I'd never imagined you in bright red before," Margaret admitted with a little giggle. "It is a brilliant color for you."

The lady laughed. "Especially with the white hair and bright red lips, I imagine."

"Indeed. You are a study in contrasts."

"Well, you look stunning as well, my dear. I do like you in pink," the duchess said.

Margaret laughed. "But you can't even see me!"

"I see you very well. I don't see your face, but that's the point of a masquerade, isn't it? Is it very hot in that mask?" she asked as they walked out the door and were handed into the carriage by the footman, Michael.

His presence—and the missing James— reminded Margaret that she'd never even said a word to James about his friend, who he was going to be visiting this evening. She felt terrible for not having sent her good wishes for a quick recovery or, at the very least, as pleasant a visit as possible. Poor thing! He was going to be having a difficult evening while she was going out to enjoy herself.

"What? Oh, it's a little uncomfortable, but I imagine I'll soon get used to it," Margaret said, recalling the question the duchess had asked her. She didn't want to sober her chaperone by reminding her of James's difficult evening, so she said nothing but determined to speak with him the following day.

As soon as they entered the magnificent ballroom rented by Lord Wickford for the occasion, they spotted Tina, who was easy to pick out from the crowd with her pure white gown and white and silver mask. Warwick, Margaret was not at all surprised to see, was dressed all in brown, his favorite color. His mask was simply gold-colored which emphasized the gold thread that ran through both his coat and waistcoat. The couple were inverses of each other —Tina so bright in silver and white, Warwick dark and sparkling gold.

Margaret and the duchess joined them. "You both look amazing," Margaret said.

"As do you!" her brother said, turning to take her in.

"That dress is as beautiful as I imagined," Tina said. Margaret could hear the smile in her voice even though she couldn't see her face.

"It's a little frillier than I usually wear," Margaret admitted.

"But that's the whole point, to wear something that won't mark you immediately, right? You want people to guess at your identity," Tina said with a laugh.

"I do beg your pardon," a gentleman said as he joined them. He was slightly rotund in an odd patchwork suit and a black half-mask. He held out his hand to the duchess as he said, "May I enquire whether you would be amenable for a promenade?"

Margaret was a little surprised to see her chaperone giggle and place her hand around the gentleman's arm. She clearly knew the man, and Margaret had a good suspicion it was Lord Gorling. He was the only person who could make the otherwise straight-laced duchess giggle in that way. "I would be delighted, sir." She briefly turned toward Margaret. "Do be good! I trust your brother to look after you." Then she simply waltzed away.

Margaret turned toward Warwick and Tina. "I imagine that was Lord Gorling, but—"

"I can't believe she just left you in our care," her brother said, clearly shocked even though Margaret couldn't see his expression.

"Well, it *is* a masquerade. I suppose rules are a little looser here," Tina said, still watching the duchess walk away.

"Yes." Warwick didn't sound very happy about it. They were all distracted by the arrival of more friends.

Two ladies approached. One was all in white, with layers of lace and gold edging matching her white and gold mask. The ensemble was topped with a white hat of tulle and lace. The other lady was all in purple and gold.

"Your Grace, you look so very elegant," the lady in white said, curtsying to Warwick, Tina, and Margaret.

"Thank you, as do you, Miss..." he said, fishing for her name.

"Ah-ah," she laughed. "I'm not going to give my identity away so easily."

He sighed but Margaret was certain he had a huge grin on his face. "Well, I know you are in some way associated with the Ladies' Wagering Whist Society." He turned to the lady in purple. "You must be Lady Blakemore."

The lady laughed. "Well done, Your Grace."

"So that means you are Miss Kendrick," he

deduced.

"Perhaps," she said with a giggle. "It's definitely going to be a challenging evening not being able to call each other by name."

"Indeed. But it's still lovely to see you this evening. And that dress looks as beautiful as I thought it would," Tina said.

"And it is thanks to you," Bel said, reaching out to squeeze Tina's hand.

"So, *you* know who's who because you made so many of their dresses," Warwick said.

Margaret could only laugh at how annoyed he sounded. Her brother did not like being out of control and not knowing anyone definitely fell into that category.

"I *designed* most of their dressed," Tina said. "Thank goodness, I didn't have to make them all. I would never have finished in time!"

"Good evening," a man in a green and blue costume said, joining them.

"Lord—" Bel began.

"Ah, ah," the gentleman said, wagging a finger. "No names this evening, but yes, it is I." He made a grand leg.

Margaret and Bel both laughed at how silly he looked doing so in his costume of alternating colors. One arm and its opposite leg were blue, the other arm and opposite leg were green, and his full mask was both colors as well. It was almost dizzying.

"This is going to be deuced confusing!" Warwick complained.

"It is Lord Conway, Your Grace," Bel whispered loudly to him.

"Thank you," he whispered back.

"Oh, now, that's not quite fair, is it?" Lord Conway complained with a laugh to his voice.

"Well, you know who he is, so I thought it would be all right," Bel said.

"All right, yes, I do," Lord Conway laughed.

A gentleman in a long green velvet cloak joined them. His mask was all swirls of gold and green, and his head was covered by his hood so his hair couldn't be seen. Margaret had no idea who he was, but clearly Bel knew—and she wasn't saying.

"Good evening, my lord," Bel said with a giggle. "You look wonderful."

"And you look quite stunning," he said with a bow. "Are you the one I'm looking for?" he asked oddly.

"No, you want the other side of the room," Bel answered. Margaret had no idea what they were talking about, but she was already having so much fun she didn't care. She did love this idea of being nearly anonymous.

"Naturally. Well, then, if you'll excuse me." The gentleman bowed to everyone and then sauntered off.

"What was that about?" Margaret asked, watching him go.

"Oh, nothing. He was looking for someone, and I told him where to find them, that's all," Bel said.

"But who was that?" Tina asked.

"I really can't say," Bel answered with a giggle. Margaret laughed too; she just couldn't help it. It was so silly not to be able to identify people who she was certain she knew.

A woman nearby gave a loud laugh and then a

little screech followed by more laughter.

"I have a feeling there's going to be quite a bit of that going on as well," Lady Blakemore said.

"What is that?" Margaret asked.

"Behavior just on the edge of propriety," her brother explained.

"Or fallen off the edge," Lady Blakemore added.

"Oh, dear." Tina turned to look in the direction of the laughter.

"Gentlemen, I suggest you keep a close eye on those you care about. This is a masquerade. People feel a great deal more emboldened when no one can see your face," Lady Blakemore said.

They all turned toward the dance floor as the orchestra began warming up. Margaret wondered if she would even have the opportunity to behave as boldly as she'd hoped.

A gentleman approached them as she was looking rather longingly at the couples who were assembling for the dance. He was dressed similarly to the gentleman who'd just left them, but his cloak was black and pinned back on one side revealing a very fine black suit. He looked incredibly elegant with no gold or silver, just a thin band of lace along the edges of his cloak and at his wrists and neck. His mask was white with black dripping eyes and black lips.

"I beg your pardon, my lady, may I have the honor of this dance?" the gentleman asked, coming forward and holding out his hand to Margaret.

"Oh! Er, may I, W... er, brother?" Margaret said with a giggle of relief. She was thrilled she wouldn't be sitting out the dance after all and titillated because she had no idea who the gentleman was.

"I suppose so, although I have to say it is very disconcerting not to know who it is you will be dancing with," the duke said with a smile for the gentleman. He looked as if he was waiting for the man to reveal his identity, but the gentleman simply bowed and held out his hand to Margaret.

She laughed again as she took it and allowed him to lead her out and join the dance.

Chapter Twenty-Four

"You seem to be enjoying yourself a great deal, my lady," the gentleman said. His voice was deep and rich with just the slightest hint of a Scottish brogue. It somehow reminded Margaret of someone, but she couldn't think of who. The fact that she didn't know any Scottish gentlemen made her even more uncertain of the gentleman's identity.

"I am. It's so unusual not to know who anyone is. It's a great deal more fun than I had even imagined," she said.

He laughed, but the movement of the dance took him away from her for a few minutes. When they came back together, she said, "Why do I have the feeling that you know who I am while I'm completely at a loss as to your identity."

He simply inclined his head and moved away from her again.

"That was not an answer, sir," Margaret said with a laugh when he took her hand for a round about.

"No, it wasn't, was it?"

Margaret laughed. "Well, then, I'm simply going to have to try to guess at your identity. I know that you can't be Lord Rosebury or Mr. Hershawn," she said, hazarding a guess.

"Why not?" He would have said more, but the dance parted them once again.

She was caught off guard by that. *Was* he one of them? But she didn't think either had had a Scottish accent—no, she was certain they didn't.

"Because neither one has a Scottish accent, while you do," she said, as they came together again. "I don't know any gentlemen from Scotland, and you are clearly from that part of the world."

He paused for a moment. "Am I? Goodness, is my accent coming through? I hadn't realized." His words took on even more of a brogue, and Margaret couldn't help but laugh.

"Are you going to go completely Scots, then?" she asked, giggling.

"Och, I might be. Who's to know?" he said, making his accent stronger still.

Margaret burst out laughing. "No, no, if you do so I can't be certain I'll understand you."

Even the gentleman had to laugh at that one. "Aye, it's true. A Scottish accent can be nearly impenetrable to a gently bred English lady such as you."

"So, you will keep it to a minimum, then?" she asked sweetly.

He paused and looked deeply into her eyes for the briefest moment. It was enough to send heat rushing through her. "I promise, I'll be sure you can understand every word I say."

"But you won't share your name?" she asked. Oddly, her voice came out a great deal softer than she had intended.

"No. My apologies, my lady, but that I cannot

do. But you don't know if the accent I have tonight is the one I usually speak with." On that beguiling note, he turned away from her with the movement of the dance, leaving Margaret completely frustrated. That meant perhaps he *could* be either Lord Roseberry or Mr. Hershawn and was just putting on the accent. It also meant he could be absolutely anyone! She shook her head at the overwhelming thought.

"Do you mean you might be putting on an accent that isn't actually yours?" she asked when he returned to her side.

"I might. Or I might be very careful with my speak at all other times, and this is my true accent." He gave a little shrug of his broad shoulders. "You never know, do you?"

"How horrendously frustrating you are!" she said with a laugh, feeling both a little annoyed and having the most fun she'd had in a very long time. "Well, then, what shall I call you?"

"What shall you call me? Hmm. It's a good question."

When he rejoined her and took her hand for the final promenade of the dance, he said, "You may call me Lord Mac. How does that sound to you?"

"Appropriately Scottish," Margaret said with a laugh. And now she knew he was a lord and not a mister, she added to herself.

When the dance ended, Lord Mac bowed and asked, "Would you care to take in some fresh air? I would offer to fetch you a lemonade, but that would be a trifle difficult with these masks."

"A stroll on the balcony sounds perfect," she said, taking his arm. It was a shame about the drink, though, she was thirsty. But he was absolutely right. She would have to unmask to drink anything, and she wasn't ready to do that. Even the hint of being anonymous was simply too much fun and too freeing!

He led her outside where the air was much cooler. It was a beautiful night. It wasn't so cold that she needed her shawl, but refreshing just the same.

Margaret looked up into the star-filled sky and felt as if the eyes of a thousand well-wishers were gazing down upon her.

"It is a beautiful evening," she said as she looked up.

"Beautiful," he agreed.

Margaret turned and saw that he wasn't looking up, but at her. She smiled. "You can't even see my face. How would you know if I were beautiful or not?"

"I know."

She tilted her head. "*Do* you know who I am, my lord?"

"I have an idea," he said slowly. "Although, if you are who I think you are, you don't... Well, you usually aren't quite so bold as you are tonight. But may I say, that if you are that person, I find your behavior this evening absolutely charming and wish you would laugh this much on a regular basis?"

Margaret didn't know what to say to this, so strangely enough she simply said what was on her mind. "I wish I would too. I wish I weren't so shy." She paused to look down at her hands resting on the stone balustrade.

"Perhaps you should always wear a mask," he

said with a laugh. "Although, it would be such a shame to hide your lovely face all the time."

Margaret could only laugh and shake her head.

"So, tell me more about the real you that no one gets to see. I can't see your face, so let me see more of *you*."

"What would you like to 'see'? I don't think there's anything particularly interesting about me."

"What's your favorite hobby? What do you like to do when you're not holding up the ballroom wall?"

Margaret laughed at the image he conjured up in her mind, then thought about it. "Well, I do love to read. I'm quite awful and like to read novels."

"That's not awful. It can be a lot of fun. I admit I've read a few by Mrs. Edgeworth."

"Have you? I don't believe I've ever heard a gentleman admit as much!"

"Oh dear, you'll keep my secret, won't you?" he asked, leaning toward her.

Her heartbeat sped up with his proximity. "Yes, of course." She then laughed. "Of course, I'll keep your secret. I don't even know who you are!"

He let out a burst of laughter. "Well, then, this *is* a good thing!"

They could hear the sounds of the orchestra starting another dance.

He grabbed her hand and started pulling her back into the ballroom. "Come, let's dance."

"Again?"

"Yes, why not?"

She paused but honestly couldn't think of a reason. She didn't know why she found this so amusing, but suddenly she just started laughing.

Lord Mac stopped pulling her forward and started laughing with her. "What is so funny?" he asked, even as he chuckled.

"I don't know!" she laughed. She was laughing so hard, her eyes began to tear. "Oh, dear." She laughed, trying to wipe at her eyes through her mask.

He pulled out a handkerchief and dabbed at the corners of her eyes with it. She giggled as she took it from him and finished the job herself. "I am the most ridiculous creature tonight."

"You are the most lovely, and we're going to miss this dance if we don't join right away," he said, grabbing her hand once again and pulling her to the floor.

She quickly tucked the handkerchief into her glove and ran along behind him.

~*~

Jamie had never had so much fun. He'd gone to a few society parties when he'd been in school, but he never thought very much of the simpering misses he'd danced with. Lady Margaret was completely different from any of them.

Not only that, but she'd clearly taken his advice and let herself be free to laugh and just have fun behind her mask. She was almost a completely different person; he could hardly believe it. Never had he seen her laugh and be as charming as she was this evening. At home she was a quiet thing— even a little sad. At the wedding ball, she'd been timid and reserved.

Tonight, she was happy and funny and... Jamie knew he was lost.

Oh, he'd known it before this, he just hadn't

allowed himself to acknowledge it—not until Wickford had insisted. Even then, his mind had warred with what his heart already knew. Tonight, Jamie Douglass knew for certain that he was madly in love. He was besotted with every side of this complicated, adorable, frustrating young woman.

And he had only this one night to enjoy her. After this, he would go back to being nothing more than a footman, and she would have to find a gentleman to marry. He was determined to make the most out of every moment he had with her and not give in to that stabbing pain in his belly which told him, if he were open and honest, he could have this woman heart and soul.

But he couldn't. He just couldn't do that to her. He couldn't tie any young lady to a broke artist and fallen nobleman who had nothing of any value to his name. It wouldn't be fair. It wouldn't be right.

No, he had tonight to be the gentleman he actually was. Tomorrow he would go back to reality—to being nothing and no one. That stabbing pain pricked him once again, this time closer to heart. He was sure it was his pride hurting, but he couldn't allow that or anything keep him from sticking to his principles.

After another dance of laughter and flirting, before they could escape yet again to the balcony outside, the Duke of Warwick caught up with them.

"You seem to be having a good time, sister," he said, strolling over to them. Jamie marveled at how he could look so nonchalant and yet be so very dominant.

"I am," Margaret said, looking up at him. "In fact, I don't think I've ever enjoyed myself more," she added with a smile to her voice.

"I can't tell you how happy I am to hear that!" the duke said. He turned to Jamie but directed his question to Lady Margaret. "And would you care to introduce your companion?"

"I would be more than happy to if I knew who he was," Lady Margaret said with a laugh. "He's asked me to simply address him as Lord Mac." She turned to Jamie and said, "My lord, my brother."

Jamie bowed. "Your Grace. It is an honor." Of course, they'd met before, but the duke wouldn't know that.

"Lord Mac. Have we met?" the duke asked with a tilt of his head.

"We have, but briefly," Jamie said.

"Where?"

"At your home, actually, and a few other places as well," Jamie said vaguely. "Have no fear, Your Grace, I intend no harm to your sister."

"Well, I should hope not!" Lady Margaret said with a little laugh.

"I as well. You are simply paying her marked attention, my lord. A brother cannot help but be concerned," the duke said.

"I couldn't agree more. I would be as well were I in your shoes. But all I want is to have a pleasant evening with the lady and then... Well, we'll see what the future brings. I am here to live for the moment," Jamie said in all honesty.

"Live for the moment—" the duke echoed.

"Oh, yes! I fully believe in living for moment," another said joining them. "*Carpe diem.* It is the *best* way to live!"

Jamie turned to find another young woman giggling next to Lady Margaret. A tall gentleman in a green velvet cape accompanied her.

"I must say that is one lesson I have learned recently, and especially tonight it is most apt, don't you agree, my lord?" the young lady said, turning toward her companion.

"I couldn't agree more." The man bowed to them all and added. "I do hope you are all enjoying the masquerade?"

"We are," Lady Margaret said before either Jamie or her brother could answer.

Lord Mac looked at her for a moment, rather shocked at how outspoken and bold she was being. It was the most incredible, wonderful thing. He nodded his approval. "I most certainly am having the most pleasant evening I've had in a very long time. It is a night of surprises and joy."

"I am so happy to hear that," another gentleman said, joining them. He was dressed all in black from his hat, to his mask, to his clothes. Jamie immediately recognized his good friend Wickford. He'd told Jamie he'd be in black. He didn't mention that was the only color he would be wearing.

"My lord, this is the most wonderful party," Lady Margaret said. She clearly recognized their host as well.

Wickford bowed. "You flatter me."

"Oh, but it is!" the other young lady agreed.

"It's a little disconcerting not being able to recognize even my closest friends," the duke said, but then he gave a little laugh. "Seeing so many people behave more boldly has been, well..." He paused and looked toward his sister. "For some, it's a good thing, for others perhaps not so much."

"On the whole, though, I think it's been a great success," Jamie said.

"I am so glad you think so, my lord," Wickford said with a slight bow in Jamie's direction. "But now, you must excuse me, the midnight dance is about to begin!"

"The midnight dance? My word, that sounds ominous!" the young woman next to Lady Margaret said with a laugh. "Well, you will have to excuse us as well. We need to take to the dance floor."

"My lady, will you join me as well?" Jamie asked Lady Margaret, holding out his hand to her.

"I would love to!" she said with a giggle.

"But that would be your third dance together," her brother objected.

"Will it? I haven't been counting," Lady Margaret said.

"I don't think it matters so much tonight, Your Grace. Now, if you will excuse us," Jamie said, giving him a bow before leading Lady Margaret onto the floor. He didn't have much time left, and he wanted every moment of it to be with Lady Margaret. Perhaps he should have led her back out onto the balcony instead, but the dance floor seemed to be an easier place for what he needed to do.

Chapter Twenty-Five

Margaret took up her position next to Bel on the dance floor. She could hardly believe how flippant she'd been to her brother. She would never behave so...normally. Of course, she knew precisely how many dances she'd had with Lord Mac. Each and every one had been sheer bliss. In fact, the entire evening so far had been wonderful.

"You know, I don't think I've ever had such a good time," she admitted to her partner.

"I can't tell you how happy I am to hear that," he said. He looked down at her as they turned about. She could almost swear she could see his eyes soften with an emotion that made her melt a little.

"Do you think we might meet again—only without our masks?" she asked hopefully.

"I'm certain that we shall, only you will not know me, and perhaps I will not recognize you," he admitted.

"But that would be too sad. I couldn't bear—" she started feeling the anguish of not being able to spend more time with this sweet, wonderful man.

"You will have to be brave and strong, my lady. It pains me as much as it does you, but as your friend said, 'Carpe diem.'"

He didn't allow her to wallow in the evening, however. Within minutes, he had her giggling once more. They chatted as they danced and having Bel next to her joining in the fun made it even more special. All too soon, Lord Wickford stood above them on the balcony and called for everyone's attention as the clock began to strike midnight.

She turned to share a look with Lord Mac but was shocked when he wasn't there! She turned and saw him working his way in between people who had gathered to listen to their host.

"Lord Mac!" she called, but he didn't hear her. Within a moment, he was swallowed up by the crowd.

She was devastated.

She was empty.

He was gone!

~*~

Alys was beyond happy to pull off her mask. It was hot and uncomfortable. Even before Lord Wickford finished reciting his poem, she was unmasking herself.

Lord Gorling, standing by her side, did the same. His was such a pleasant countenance, it was really a shame to cover it with a mask, she thought as he revealed himself.

He turned to her, smiling. "That is so much better. You are so much more lovely than that mask."

Alys giggled. "You know, I was just thinking the same about you."

He raised his eyebrows and was about to say something when a screech was heard throughout the ballroom.

Alys turned and was shocked to see Margaret standing in the center of the ballroom, looking from one of the Kendrick twins to the other. They flanked her in identical dresses. They'd removed their masks and hats along with everyone else to show the world their true, identical faces. It was a very clever trick, but sadly, Margaret hadn't known that the twins existed and was clearly overwhelmed.

Alys rushed over.

"What is this? What's going on?" Lord Wickford asked, his voice loud enough for everyone in the vicinity to hear. He stopped the moment he saw the girls and burst out laughing. "Twins! Miss Kendrick, you did not tell us you were a twin!"

Alys reached in from behind Margaret and gently pulled her away from the twins. The girl seemed to be in a trance; she just stumbled backward not taking her eyes off the Kendrick girls.

The sisters laughed out loud.

"But wait, which one of you is the Miss Kendrick we know?" Lord Wickford asked.

"I am the one who has been here for the past month," Isabel said. "Beatrice and I are mirror twins—we look identical, but are opposites."

"Twins," Margaret whispered.

"You can remove your mask," Alys told her.

That seemed to snap the girl out of her shock. She turned toward Alys. "What? Oh! Yes." She pulled off her hat and mask and gave her head a little shake. "That feels so much better."

"I'm sure it does," Alys said, but Margaret had turned back toward Isabel and Beatrice.

"I just can't believe... Why didn't they tell me? I thought we were friends," Margaret said. She seemed to be much more upset by this than was warranted.

"Beatrice only just arrived in Town," Alys said, perpetuating the lie the ladies of the Wagering Whist Society had agreed upon. She hated lying to her good friend, but the truth wasn't hers to tell.

"Oh." Margaret pulled a large, white handkerchief from her glove and wiped her face with it, dabbing at the corners of her eyes. Had there been tears there? Surely, the girl wouldn't cry over the fact that her friend hadn't told her she had a twin sister.

"Is everything all right, my dear?" Alys asked. She put her arm around Margaret's shoulders and led her away from the dance the floor to where Lord Gorling was still standing and watching.

"Yes, I suppose...well..." Margaret dithered. She seemed unable to make up her mind.

"Where is that young man with whom you've spent the entire evening?"

The girl turned toward her, actual tears beginning to make their way down her softly flushed cheeks.

"Margaret! My dear! I'm so sorry I asked. Did he do something? Say something inappropriate?" Alys was horrified to see the girl cry, especially in public!

"Come, come," Lord Gorling said, approaching quickly. "I think you just need some fresh air, my dear. It'll be all right. You'll feel much more the thing in a moment." He put a fatherly arm around Margaret's shoulders and led her toward the French doors. "Excuse me, pardon me," he said to people in their way. "We're not feeling well here. Need to get out. Excuse us."

He worked their way out of the crowd and finally onto the balcony. Tears were still sliding down Margaret's cheeks, and she was sniffling into her handkerchief.

"I'm sorry. I don't... I don't mean..." she tried to apologize.

"Now, now, it's all right," Alys said, taking and patting Margaret's free hand.

"What did that cad say to you, Lady Margaret? I'll thrash him like—" Lord Gorling started.

"No, no," Margaret shook her head and then turned pleading eyes up to his lordship. "Don't hurt him. He didn't say anything. It's just... He just...disappeared, that's all."

"Disappeared?" Alys asked.

Margaret nodded as more tears began to stream down her face. "Before...before the unmasking. Just as the clock started to strike, he bolted from the dance floor. I...so wanted to see who he truly was, but...but he left!"

"Huh! Didn't want to be found out," Lord Gorling said, looking as stymied as Alys felt.

But that wasn't all the duchess was feeling. No, indeed, indignation, nay, anger was quickly overcoming her. "Why that horrid man! He was sweet on you all evening, and when it came to revealing his true identity he vanishes!"

Margaret could only nod as she tried her best to hold back her tears.

Alys took the poor girl in her arms. "There, there, my dear. He clearly wasn't worth knowing."

"No, he *was*. He was so sweet. So...so wonderful," Margaret managed between sobs.

Lord Gorling reached out and awkwardly

patted the girl's back as well. "Couldn't have been all that wonderful if he didn't want his true identity known, now, could he?"

"But he was," Margaret insisted. She pulled away and did her best to stem the flow of her tears. With a hiccough and a gasp, she looked down at the handkerchief in her hand. "This is all I have left of him."

"What?" Alys asked. She looked at the scrap of cloth. Some color on the material caught her eye. She reached out and turned it over to see initials carefully embroidered onto a corner. There was a large R with a smaller J weaving in and out of it. She looked up at Margaret. "His initials are JR. Is that right?"

Margaret also looked at the embroidery. She shook her head. "No. He told me to call him Lord Mac. He was a Scot."

"Well, either he has someone else's handkerchief or he was telling a fast one," Lord Gorling said.

"Most likely the latter," Alys commented. "Are you certain he was a Scot?"

Margaret lifted one shoulder and dropped it again. "He spoke with a bit of a brogue that sounded Scottish, and when I asked him about it, he seemed embarrassed to have been caught out. But he also admitted that he doesn't normally speak with an accent, so I don't know. Perhaps? Are there any gentlemen of Scottish ancestry who don't speak with a Scottish accent normally?"

"Hmmm. I don't think I know any Scottish noblemen," Alys said, searching through her mind. "Well, there's Perth and Selkirk."

"Glasgow and, of course, Roseberry," Lord

Gorling added.

Both she and Margaret looked up when he said Roseberry.

"What?" Lord Gorling asked, looking from Alys to Margaret and back again. "Rose... oh! JR! Of course! Er, don't know what Roseberry's given name is, to be honest. Fellow's constantly with my Henry, though, so shouldn't be too hard to track down. I'll go find him now," Lord Gorling said before stalking off.

"Lord Roseberry doesn't have a Scottish accent," Margaret pointed out to his retreating back.

"But he *is* a Scot. As you said, he could have put one on if he didn't want to be recognized," Alys pointed out.

They stood in comfortable silence for a few minutes while waiting for his lordship to return.

"You seem to have had a wonderful evening," Margaret said quietly while they waited.

Alys could feel the heat rising in her cheeks. "I have. I looked to see how you were doing a few times, but you were always so happy in this man's company that I didn't bother to interrupt."

Alys knew she'd been remiss in her chaperoning duties, but indeed, she'd been having much too much fun to worry overmuch about Margaret. It was bad, but she hadn't ever thought she could be so happy in the company of a gentleman other than her dear Kendell. She was pleased she'd been wrong, but she also knew it wasn't right for her to abandon her duties in this way.

"I *was* having a good time with Lord Mac, or whatever his real name is. And I'm glad that you and Lord Gorling enjoyed yourselves."

"I feel as if I should have been more diligent," Alys admitted.

"Oh, no. I'm certain you wouldn't have been able to discover his identity any more than I," Margaret said.

"I don't know. I do know a great many more people. Maybe I could have—"

"Henry says he hasn't seen Roseberry since they came in together," Lord Gorling said, joining them once again. "Been suspiciously absent—his words, not mine."

Alys looked to Margaret.

"Did he say what Lord Roseberry was wearing this evening?" Margaret cleverly asked.

"A black cape and tricorn, but that could describe any number of men," Lord Gorling replied.

"Including my mysterious Lord Mac," Margaret said, turning toward Alys. "Perhaps he *was* Lord Roseberry."

"But then why go to the trouble of hiding his identity. You know each other quite well."

"I don't know," Margaret said, thinking about it. "He did pay a call on Warwick last season to ask for my hand. Warwick turned him down, though. He said Roseberry hadn't thought I should have a say in who I married, that it should be up to my brother."

"Could it be he was trying to get back into your good graces and will reveal himself at a later time?" Alys asked.

"That *is* possible," Margaret said, perking up.

"Sounds quite likely to me," Lord Gorling said. "Just the sort of thing a man in love might do."

Margaret turned widened eyes to him. "Do you... Do you think so?"

He gave a decisive nod. "I do. I would if I were in his position. Wants to make amends, doesn't quite know how. Easiest thing in the world to do so behind a mask where you wouldn't have any preconceived notions."

"It does make a good deal of sense," Alys agreed.

"Your Grace, do you think you could ask the Ladies' Wagering Whist Society if they know any other men with the initials JR—just to be certain?" Margaret asked.

"Of course! I would be happy to. We don't meet again until Wednesday next, naturally, but I don't think much is going to happen between now and then," Alys said, giving Margaret as comforting a smile as she could. She was so relieved that this mystery was most likely solved, and her dear friend was in a better mood. She worried about this girl!

Chapter Twenty-Six

~April 28~

"**I** don't understand the meaning of this, Mr. Douglass, and I *don't* like it," said Holton the butler, tossing a note onto the table next to Jamie who was finishing up his breakfast.

It was his morning off, but for once he had nothing planned. He had no painting to work on, no excursions or chores outside of the house that needed to be done. He was actually thinking of relaxing with a book in his room for change.

"I beg your pardon, sir?" Jamie asked.

"Receiving personal missives," the butler said, raising his eyebrows at the note as if it were something evil.

"At least it doesn't smell feminine, or does it?" Harold, another of the footmen sniggered from across the table. He grabbed the note before Jamie could do so and gave it a sniff. "No. Just an ordinary note. How boring. If you're going to get secret notes, at least make them interesting for us, James."

Jamie laughed and popped the last piece of toast into his mouth. "If it were a secret note, I don't think it would have been handed to Mr. Holton," he said around his food.

Harold frowned. "No, I suppose not. Even more boring."

Both Harold and Holton stood there waiting, watching Jamie. He looked at them both. "Is there something else, sir?" he asked the butler.

"You're not going to open the letter?" he asked.

"Oh, yes. I will. Good morning, sir. Harold." Jamie picked up his plate, tea cup, and the note. The first two items he put onto the counter with the other dirty breakfast dishes. He then took the note upstairs with him to his room, knowing full well the disappointment he was leaving in his wake.

On his way up the stairs, he opened the letter. It was from Wickford, requesting his presence that morning. Oddly, he asked Jamie to bring any and all completed paintings he had. Could his friend have a client for him? That was an exciting thought.

Jamie grabbed his work, which was all neatly stored in a rolled tube of brown paper and headed back down and out the door.

Wickford was actually up, although not yet dressed, when Jamie knocked on the door to his private rooms. He was sipping at a cup of coffee and reading the morning paper when Jamie was shown into the drawing room.

"Well, look who's up with the chickens," Jamie said with a laugh.

Wickford just frowned at him. "Not terribly happy about it, but I remembered you only had the morning off. For you, I roused myself at this ungodly hour. Do have a cup of coffee," he added as he watched Jamie helping himself before he'd even been asked to do so.

"Thank you." Jamie sat back on the

comfortable chair he'd sat in the last time he'd been here.

Wickford raised his eyebrows. "Care for something to eat? Shall I have some eggs and a steak prepared for you?"

"Oh, no, thank you. I just ate."

"Ah." Wickford stared at him, one corner of his mouth twitching with a smile.

"What? Do you object to me making myself comfortable in your home?"

"No! No. Not at all. I'm very happy you are doing so." His friend laughed.

"We've been friends a very long time, Joshua," Jamie pointed out.

"And we shared rooms for many years. Honestly, I have no problems here."

"Good. So, why *did* you rouse yourself at this, as you say, ungodly hour?" Jamie asked before taking another sip of his coffee.

"Ah, yes, right. Did you bring your paintings? Yes, I see that you did. May I see them?"

Jamie nodded, put down his cup, and pulled out the work he'd brought. He opened the painting of the old man, his mother, and two more which he hadn't shown to the Duchess of Kendell or the Duke of Warwick. They weren't his best pieces, but they weren't all that bad either. He grabbed knickknacks and candlesticks from around the room to hold the paintings open.

"Hmmm," Wickford said, examining the paintings. "They'll need to be framed, naturally," he commented off-hand.

"I suppose so."

"Is this your mother?" Wickford asked,

pointing to one.

"Yes. Just before she passed," Jamie explained.

Wickford nodded and rolled that one up and handed it back to Jamie. "You'll be keeping that."

Jamie nodded and then asked. "And what are you planning for the others? Do you have a client to whom you'd like to show them? If so, then I think the one of my mother is a very good representation of—"

"No, I don't have anyone in mind," Wickford said, interrupting him. "I'll get them framed put them up on the walls of my club. I expect they'll sell quickly."

"Really?" Jamie was surprised..

"Yes. A few gentlemen have inquired into purchasing some of the paintings I already have up. I've even sold a few I didn't particularly like. But yours... I think they might garner some real interest, especially the landscapes. I don't know about the portrait."

"If they sell, I'd be happy to do some more for you," Jamie offered.

Wickford looked up from studying one of the paintings. "Yes, I'd like that. Can you do so without leaving London? Don't you have to be..." He waved a hand around randomly. "I don't know, at the place you're going to paint?"

"It's easier, but I could just do it from memory. I can't exactly just up and leave London right now."

Wickford smiled. "No, you can't. Not when there's a beautiful young lady..."

Jamie just shook his head. "She's not for me. I can't... I'm a footman and a painter, Wickford. She's the sister of a duke!"

"You're a bloody marquess!" his friend protested.

"Yes, but—"

"No but. There are no buts here. You *are* a marquess. She's a lady. I see no problems here."

Jamie looked at his friend for a moment. There were so many feelings ramming their way through him. Agreement. Anger. Longing. Frustration. Finally, he said, "I may be a marquess, but I'm a poor one. Broke, in fact. I've got an estate that needs more than I could ever afford to put into it."

"You said you were renting it out," Wickford pointed out.

"I am renting the land. The money is going to support those who've worked that land for generations and upkeep for the house so it doesn't fall down on the heads of the retainers living there—and believe me, it's a real threat."

"So, you're not seeing a cent of what you're earning?"

"Not one. If I were, I assure you, I would not be working as a footman. It's bloody hard work!" Jamie said with more feeling and volume than he'd intended. He rubbed a hand down his face and leaned back in his chair. "I'm sorry. I'm tired."

"No need to apologize. I'm sure it is difficult work, and I'm trying to do everything I can, so you won't have to do it for much longer."

"I know. I appreciate that, really, I do."

"But I don't understand why you won't follow your heart and go after the girl with the enormous dowry, which would solve all your problems," Wickford said, leaning forward.

Why didn't he? It would make his entire life so

much easier. But no, he couldn't. He shook his head. "I won't marry for money. I wouldn't demean Margaret that way. She deserves so much better."

"You're a stubborn mule, you know that?" his friend said with true kindness in his voice.

Jamie knew he was just trying to help. Trying to look out for him the way Jamie had done for Wickford when they'd been in school. Jamie deliberately didn't mention his battered pride. He didn't mention the fact that he was coming to realize he actually liked being a gentleman, and it wasn't just the long hours on his feet. And he most certainly didn't mention the fact that he'd already thought through everything that Wickford was telling him. He didn't say any of that. Instead, he simply sighed, "I know."

~April 29~

Alys neatly folded her hands on top of the green baize table, having lost her second hand that day. This was becoming a bit of a habit, she realized. She began to think about what secret she might be revealing soon when the game finished. She was certain that this time it was she who will have lost.

Thoughts of secrets turned her mind to the gentleman Margaret had been dancing with at the Venetian ball. She'd promised her young friend she'd ask the ladies if anyone knew his identity, although she was certain they wouldn't have an answer.

"Is there anything wrong, Your Grace?" Lady Welles asked. She was such a sweet, thoughtful girl.

"No. I was just thinking of the Venetian ball," Alys said, giving the girl a smile. "There was a man there... I wonder if you noticed. He spent just about the entire evening with Lady Margaret."

"Oh, yes! I *did* notice," she said, perking up in interest. "Who was he?"

"That is precisely my problem. I don't know. Neither did Margaret," Alys admitted. "He said she should call him Lord Mac but then left her with a handkerchief with the initials JR on it. Might *you* have any ideas as to his identity?"

"Lord Mac?" Lady Sorrell asked.

"He said he was a Scot," Alys explained.

"And his initials are JR," Lady Welles said, thinking about it.

"Apparently," Alys nodded.

"Well, which noblemen who might have been in attendance have the initials JR?" Lady Sorrell asked, always so practical.

There was silence at the table for a moment while they all thought about it.

"There's Lord Roseberry," Lady Moreton said. "Doesn't his first name begin with a J?"

"Yes, Joseph," Lady Welles said.

Alys looked at her. "How do you know that?"

The girl shrugged. "I read Debrett's." She gave Alys a pleased smile.

The duchess could only laugh. "I suppose it's been too long since I've done the same."

Lady Ayres came over to their table. "Have you finished your game, ladies?" she asked.

"Yes. We're just trying to think of noblemen with the initials JR who might have been at the Venetian ball," Lady Moreton explained. "Do you know of any?"

Lady Ayres thought about it, "There was Lord Rexford."

"No, his given name is George," Lady Sorrell said with a shake of her head.

"And this gentleman claimed to be a Scot—or he spoke with a Scottish accent according to Margaret," Lady Welles added.

"Oh, a Scotsman. What about Lord Ranelagh. What's his name?"

"I believe it's Jonathan," Lady Ayres said.

"Yes, it could have been him," Lady Sorrell said.

"He's Irish, not Scot, but otherwise, he does sound quite likely," Alys agreed.

"And there's Lord Rogan. I don't know that he's a Scot, though," Lady Ayres said, continued to think about it.

"His given name is Francis," Alys said. That one she knew. Her husband had had dealings with the man. She'd never really liked him very much.

"And I don't think he could have jumped about and danced as gracefully as the man Lady Margaret danced with," Lady Welles added with a giggle.

"Goodness, no! Lord Rogan is rather old and plump," Lady Moreton agreed with a little laugh.

"I can't think of any more than that, can you, ladies?" Lady Ayres asked, turning around to Mrs. Aldridge, Lady Colburne, and Lady Blakemore, who were holding a conversation by the other card table.

"What's that?" Mrs. Aldridge asked.

"Do you know of any gentlemen with the initials JR who are young and Scottish?" Lady Welles asked.

They all thought about it for a moment, but could only suggest the men who had already been discussed.

"Are you trying to figure out who danced attendance on Lady Margaret at the Venetian ball?" Lady Colburne asked.

"Yes, that's it, precisely," Alys said. That girl was always quite clever and quick.

Lady Colburne nodded. "I saw them off and on all evening. I don't think they left each other's company even once."

"No, I don't believe they did either, which is why we're quite desperate to figure out who he was," Alys said, standing. Her joints were becoming stiff sitting for so long.

"You mean Lady Margaret didn't know?" Mrs. Aldridge asked.

"If she did, we wouldn't be having this discussion," Alys said, frowning at the woman. She was standing there, holding her little dog with one hand and absent-mindedly petting it with the other. Alys repressed a shudder.

"He disappeared before the unmasking and simply left Lady Margaret with a handkerchief with his initials on it. Isn't that romantic?" Lady Welles asked with a broad smile.

"It may have been romantic, but it's also quite annoying," Alys commented dryly. She appreciated the girl's romantic sensibilities, but it didn't help Margaret.

"Well, yes, I suppose so, but now she gets to look at every gentleman she sees and wonder if it was him," the girl said with a giggle.

"If only Lady Margaret weren't so shy," Lady Ayres commented.

"And there we have the crux of the matter. If she weren't so shy, she might be able to figure out who he was by dancing and speaking with various gentlemen, but she has such a difficult time doing so," Alys said with a little shake of her head.

"Oh, poor thing! Well, perhaps if she just focuses on the two gentlemen we determined could be him, it will be easier," Lady Colburne said.

"Yes, I'll tell her so this evening."

Chapter Twenty-Seven

~April 30~

"**J**ames!"

Lady Margaret's enthusiastic greeting took Jamie by surprise. "My lady?"

She sat back in her chair at the breakfast table. "I feel like I haven't seen you in ages."

He could only smile. He filled her cup and then placed the tea pot, which he'd just carried up from the kitchen, in front of her. "I've been here as always."

"But you're here in the breakfast room this morning instead of at the front door. I suppose that's why I haven't seen you," she said, sprinkling a little sugar into her cup.

"Yes. Mr. Holton decided to try the new footman, George, on the front door today. For some reason, he believes that's a good place to start someone," Jamie explained.

"Maybe so he can ease into learning how we like things done. The front door is a basic, simple duty. All you have to do is answer the door and ask who's calling," Margaret commented.

"And know who is at-home and who is accepted in even when you or the duchess are not available to others," Jamie added.

"Yes, but it's still pretty simple information to know rather than how we prefer to be served at table."

Jamie nodded. He'd had to learn how the duchess preferred to be served, which wasn't the same as his mother's preferences, for example. He'd never thought of it before. "Yes, I suppose it does make sense." He gave her a smile. "I guess that's why I'm a footman, and Mr. Holton manages things so well."

She gave a little laugh. "There are little tricks one needs to know, like that." She took a sip of her tea and then asked, "How is your friend? I meant to ask earlier."

"My friend?" Jamie had no idea what she was talking about.

"The one you visited the night of the Venetian ball? You said he was ill?" she reminded him with a curious tilt to her head.

"Oh, yes!" He'd completely forgotten the lie he'd made up so he could have that evening off to attend the ball. He schooled his face into a serious expression and lowered his eyebrows in concern. "He's doing a little better. Progressing, but slowly."

"But he *is* getter better. That's wonderful," Lady Margaret was so enthusiastic and happy for his made-up "friend."

James replaced his smile. "Yes. It was a little difficult seeing him so ill, but yes, he's doing better. Did you enjoy the ball? Did you manage to have fun like we discussed?"

Lady Margaret's smile broadened. "Yes! It was the most wonderful night of my life," she said with a sigh that just made Jamie's heart dance with joy.

"I spent the entire night dancing and talking with a gentleman who called himself Lord Mac, but I think I've figured out who he truly is. We were all in masks, of course, so I couldn't see his face at all."

James' heart stuttered. "But you know who he is?"

"Yes." Lady Margaret giggled. "You see, he accidentally left me with his handkerchief! It has his real initials on it—JR. So, it could only have been one of two gentlemen—Lord Roseberry or Lord Ranelagh. Lord Ranelagh is Irish, not a Scot, and I don't believe he could have been as wonderful as this man was, so it *has* to be Lord Roseberry. I'm going to be seeing him tomorrow night, so I'll find out."

Jamie could breathe again; he just wasn't sure he wanted to. He'd completely forgotten that he'd given Lady Margaret his handkerchief during the evening. It was both a good and a terrible thing the tailor had sewn on the wrong initials.

Lord Roseberry? Jamie didn't really know very much about the man. "Well, that's excellent!" he said, swallowing a bit of bile down his throat as his stomach protested the lie. "I'm thrilled and amazed you will ask him about it. It will take great courage to face him directly."

"Oh, well..." Margaret hesitated. "We did become remarkably close that evening. I can't explain it, but somehow I felt so comfortable with him—almost as if I knew him." She gave a little laugh. "Which is why I believe that I must! It's got to be Lord Roseberry, who I *do* know and have found to be quite a pleasant gentleman. And I won't need to actually ask him outright. If I dance with him, I'll know."

"Really? You can tell just by dancing?"

"Oh, yes. I tell you, I connected with him in a way I've never done with a gentleman before." Her gaze shifted out the window behind Jamie. "He was so wonderful. I do so want to see him again to, to be with him." She looked back at Jamie. "Truly, he was the only man I've ever met who I could see marrying and being happy with."

"James!"

Jamie nearly jumped out of his skin at the interruption; Lady Margaret did actually jump.

"I *do* beg your pardon, my lady," Mr. Holton said, giving her a slight bow. The look he gave Jamie wasn't nearly as kind. It clearly said, "*You're in trouble.*" He gave a jerk of his head toward the door, so Jamie followed him out after giving Lady Margaret a bow.

He followed the butler all the way down to the kitchen before the man turned on him. The look of fury in his eyes didn't bode well. "I know you have taken liberties in speaking with Lady Margaret while you were allowed to paint her portrait, but that does *not* give you the right to hold a conversation with her now. You are *not* her equal. You aren't even as noble as her smallest toe. Do not presume!"

Jamie pulled back his shoulders and opened his mouth to tell this imbecile just how noble he really was but quickly stopped himself. He couldn't lose this job. Not now. And besides, if he told Holton the truth, both the duchess and Lady Margaret would learn of it too. Of course, then he could tell Margaret it had been he who she'd danced with at the ball, but then what? She was finally happy—happy with the idea that it had been

Lord Roseberry with whom she'd spent an absolutely perfect night. Would she be as happy if she learned it had been a footman who'd been lying to her for the past month?

No. She'd probably hate him—and rightfully so. No, she could never find out the truth. He couldn't bear it if Margaret became angry with him.

So, Jamie closed his mouth again and said nothing.

"Right. If I catch you speaking anything more than a 'yes, my lady,' you *will* be turned off. Is that understood?"

"Yes, sir," Jamie replied.

Holton nodded. "Now, go relieve George at the front door. Clearly that is the place for you. You cannot be trusted anywhere else."

Jamie walked out without another word. Anger, humiliation, and frustration warred within him. He didn't know how much more of this he could take. He was a marquess for God's sake, raised as a member of the nobility. Poverty and the desire to be an artist had put him in this position, but his father had drilled pride into him from the time he was born. No matter how hard he tried, he just couldn't put that aside.

~May 2~

Margaret had never been so excited to go to a party before. She was going to see Lord Mac, she just knew it! She could hardly wait.

She was downstairs, ready to go nearly a quarter of an hour before they were scheduled to leave. As usual, James was on duty at the front door.

"You look beautiful," he said so softly Margaret wasn't sure he'd actually spoken.

She clasped her hands together. "I look all right? Oddly enough, I'm nervous. What if he decides he doesn't like me without my mask? What if he was only kind because he didn't have to look at my face?"

James chuckled. "You have a beautiful face. There isn't a man alive who wouldn't want to look at it."

Margaret felt her cheeks heat. She found herself stepping closer to the footman, looking up into his warm, smiling eyes. "You are so kind, James."

He shook his head as he smiled down at her. "Not kind, just honest." He paused for a moment and then stepped away with a sigh. "Perhaps too honest. It's not my place—"

"Your place? I asked you!" Margaret said, suddenly angry that he was behaving as if he were a servant. He *was* a footman, but she hated being reminded of the fact. She was much happier simply thinking of him as a friend...who also worked for the duchess.

"Yes, but I shouldn't..." For the briefest moment, there was a pained expression on his face. He quickly hid it, though, and schooled his expression into nothing. "My lady, perhaps it would help with your anxiety if you went into the drawing room and had a glass of wine before the duchess joins you," he said in a near monotone. Margaret hated it.

She didn't want to speak to James the footman. She wanted her friend James. She wanted his advice and his reassurance, but it didn't look like she was going to get that. The footman was on duty, so she gave him a brief nod and did as he suggested.

She'd taken only one sip of the wine she'd poured for herself when the duchess joined her. "You're ready early."

"Yes. I was anxious," Margaret said. She indicated the sideboard where the wine and some glasses were laid out. "Can I pour you a glass of wine before we go?"

"No, thank you. Since we're both ready, perhaps we should just leave. I don't believe it will hurt to be a little early."

Margaret emptied the wine into her mouth, drinking it much more quickly than she'd intended, but she needed the courage it would give her. With a slight cough, she touched her handkerchief to the corners of her mouth. She gave the duchess a nod to indicate she was ready.

The older lady simply stared at her for a moment, perhaps making sure she wouldn't keel over from drinking so fast. Once she was satisfied Margaret was all right, she turned on her heel and headed toward the door.

Happily, there were a number of others who'd decided to join the party early. Even more strangely was the fact that soon after they'd entered the drawing room, Margaret found no fewer than three gentlemen interested in speaking with her. That had never happened before, except perhaps at her coming out ball.

For a just moment after the men had joined her and the duchess, she'd had her usual gut reaction to flee, but she held herself firm and reminded herself that she could do this. She could be just as interesting and charming as Lydia—who was, without a doubt, the best person to model herself after when it came to flirting with men.

How she wished James was here to give her his silent encouragement! But then again, maybe she didn't need him. Maybe she could do this on her own.

She remembered James's words before she'd gone to the Venetian Ball. He'd told her that with her mask on she could be anyone she wished to be. Well, tonight she didn't have a physical mask, but there was still no reason why she couldn't be that laughing, charming person who'd danced all night with Lord Mac. She could simply put on an invisible mask and pretend to be someone else—no one would be the wiser.

Except the duchess.

As Margaret spoke and laughed with the men who'd come to greet her, she kept noticing side-looks from her chaperone. After the gentlemen had departed to seek out other young ladies to charm, she turned to Margaret.

"*Why* have you never behaved as such before this?" the duchess demanded.

Margaret lifted a shoulder and let it drop. "I... I couldn't."

"But you could tonight? What's changed?"

She gave the duchess a little smile. "James. He told me before the Venetian Ball that I could be anyone I wanted behind my mask. Tonight, I decided to be that person again, only without the mask. I'm simply pretending to be someone else."

"If I'd only known that's what it would take," the duchess said with a shake of her head. "You could be an actress," she added with a laugh.

Margaret giggled but agreed.

Chapter Twenty-Eight

It turned out to be quite a wonderful evening after she'd decided to wear her invisible mask. The only thing that was missing was Lord Roseberry.

At one point, she found herself with her good friends Diana, Lydia, and their respective husbands. They had been speaking for a few minutes when the duchess gasped lightly.

"Mr. Hershawn is here," she murmured.

"Is Lord Gorling with him?" Lydia asked with a giggle.

"It doesn't... Oh, yes, he is," the duchess said, sounding relieved. "You never know. I think Lord Roseberry and Mr. Hershawn frequently have other plans before attending parties that don't always include Lord Gorling."

"Well, it's not entirely surprising. I can't imagine you'd always want to have your father about," Lord Welles commented.

"No," Lord Colburne agreed with feeling.

"But Lord Gorling is still pretty new to Town. I don't imagine he has many friends of his own quite yet," the duchess said.

"He's actually made quite a name for himself in the clubs," Lord Colburne commented.

"And in Parliament," Lord Welles added.

"Really?" The duchess turned a surprised expression on the two gentlemen.

"Oh, yes. He speaks with everyone," Lord Colburne told them. "Gets into some heated discussions too."

"As he does on the floor of House," Lord Welles agreed. "Quit an opinionated gentleman."

"Do you agree with his opinions?" Lydia asked, turning to her husband.

"Sometimes," he said with a shrug. "Other times, he's...well, quite radical actually. He's very pro-democracy. Thinks the American have got it right."

"He's not suggesting we get rid of our monarchy, is he?" the duchess asked with some surprise.

"Oh, no! Nothing so extreme. He'd just like to see some suffrage reform, that's all. Not a terribly popular opinion amongst the lords, I have to say," Lord Welles added.

"No, I can't believe it would be," Diana said.

"And here he comes," Lydia said. She giggled and then added, "If I'm not mistaken, he's headed straight for the duchess without an eye for anyone else."

"How could he possibly notice anyone else? Her Grace is looking quite fetching this evening," Margaret said with a laugh of her own.

The lady in question gave her a mock scowl before turning a broad smile onto Lord Gorling. "My lord, how lovely to see you this evening."

"And you, Your Grace," he said, bowing over her hand. If his lips lingered a little longer than they should have on her fingers, no one said a word. "You are looking stunning tonight. That color suits you very well."

"As well as the red that you were exclaiming over at the Venetian Ball?" the duchess asked with a giggle—a giggle! Margaret had to work to keep her own titters inside.

"Well, no. I am sorry to say, you looked positively ravishing in red," the gentleman said.

The lady simply *harrumphed* before breaking into more giggles.

Lydia and Diana were laughing as well, and even their husbands were smiling at the banter between the older couple.

"Oh my, I don't know—" the duchess began.

"Come, promenade with me, Your Grace. We'll leave these young people to their own pursuits," Lord Gorling said, pulling her hand around his arm.

"How can I say no?" A moment later, though, she did actually pull back. "Oh, wait, I must say no! I can't just leave Lady Margaret here on her own. Not again." The duchess turned a stricken look onto her protégé.

"It's perfectly all right, Your Grace, Diana and I will look after her," Lydia said, putting a hand on Margaret's shoulder. "You go on and have a good time."

"But you aren't any older—" the duchess began.

"No, but we are both married, which makes us perfectly well qualified to be her chaperone for the evening," Diana said with a broad smile.

"Are you sure…?" The duchess looked very hesitant.

"Absolutely!" Diana, Lydia, and Margaret all

said at once. They turned to each other and burst into laughter.

Even the duchess laughed. "Well, since you are all so certain, I suppose I have no choice."

"None," Lord Colburne said, echoing the prevailing opinion.

The duchess and her beau walked off, looking so happy Margaret turned back to her friends with a big smile. "Thank you."

"Whatever for?" Diana asked.

"We just love seeing her so happy," Lydia said.

"She is a very kind lady," Lord Colburne said.

"And she deserves to find love too," his wife said, looking up at him happily.

Margaret felt a little hitch in her breathing and an unusual tightness in her throat. Seeing her friends so happily married was wonderful...and yet painful. They'd all started out together in their first season only the year before, and already both Diana and Lydia were happily married while Margaret didn't even have one gentleman seriously interested in her.

Well, that wasn't true. She did have the mysterious Lord Mac, but that was probably just a one-time thing, a lark some gentleman had played on her. How she wished she had someone...

Strangely, James's smiling face hovered in her memory. He was so handsome and joyful. He made her happy, and oddly, he seemed to care for her. At least, she didn't think he'd said all those sweet things this evening because he *had* to, because he worked for the duchess. No, it couldn't have been that. And he'd helped her before. In fact, a number of times.

She shook the fancies from her mind. She was being ridiculous. James was a footman! He could never be anything more than a friend, and even being that much was beyond common. How she wished he were anything but a footman.

"Margaret, did you want to speak with Lord Roseberry?" Lydia's voice jolted her from her thoughts.

"What? Lord Roseberry? Oh, yes," Margaret said. He was standing quite close by, speaking with Mr. Hershawn and Lady St. Vincent.

"Come, why don't we say hello," Lydia said, taking Margaret's arm so she had no choice but to go along.

"Good evening, Lady Welles, Lady Margaret," Lady St. Vincent said, seeing them approach.

The two gentlemen turned around to greet them as well.

"Good evening," Margaret said, giving them all a little curtsy. "Lord Roseberry—"

"Good evening, Lady Margaret. I don't mean to be rude, but will you please excuse me?" Lord Roseberry gave them all a quick bow, turned around, and walked off.

"What was that?" Lydia asked, clearly as shocked as Margaret.

"I, I can't say," Mr. Hershawn said. He was as flummoxed as well. "If you'll excuse me, I'll see if I can't find out." He too gave them a bow and went off in his friend's wake.

"That is the oddest thing I think I've ever seen," Lady St. Vincent said, also watching the gentleman's back. She turned toward Margaret and Lydia. "Neither of you have quarreled with Lord

Roseberry, have you? I mean, I can't imagine that you would have."

"Even if we had, he couldn't be enough of a gentleman to face us?" Lydia asked with an awkward little giggle.

"I wonder…" Margaret said, quietly voicing the thought inside her head.

"What? Do you know something?" Lydia asked, turning to her.

"No. It's just… I wanted to speak with him because I think he might be the gentleman I danced with at the Venetian Ball. If he is, then maybe he's avoiding me so I don't learn of his identity. Is that too farfetched?" Margaret asked the women.

"I heard you spent the evening with just one gentleman. You think it was Lord Roseberry?" Lady St. Vincent asked, looking in the direction the men went.

"I don't know, but…"

"Oh, yes, we discussed this at the last Ladies' Wagering Whist Society meeting. You were left with the handkerchief with the initials JR, weren't you?" Lydia asked.

"Yes. I asked the duchess to inquire whether any of the ladies could think of any gentlemen of the *ton* with those initials," Margaret said.

"JR?" Lady St. Vincent said, thinking about it.

"The only men we could think of was Lord Roseberry and Lord Ranelagh," Lydia said.

"Yes, but I'm certain it isn't Lord Ranelagh," Margaret agreed.

"The only other person I can think of is Lord Redenton," Lady St. Vincent said.

"Isn't he about eighty years old?" Lydia asked with a giggle.

"Sixty, but yes, he is an older gentleman," Lady St. Vincent said with a broad smile.

"I don't think he could have danced as much as the gentleman in question did," Margaret said, also giggling.

Lady St. Vincent laughed. "No. I don't suppose he could. Well, then, perhaps you're right, Lady Margaret. And it looks like you might have a difficult time pinning the man down, oddly enough."

There was a commotion at the door just then, and they all turned to see what it was about. Margaret could see Lord St. Vincent quickly making his way over and gave a laugh. "I believe it's your step-son, my lady."

Lady St. Vincent nodded, her smile growing. "Yes, he must have gone to greet Beatrice and Bel. I think those girls are going to cause a stir wherever they go for some time," she said with a laugh.

"Oh, and there's Lord Roseberry again," Lady St. Vincent pointed out.

"Thank you! If you'll excuse me." A spark of nervous excitement lit in Margaret's belly as she strode off to try to intercept the gentleman. "Lord Roseberry, Lord Roseberry," she called after him as he tried to escape yet again.

"I beg your pardon, Lady Margaret," the man said, unable to do anything but turn around to speak with her.

She put a hand to her hip. "May I ask why you keep running away from me?"

His eyes darted this way and that. "It's

just...spies," he whispered. "My mother has spies everywhere!"

"Spies?" Margaret was completely confused.

"Yes. The other ladies of society. I've recently learned that they are spying on me and then going and reporting to my mother. I do beg your pardon, my lady, but she has determined that *you* are the right one for me. I don't wish to put either of us into an awkward situation. If she hears I spoke with you for much longer than a few minutes, she's going to get the wrong idea, and I'll never hear the end of it," he explained.

"Oh!" It was all Margaret could think of to say. It was so odd. His mother was bound to find out anyway if he cared for her. Maybe he was worried she would gloat over being right. That might prick a sensitive male ego.

"Thank you for understanding, my lady." He gave her a quick bow and darted off again.

Well, at lease she had an explanation, no matter how odd it was. It still didn't help her in discovering whether it was he who had spent the evening with her at the Venetian ball, though. How very frustrating!

~May 4~

Monday afternoon, Jamie opened the duchess's front door to Wickford.

"Wick—er, good afternoon, my lord," Jamie said, bowing his friend into the house. "I don't believe either the duchess nor Lady Margaret are at-home to visitors, I'm afraid. Did you have an appointment?"

"Here." His friend slipped him a small leather purse which Jamie immediately hid in a pocket. "Two of your paintings have sold."

"Two? But it hasn't even been a week!" Jamie couldn't believe it.

His friend just shrugged. "I want more. Can you do more?" Wickford asked, a sly grin lifting one side of his mouth.

"I...I don't know. I'll try. It's hard while working," he admitted.

"Well, quit!"

"I can't. You know I can't," Jamie said.

"My Lord Wickford," the butler said from behind Jamie. "I am so terribly sorry, I don't believe the duchess is at home to callers this afternoon."

Wickford turned and looked down his nose at the man, which made Jamie disturbingly happy. "I am well aware of that," Wickford snapped. "This man, here, was just informing me as much. I was sure it was today that they were open to callers."

"I do beg your pardon, my lord, but it is Thurdays that they are at home."

Wickford gave an exasperated sigh. "Very well. You will give Lady Margaret that message, won't you?" he asked, turning back to Jamie.

"Er, yes, my lord. Of course, my lord. It will be my pleasure," Jamie said, bowing.

"All right, then." Wickford turned and went back out the door.

"He left a message for her ladyship?" Holton asked.

"Er, yes, sir. A verbal message. Would you mind very much watching the door while I deliver it?" Jamie asked.

Holton frowned but reluctantly shook his head. He clearly wished to know the message but couldn't very well ask straight out what it was.

With completely inappropriate satisfaction at keeping the man guessing, Jamie went off to find Lady Margaret. Only when he was halfway to the private drawing room did he realize he should first put away the money that was bulging in his pocket.

He didn't actually need to deliver a message to Lady Margaret. If he returned to his post right away Holton would never know the difference and neither would Lady Margaret. On the other hand, delivering something he made up on the spot would give him an opportunity to see and speak with the lovely young lady, who was always on his mind and who never failed to brighten his day.

He was standing outside of the drawing room with the door slightly ajar, trying to quickly think of something to tell her, when he couldn't help but overhear Lady Margaret talking inside the room. Of course! He'd forgotten that the Duchess of Warwick was visiting.

Chapter Twenty-Nine

Margaret laughed. It was silly what she was feeling—so hopeful, yet embarrassed. Whenever she thought of the night of the Venetian ball, she felt so happy. That was it. Happy. No, maybe delighted was a better word. Or ecstatic. Yes, she liked ecstatic because it was definitely more than simple happiness.

She shook her head and laughed again. Whatever it was, it was wonderful.

"I don't think I've ever seen you like this," Tina said, laughing. Margaret was sure she was laughing at her and not with her, but she didn't care.

"I've never been like this! I've never felt this way," Margaret admitted.

"And you think it was Lord Roseberry?" Tina asked.

"I do. He did propose to me once before last year, but Warwick scared him off, and he's hardly said a word to me since," Margaret told her sister-in-law. "And besides, who else could it be? His initials are JR, and I know for certain it's not Lord Ranelagh."

Tina thought about it for a moment and then shrugged. "It does make sense, except for the part that he's been avoiding you."

"That's because of his mother. He told me so last night. She puts such pressure on him to marry. He hates it and wants to take his time making his own decision. She has spies everywhere watching him all the time, he said. I'm certain that it's why he was able to pay so much attention to me at the Venetian Ball when we were all masked, and no one knew the identity of anyone else. But last night, he could barely say two words to me for fear that word would get back to his mother."

Tina just shook her head. "How awful to have so much pressure put on you in that way."

Margaret could only stare at her good friend. "Tina, how can you say that? You and Warwick have been doing nothing but putting such pressure on me for over a year!"

"Well, yes, but that's different," Tina argued.

Margaret waited for more of an explanation.

"You have to marry or else you're going to lose your inheritance!" Tina continued.

"Which means I've had even *more* pressure put on me," Margaret pointed out.

Tina was silent for a moment as she thought about this and took a nibble of the cake that had been sitting on her plate for the past fifteen minutes. "I can't say that I've *liked* putting such pressure on you, especially when you were already having such so much trouble trying to put yourself forward, but... You know, it's because we love you."

Margaret sighed. "Yes, I know. And you do it only because you are looking after me, but it's been extremely difficult."

Tina nodded. "I'm sorry." She took a sip of her tea and then said in a much more enthusiastic voice, "But now you've got Lord Roseberry."

"Well, I don't have him yet, but I certainly hope to!" Now if she could only figure out why that didn't make her as happy as it should have. Every time she thought of a life with him… James would pop into her mind. It was wrong. It was so very, very wrong. Not only that, but it was impossible.

No. Roseberry, if he were indeed the man from the Venetian Ball, was unquestionably the right man for her. James was a footman and, no matter how she looked at it, absolutely ineligible. He was a friend and would never be anything more.

~*~

Jamie leaned silently against the doorframe feeling horrendously guilty for eavesdropping. All right, if he had to be honest with himself, he felt worse about *what* he heard than how he'd heard it.

But he shouldn't, he reprimanded himself. He should be happy for Margaret. She was doing the right thing—no, it was even better than that—she was doing what she should have been doing all along. She was going after a man who would make her happy.

Jamie just had to accept they could never be together. He'd always known it. He'd *said* he accepted it, but then again, he'd said a lot of things in his life. He'd said he'd become a painter. He had put aside his estate, his heritage, his own identity to fulfill that dream. And here he was, a footman doing nothing but longing for someone he could never have.

He was an idiot, but he really should—

Someone cleared their throat just behind him. James jumped from where he'd been leaning against the door frame. Mr. Holton stood just behind him frowning fiercely. Slowly the man crossed his arms in front of his chest. His meaning was abundantly clear; James was in serious trouble.

~May 5~

Tina gave a little gasp as she and Margaret were standing side-by-side at Lady Hallburn's party. The duchess hadn't even had to worry about staying with Margaret most of the evening. She had had a partner for every single dance so far and even had been asked in advance for the supper dance. It was so completely unusual; it was a little disconcerting.

However, after her last dance had ended, Margaret's chaperone was nowhere to be found, so she'd asked Lord Michael to leave her with her sister-in-law. Happily, Tina didn't mind a bit as she still wasn't very comfortable dancing yet, despite the lessons she'd been taking.

"What is it?" Margaret asked.

"There's Lord Roseberry, and there's a set just forming," Tina said. "You don't have a partner for this dance, do you?"

Tina had never had to ask her that before, Margaret thought with a little giggle. "No, this is one of the few dances all evening I have free. I would love to dance with Lord Roseberry but—"

Tina didn't wait to hear what was stopping Margaret. She simply raised her fan in order to discreetly call Lord Roseberry over to them. He wasn't watching, however. Mr. Hershawn was with him as always, and happily he did see the duchess's summons.

It looked like the two men had a word before Mr. Hershawn practically dragged his friend over to them. Margaret hated that Lord Roseberry had to be forced to join them. On the other hand, how else was she going to find out if he was, in fact, Lord Mac?

"Good evening, ladies," Mr. Hershawn said with a bow. Lord Roseberry bowed as well.

"Good evening, gentlemen. Lord Roseberry, I don't believe you've danced once this evening," Tina began.

"Your Grace," Lord Roseberry bowed, giving her a smile. "Is His Grace not here this evening?"

"No, my husband is not. However, I don't dance. Lady Margaret does," Tina said, with no subtly whatsoever. Margaret closed her eyes for a moment and tried not to cringe.

"Indeed, I, er, I—" Lord Roseberry stammered. He looked pleadingly at Margaret, who immediately felt terrible for him. She was certain he was thinking of his mother and what she might say were he to lead her out.

"You know, my lord, perhaps tongues would not wag quite so much if you danced with other young ladies as well," Margaret suggested.

He looked at her in surprise, but his eyes were also darting to Tina.

"My sister-in-law is completely in my confidence and would never say anything, I can assure you," Margaret reassured him.

"Oh, er, yes. Well..." Lord Roseberry began.

"She's got an excellent point," Mr. Hershawn agreed. "Perhaps if you danced with a few young ladies, in addition to Lady Margaret, your mother wouldn't say anything."

Margaret gave him a hopeful look.

Lord Roseberry smiled politely, but Margaret couldn't tell if he were actually convinced. He did the polite thing, however. "Very well." He bowed and offered her his hand. "If you would do me the honor, my lady?"

"Thank you," Margaret said. Excitement built up quickly within her. She was finally going to get to dance once again with the sweet and wonderful, thoughtful and kind Lord Mac.

Strangely enough, Lord Roseberry didn't take her hand in quite the same way as Lord Mac had. She didn't know what it was or how he'd done it, but the gentleman at the Venetian ball had made her feel cared for when he'd taken her hand. Lord Roseberry barely touched her. Maybe he was still feeling worried about his mother.

"How long has it been since you've been back to Scotland, my lord?" Margaret asked.

He looked startled. "Scotland? I haven't been since I was a child, my lady. Why do you ask?"

"Oh, I was just wondering. I know your title is Scottish, is it not?"

He gave a hesitant nod. "It is. But I also own an estate in England, which is where I grew up when we weren't here in London."

The dance took them apart for a moment. When they came back together, she said, "I see. So that's why you don't have an accent."

"Er, yes."

"But you could if you wanted?" she asked.

He looked at her oddly as they moved away from each other as the dance prescribed. "I'm afraid I do a very poor approximation of a Scottish brogue," he admitted when they stood next to each other once again. "As I said, I grew up in England."

"Oh." Now Margaret was confused. If he couldn't speak with a Scottish accent... Was it possible that he *wasn't* Lord Mac?

They danced in silence for a little while before Lord Roseberry began a polite conversation about the weather. Margaret didn't understand this. Lord Mac *had* to be Lord Roseberry. If he wasn't...then who was? No, no, he had to be funning her. He had to be continuing his ruse.

As the dance ended, she gave him a bright smile. "I am so dreadfully warm, would you mind very much coming with me into the refreshment room for some lemonade?"

"Of course!" He gallantly held out his arm for her to take.

After she had slaked her thirst, she was even more determined to be certain that Lord Roseberry was Lord Mac. She was beginning to worry that he actually wasn't—he just didn't feel right. There was no way to explain it, but he didn't feel like the man she'd danced with at the Venetian ball. She still had one trick up her sleeve, however.

She pulled out the handkerchief Lord Mac had left with her. "I do believe this is yours, my lord."

He looked at it, immediately lifting the corner with the initials on it. He gave her a little smile. "No, I'm afraid it isn't. All of my handkerchiefs have a rose embroidered on them." He pulled one from his pocked and showed her the pretty red rose that was delicately stitched below his initials.

"Oh, but then... Are you certain?" Margaret asked. She hated the hollow feeling that was slowly enveloping her stomach.

"Absolutely."

"But then, who's handkerchief is this?" she asked, completely at a loss.

"I'm afraid I have no idea. I don't think I know anyone else with my same initials," he said, thinking about it. "There's Lord Redenton, but he's not in London, I don't believe. And, of course, Lord Ranelagh," he suggested.

Margaret shook her head, feeling tears beginning to burn her eyes. It couldn't be Lord Ranelagh. It just *couldn't*!

~May 6~

Lady Welles, Colburne, and Sorrell all jumped when Alys entered Lady Ayres' newly redecorated drawing room that Wednesday afternoon. She paused just inside the door as the three women looked at her with matching guilty expressions.

"Good afternoon, ladies," Alys said, coming farther into the room. "My, Lady Ayres, what a difference your new furniture makes to this room. It's absolutely lovely!"

"Thank you so much, Duchess," Lady Ayres said with a touch of pink coming to her cheeks. She was clearly proud of the room, as she should be.

The new gold damask furniture matched the framed tapestry on the wall just above the sofa, picking out the colors within the stitching and the frame elegantly. Much more so than the previous sofa, which had had a matching tapestry back. It had been too much of the same in Alys's opinion. The wooden arms and scroll-top back also picked up on the wood of the card tables situated nearby. It was all quite lovely.

Lady Ayres and Lady Blakemore were standing just beyond the younger women by the fireplace with its new gold-framed mirror above it. They turned toward her, nodding their greetings. Lady Ayres, Alys noted, was holding her tallying book.

Lady Ayres came forward to greet her properly. "I do hope you are well this afternoon?" she asked with a welcoming smile.

"I am, thank you. And yourself?" Alys asked, feeling more comfortable as they went through the usual routine.

"Very well. We are just awaiting a few more—ah, here are Mrs. Aldridge and Lady Moreton, perfect," Lady Ayres said, turning to the two other newcomers. "Ladies, please do come in and help yourselves to a cup of tea."

The other ladies exclaimed over the new furniture before greeting the newcomers. Soon they were all comfortably sitting around the tea tray, enjoying the fine buttery biscuits. Alys particularly liked them and had to remember to ask for the recipe, so her own cook could make them as well.

She was just biting into her second when Lady Ayres called the meeting to order. "Ladies, your attention, if you please?"

The chatter quickly died away as all eyes turned to their hostess.

"I'm afraid it is that time again when one of us must divulge a secret," Lady Ayres said, letting her eyes roam the group. She landed, finally, on Alys. "Your Grace, I am very sorry to say it will be you this time."

Alys started. "Me? Really?" She didn't know why she was so surprised. She had known this was coming. And yet, she suddenly found herself rather at a loss.

"I'm afraid so," Lady Ayres said. She then sat down and waited.

Chapter Thirty

Everyone turned to Alys. It was extremely disconcerting. "Well, I... I don't know that..." She gave a little embarrassed laugh. "I hadn't anticipated this would come quite so soon, to be honest." Were there any secrets about Margaret she could divulge? So many of the others who had had to tell their secrets related theirs to some love affair that was going on in their life. But, no, there was nothing. She could tell them about her romance with Lord Gorling, but not only was it none of their business, she was pretty certain they all knew of it in any case. They hadn't exactly been discrete.

Mrs. Aldridge's nasty little dog came sniffing around her feet.

"Might it have something to do with Duchess, Mrs. Aldridge's dog?" Lady Ayres prompted.

Alys looked down at the disgusting creature and then back up at the lady. "No. Not at all. I..." What could she say? What could she tell them? Certainly not the truth of her parentage, could she? Well, Lady Ayres, herself, had divulged to them that she had had a child out of wedlock. She supposed her story wasn't any worse than that. And honestly, she had no other secrets to tell.

She took a bracing sip of her tea. "I don't know

if you noticed that I was particularly interested in Lady Ayres's daughter's relationship with the Duke of Warwick," she began hesitantly. "There was, er, a reason for that."

"I thought you were very close friends with the duke," Lady Welles said.

Alys gave a hesitant little nod. "Well, we were certainly acquainted, but we weren't what you might call close until that time. His mother and I knew each other when we were first brought out into society. But I was most interested in Tina becoming engaged to Warwick not just because...because they were in love and should be together, but for other, more...personal reasons."

The women all waited patiently for her explanation. There seemed to be nothing for it, but to spill, as the young people said. She swallowed. "You see, my own mother was... Well, she was not of the nobility. She was a governess."

She paused to let that settle in. "She and my father had an affair. She was governess to his two boys—he'd lost his wife a few years earlier. It was highly inappropriate, but apparently, they fell in love. As soon as she realized she was expecting, she told him and he did the right thing and married her. But... Well, she never was accepted by society," Alys said, finding the freckles on the back of her hands unusually interesting.

"Were you born before they were wed?" Lady Ayres asked gently.

Alys looked up. "Oh, yes! He got a special license, and they married right away. I am legitimate. My half-brothers, however... They knew, or suspected. They were eight and ten when I was born, but somehow, they knew. They never let me forget my mother was nothing more than a governess," she added.

Somehow her voice had stopped working quite right. She cleared her throat and looked up. Oddly, her gaze landed on Mrs. Aldridge. "So, you see, I know very well your position," she said to the lady. "Trying to fit in where you only have a tenuous hold. I don't mean to be rude, but despite the fact that my parents were married and my father an earl, I too was called a mushroom." She could feel her face grow warm with old anger and hurt. "I was told on many, many occasions that I was pretending to be better than I was. My half-brothers threatened to tell society my dirty little secret, as they called it."

"How awful!" Mrs. Aldridge exclaimed.

Alys gave her a little smile. "I even changed the spelling of my name to seem more noble."

She received some curious looks at that, so she laughed. "My given name is Alice, spelled the usual way. I changed it to A-L-Y-S, thinking it sounded more prestigious."

Some of the ladies laughed or smiled.

"But what about the dog?" Lady Colburne asked.

Alys was confused. She looked at the young lady. "What dog?"

"Mrs. Aldridge's dog, Duchess. Why do you hate her so much?" Lady Welles asked.

"Is it because of her name? Or something else?" Lady Sorrell added.

"No, no, the name is confusing and stupid. I've always disliked dogs. My half-brothers would keep their enormous hunting dogs with them at all times in the house and out. They never failed to growl at me and threaten me. The boys thought it hilarious. I suppose, as a result, I dislike all dogs, even little ones like…" She gestured to Mrs. Aldridge's pup, which honestly couldn't be less intimidating with its big brown eyes and long floppy ears.

"Well, that's simply awful," Mrs. Aldridge said. "Did your mother never say anything to them?"

"No, no! She never felt she could reprimand them—especially not after she married their father. She wasn't a very strong person, I'm afraid," Alys explained. "She was always very well aware of her position and felt as if she were encroaching as the lady of the manor." Alys gave a little smile. "She told me never to forget where I came from—good, hearty common stock, she said. Well, I can tell you, I have tried my entire life to do to forget that she wasn't of the nobility."

"You did very well, considering," Lady Blakemore commented.

"Yes, I did," Alys said, smiling at her. "My husband, Kendell… He knew who I was—my brothers felt no compunction about telling him as soon as they saw that he was interested in me. He didn't care, though. So long as I knew how to behave, how to be a duchess, which I did. Despite my mother's low beginnings, she had read a great deal and taught me all I'd need to know to be a nobleman's wife." She took another sip of her tea, beginning to feel…quite well, surprisingly. "I had a very happy marriage, and in the end, I believe my mother did as well."

"Well, that is something," Lady Moreton said. "I suppose it really doesn't matter where people come from so long as they know how to behave."

"Precisely," Alys agreed with a little smile.

~May 7~

It took Jamie a couple of tries throughout the day, but finally he managed to be in the kitchen at the same time as Mary. He was sitting at the table, nursing a cup of tea, when she came in looking exhausted.

"You look like you need a break," Jamie said, standing and taking the ash bucket from her.

She smiled at him as she wiped her forehead with a filthy hand, smearing soot across it. "Thanks."

"Why don't we go out into the garden for a moment?" he suggested as he dumped the contents of the bin.

"Ugh, what I wouldn't do for a bit o'fresh air!" Mary said with a sigh.

"Then come on." He started toward the door.

"But I got floors that need swabbin'," she protested weakly. She didn't look like she could clean a floor even if she wanted to.

"They'll still be there when you get back." He took her dirty hand and led her out the back door before Mr. Holton or the housekeeper could discover them.

Mary followed with a little giggle.

Jamie finally let go of her hand when he reached the wall near the back gate. "I've got something for you," he said, hardly able to contain his own excitement. He'd had to wait all day, and his patience couldn't wait another moment.

She looked up at him with her big brown eyes. "What is it?"

Jamie pulled out the purse Wickford had given

him earlier. He'd set aside a little to buy more art supplies, but there were still enough coins in it to clink very nicely.

Mary's eyes widened at the sight of it. "What's that?" she asked on a breath.

"It's your ticket home."

Her gaze shot back up to his face, and her mouth dropped open.

He took her hand to place the bag into it, but she snatched it back again. "I can't take that!"

"Why not?"

"'Cause! It's yer money, not mine."

"But I want you to have it," James argued.

"Where'd you get it?" Mary asked skeptically.

"I sold a painting." It was mostly the truth. He hadn't sold it himself, and it hadn't been just one, but she didn't need to know the details.

"Oh, but...but I can't... That's yer money!" she protested again.

"And I want you to have it. You want to go home, and so you should."

"An' what about you?" she asked, pulling her gaze from the bag where they'd rested once again, as if she couldn't stop staring at it.

"I don't need to go home," he said with a shrug.

"Don't ye want to?"

Jamie thought about it. Oddly enough, while he'd thought a few times about leaving his post here, he'd never once actually thought of going back to Scotland. He didn't know what sort of home he had to go to. He'd rented out all of his land, although the manor house was still vacant except for the old retainers left to watch over things. He supposed he could go there, but to do what? Become a farmer? He had no skill or knowledge and very little desire to do that.

For now, he just shook his head. "I've got no one to go to. You do. You need this. I don't."

"But—"

"No, Mary, please. I want you to have it," he insisted.

Slowly, she took the pouch. "I'll pay ye back. Every cent!"

He just smiled at her and nodded. "I know you will."

Her hug caught him off-guard, but he gently squeezed her back. "Be happy, Mary."

"It'll be hard without ye, but I'll do my best."

~*~

After Jamie had gone back inside, Harold called out to him. "Her Grace wants to see ye. Askin' for ye, personally. Yer either a favorite or yer in for it. Either way, I wouldn't want to be you," the fellow said with a laugh.

Jamie had no idea why the duchess was asking for him. He could only hope that it had something to do with a painting. He didn't *think* it would be that, but he *hoped* it would.

"Come in," the duchess said after he'd tapped lightly on the door to her private sitting room.

"Good afternoon, my lady. You needed me?" he asked, bowing to her.

"Yes." She took in a deep breath and didn't look happy. "I have had strange reports of you from Mr. Holton. He is finding your behavior disturbing." She paused and looked up at him to see if he had anything to say.

He didn't, so she continued. "You have apparently been having intimate conversations with Lady Margaret?"

James thought of the conversation he'd had with her the other morning when Holton had caught them. There couldn't have been anything more innocent, and yet... Jamie was a footman. He wasn't *supposed* to be having a conversation with a young lady of the house. It wasn't proper behavior, but it was Margaret. He'd been helping her. Encouraging her. Doing all he could to make her happy.

"And then the other night," the duchess continued, her voice sharpening. "She, herself, told me of some advice which you gave her just before the Venetian ball. *You* gave her advice." A hint of disgust flavored her voice. She took in a deep breath. "I appreciate that you are trying to help a young girl overcome her shyness, but I must remind you of your place. I am surprised I need to remind you of this, but you are a footman." She lifted her chin as she continued, "I can't imagine what you think you know of society. Just watching your betters doesn't make you one of them or give you knowledge of how they should or shouldn't behave."

Jamie felt his gut tightening. Betters. *Betters*! As if he were nothing. Nobody. His breathing had quickened, but mentally he gave himself a shake. She didn't know—and she couldn't. Do nothing; say nothing; show nothing, he reminded himself as he literally bit his tongue. He kept his face frozen and bland, his gaze directed over her left shoulder.

"I worry that you believe yourself to be on par with Lady Margaret and myself because you have painted some pictures, but you need to be cognizant of your place, young man. You are nothing more than a servant in this household, and I expect you to remember that. You may have been given special access to Lady Margaret when you were painting her portrait, but that doesn't mean you continue to have such privileges. You are *not* her friend nor qualified to advise her. You leave that to me, do you understand? Lady Margaret is not your concern."

Jamie didn't know when he'd lowered his gaze to the floor, but he kept it lowered now, not even looking up when the lady had stopped speaking. He knew without a doubt if she saw his eyes, she would know just how furious he was. What he didn't know was whether he was angrier at her or himself.

"I must keep order in this household, James. It was exceedingly generous of me to give you the special permission I did, but I cannot have you continuing to behave as if you were better than any other footman in my employ."

His nails dug into his palm while he considered the fact that *he* was the one who had put himself into this situation. He was the one who'd kept himself here even when Wickford had tried to convince him to leave. But for the duchess to shove his position in his face and tell him that he was nothing and not to even presume? It was too much.

No, he couldn't trust himself to speak for fear of what might inadvertently come out of his mouth.

"Do you have nothing to say for yourself?" the lady asked.

Jamie didn't move. Didn't open his mouth or lift his eyes.

She sighed loudly. "Very well. Consider this your first warning. If I have to speak with you again, you will be dismissed. Is that clear?"

He gave a nod.

"You may go."

Jamie got out of there as quickly as he could and went straight back to his post at the front door. The monotony of the job would calm him down—he hoped.

He just wished Mary's queries of why he didn't want to go home would stop sounding over and over again in his mind.

Margaret. He had to think of Margaret because it was for her that he'd kept this job. If it weren't his ridiculous feelings for the girl, he could have left. He could be somewhere in the countryside, painting right now. He could be producing work that Wickford would sell for him. Hell—when did he lose sight of his desire to be an artist? When had it become more important that he stay close to Margaret rather than follow his dream?

Chapter Thirty-One

Margaret turned this way and then the other. "What do you think? Is it appropriate? Is it all right?"

The duchess smiled at her indulgently. "You look lovely, my dear. Lord Bertram will no doubt be honored to have you next to him."

Margaret took in a deep breath, trying to calm her nerves. She had never gone out for a drive with a young man on her own before. She'd never been asked.

She was still reeling over the fact that *three* gentlemen had sent her flowers after Lady Hallburn's party the previous week, and the number of gentlemen who'd shown up at the duchess's at-home the previous Thursday was simply unprecedented! It was all thanks to James and his wonderful advice, she was sure of it. She wished she knew how to thank him, but somehow, recently, she'd simply found herself too tongue tied around him.

It was the oddest thing! They were friends. Why would she feel awkward about speaking with him? And yet, every time she looked at him all she could see were his eyes growing soft and warm as he'd looked at her before she'd gone out last week;

how he'd told her that she was beautiful in that sweet, soft lilting voice of his. It had made her grow warm then, and it still did now.

But he was a friend! She couldn't possibly feel anything for him. And he was a footman, so it would be wrong for her to feel anything. As if she had conjured him with her thoughts, James came into the room after a brief knock on the door.

"I beg your pardon, my lady, Lord Bertram is here to see you," he said. He then stood aside as his lordship strode into the room.

"Your Grace." The gentleman bowed toward the duchess. "Lady Margaret." He bowed to her, giving her a sweet smile. "You are looking beautiful this afternoon, if I may be so bold as to say so."

Margaret curtsied, hiding her smile as she did so. "Thank you, my lord. I have my wrap and parasol right here, so I'm ready to go when you are."

"Brilliant! Your Grace?" he said, asking her permission.

"Of course, you go on. Have fun!" the duchess said with a little laugh.

James held the door open as Margaret and Lord Bertram left the house. Usually she would give him a smile or a nod of her head as she passed him. Today, with all the mixed feelings she'd been having, combined with Lord Bertram's presence, she simply kept her gaze straight ahead as she walked past.

She felt bad, but she just couldn't bring herself to look at him.

"It is a fine day for a drive, my lady, and I am going to be envied by all we see. I'm sure of it," Lord Bertram said, as he handed her up into his phaeton.

Margaret giggled. "La, you exaggerate, my lord."

He stopped. "You do not believe it's a fine day? But the sun is shining, at least it is in my heart," he said with mock hurt.

The sky *was* overcast, but Margaret just laughed. "It wasn't that part I was questioning, my lord."

"Ha, pish tosh," he said with a negligent wave of his hand before going to walk around his horse's head and climb up on her other side.

Margaret could only laugh. This was going to be an enjoyable outing; she was certain of it!

~May 11~

"Lord Wickford, if you please," Jamie said Monday evening as he entered Powell's Club for Refined Gentlemen, or whatever the place was called. He'd had the entire weekend to try to calm himself down after the duchess had spoken to him, but somehow the longer he stewed on it, the more certain he was that he had to do something. He wasn't certain yet, but maybe speaking with Wickford would help—goodness knew he couldn't hold this inside for much longer.

The footman at the door bowed. "Your card, sir?"

"Just tell him the Marquess of Rossburke is here," Jamie informed him, not having a visiting card to give. But no longer would he hide his identity. He was done with it.

The footman bowed again and left to find his employer.

A few minutes later, Wickford came sauntering out of the gaming room. "Well, well, well... Rossburke is it tonight?"

Jamie just scowled at him. "Is it possible to get a drink in this damned place? If so, I want one, now!"

Wickford's eyebrows rose. "I think that might be possible. The cost, of course, is that you spill every last detail of what's bothering you to the one buying you that drink. Can you do that?"

"Every detail," Jamie growled. "I am done playing games, Joshua. Done!" He'd held on to his anger for nearly twenty-four hours and now it wanted out. He was just going to have to be careful and let it out slowly, and in a measured way, so as not to jump down his friend's throat. Especially since that friend had done so many very good things for him recently. No, Wickford didn't deserve Jamie's anger.

His friend nodded and led the way into the reading room. "I knew this day would come, you know. It's a very fine line you've been walking. Will you give me a hint—is it the young lady, the old one, or the job that has finally sent you reeling?"

"All of them!"

A whoosh of air came out of Wickford, and he could only shake his head in wonder. "All right, then. I look forward to hearing all about it, but first, let's get you that drink."

They sat in silence for a few moments while they waited for a bottle to be brought to them.

Jamie looked around and appreciated what Wickford had built here. The members looked comfortable in their surroundings, either reading quietly with a drink at their elbow or talking with friends and sharing a bottle. He knew in the other room Wickford was raking in the pounds as men gambled away their fortunes over the turn of a card.

It was all oddly soothing, so he let it all just wash over him, taking in a deep breath of calm.

"Here you are," Wickford said, handing Jamie a glass of rum. "I can make you a member if you're interested," he offered.

Jamie gave him a little smile. "I appreciate that, but no. Not now. Perhaps in a few years, I'll have the wherewithal to pay the dues on my own."

"Well, here's to that day," Wickford said, raising his glass.

Jamie followed suit and took a sip of some very fine rum. It felt good—the sweet, smooth flavor sliding across his tongue, the slight burn of the alcohol as it made its way down his throat.

"It's good, isn't it?" Wickford asked, watching him.

"Very. And much needed, thank you."

His friend nodded. He was clearly waiting for Jamie to start his tale, so he took another sip of his drink.

"The duchess called me into her drawing room yesterday and informed me that I have been out of line—presuming to know much more than I possibly could, being a footman."

"Really?"

"Yes. The butler told her that I had a conversation with Lady Margaret, and we were speaking together as if we were friends."

Wickford's eyebrows rose a touch. "And were you?"

"Yes, because we *are* friends."

Wickford nodded. "And that's not appropriate in the eyes of either the butler or the duchess."

"No. Not only that, but apparently Lady Margaret told the duchess that she was following my advice and trying to be more outgoing. It's working too. Since your ball, she's been much bolder, seeking out Lord Roseberry because she thinks he's the one she danced with that night. Seeing her behaving this way has inspired other gentlemen to seek her out as well. She's received bouquets of flowers, had at least half a dozen fellows come visit when the duchess was at home, and has gone out driving with Lord Bertram."

"Where does all that leave you?" Wickford asked, lowering his eyebrows and beginning to look concerned.

"Reprimanded by the duchess for giving advice, oddly enough."

"Because you're a footman and can't possible know how a young lady should behave?"

"Because I can't possibly know how one should behave in society," Jamie corrected him.

"Ah, of course." His friend nodded. "And what about Lady Margaret?"

"She's followed my advice, and it's doing her good," Jamie said.

"Yes, I got that, but how do *you* feel about her newfound success?"

"Oh, well…" Jamie took another long sip of his drink. "To be completely honest?" he asked, watching the thick amber liquid swirl around his glass.

Wickford nodded. "That was our deal."

"Like something she stepped in while crossing the street."

"Shit."

"To put it bluntly, yes," Jamie said. He tipped the contents of his glass into his mouth.

Wickford held the bottle out to him. Jamie took it and refilled his glass gratefully.

"Oh, and in all of her social success, the good lady has decided I'm no longer worth her time," Jamie added before lowering the level of liquid from his overfull glass.

"What?"

"Lady Margaret hasn't spoken directly to me in days. When she went out driving with Bertram, she gave me the cut direct as she walked out of the house—usually she smiles or nods to me as she's going out, but yesterday I got nothing. She just walked right on past as if I wasn't there."

"As if you were a footman?" Wickford asked with dry irony.

"Very funny."

"Hey, you're the one who chose the profession," Wickford said, raising a hand in surrender.

"I did so because I was starving!"

"You could have come here. I would have fed you," Wickford said.

Jamie just scowled. "I wasn't looking for a hand-out. I needed employment."

"No, you needed to eat and find a way to sell your paintings. I could have helped you with both."

"Yes, you could have," Jamie acknowledged as the odd dichotomy of the warmth of friendship and anger at Wickford for being right warred in his gut.

"But that was last hand, we're playing a new game now," Wickford said. "So, your love is ignoring you, your employer is reprimanding you for being uppity, and your paintings are beginning to sell if you would get me more…"

Jamie just shook his head. "I appreciate that you've managed to sell some, but I don't…" He stopped, the words catching in his throat. He cleared it and went on. "I think it's time I returned home."

"To Rossburke? I thought you'd leased it?" Wickford asked.

"I did. I leased the land, but I can probably get some, if not all of it back. And I was clever in one thing—I only leased it for a year on a tentative basis."

"You weren't certain this would work out. That *was* clever," Wickford nodded.

Jamie just shrugged. "Sometimes I have my moments."

Wickford laughed but sobered quickly. "So, you'd do what? Become a farmer?"

Jamie gave him a frown. "I don't know. How hard can it be?"

Wickford raised his eyes to the ceiling. When he lowered them back down again, he said, "Hard!"

"Well, I'll learn! I can't stay here, Joshua. I can't go on working as a footman. I thought I could do it, but I'm just not cut out for servitude. I hate it, but I'm a nobleman. I was raised to be a marquess, and no matter how hard I try, I just can't remove that part of myself—my damned pride. My father instilled it in me from the moment I was born, and I can't just push it aside."

Joshua began to laugh. Within a moment, heads were turning; he was laughing so hard.

Jamie just sat there, confused as to what his

friend had found so funny.

When Wickford finally caught his breath, Jamie merely said, "Care to share the joke?"

"You're a marquess," Wickford said, still chuckling a little.

"Yes, I think I just said that."

CHAPTER THIRTY-TWO

"You've been trying *not* to be a marquess ever since I met you when we were, what, eight? Nine years old?" Wickford asked.

"Eight. We met when we were eight," Jamie reminded him.

"Right. I remember it. The headmaster called you Lord Rossburke, and you shouted at him that you were *not* the marquess. Your name was Jamie Douglass and he'd do well to remember that!" Wickford burst out laughing again. This time at the memory of the bold, angry little boy Jamie had been.

"I'd just lost my father," Jamie explained.

"I know," Wickford said, sobering up quickly. "I know, and it was terrible, I'm sorry. But still, you have *never* wanted to be the marquess, and now that you're not—at least in the eyes of the duchess and her protégé—you want to be." Wickford leaned forward toward Jamie. "Deep down in your soul, you are a nobleman, Jamie Douglass, and you always have been." He sat straight again. "And may I add, I've always reminded you of this."

Jamie could only frown. "I know. You're right. You've always been right, and I've hated you for it ever since we met."

Wickford gave a little laugh and shook his head. "So, what are you going to do, my lord?"

"I'm going to quit my job and go home," Jamie said, knowing that no matter how hurtful, the decision was the right one.

He'd wanted to be an artist. He'd wanted it so badly, he given up everything to do that. But no matter how hard he tried, he simply could not give up what he was raised to be. His father and his grandfather had both failed miserably at making their estate profitable, and maybe he would as well, but it was *his* estate. He needed to be there. And watching Margaret fall in love with someone else wasn't exactly high on his list of things he enjoyed doing either.

Wickford had sat back, sipping from his glass. He seemed to be contemplating something.

"What?" Jamie asked.

"Don't do it yet. Not just yet. I may... No, I won't say any more. Just...just wait."

"What am I waiting for? I need to go back and see if I can untangle the contracts I signed, giving my land away. I need to see if my house is even livable, and I need to learn how to be a bloody farmer. I'm finally taking your advice and trying to get my life back on track, and now you're asking me to wait?"

"I know. I know." Wickford even went so far as to stroke his chin. He always did that when he was conjuring some sort of plan.

Jamie had no idea what his friend was putting together in his devious mind. His ideas were usually very good but sometimes very bad. Jamie didn't know which one it was going to be this time. The thing was, when they were very good, they could be very, very good.

"You want me to wait," Jamie clarified.

"Yes. Just wait. I'll let you know." It made no sense, and it was all Jamie could get out of him. So, he'd wait—but not for long.

"Fine. You've got a week. No more," Jamie said.

~*~

"I just don't understand why you're so upset about this, Margaret," Tina said, pouring out a second cup of tea for herself.

"Because if Lord Roseberry isn't Lord Mac, then it worries me that it might have been Lord Ranelagh," Margaret explained. She'd been worrying about this for nearly a week now.

"No, it wasn't him," Tina said with a shake of her head. "I discussed it with my father, and he told me that Ranelagh had already left London by then—he'd only come for the wedding."

Margaret sat forward in her chair. "Really? It *couldn't* have been him?"

"I'm afraid not."

"No, no, don't be afraid. This is good news...although...if it wasn't Ranelagh and it wasn't Roseberry, then who could it have been?" Margaret was now completely flummoxed.

Her sister-in-law couldn't help though. "There's no way to know. I'm sorry."

Margaret sat back again and took a sip of her now-cold tea. It wasn't either of the two men she thought it might be. That meant she might never learn who Lord Mac was. How could she live without knowing? That had been the most wonderful night of her life!

The more she'd thought about it, the more she realized she'd completely and ridiculously fallen in love that night. How it was possible to fall in love in one evening, she had no idea, but she ached for Lord Mac. She thought of him constantly. No other man could or would ever live up to him.

In one evening, a stranger came into her life and both made it and destroyed it. She was now, finally, being able to put herself forward. As a result of that, and the fact that gentlemen now saw her as someone coveted by another, they were interested in her—in this way Lord Mac had helped her. But he'd destroyed her by being wonderful. No man could ever live up to Lord Mac's perfection. Perhaps she was putting him too high onto a pedestal, making him even more special than he'd been, but it didn't matter because she'd never see him again. No matter what, she would simply have to make do with whoever she married.

"Be happy, Margaret. You're doing so well now, and you've got gentlemen interested in you," Tina said, reaching across and taking Margaret's hand.

"I know. I'm trying."

~May 12~

Alys was sitting in her private drawing room enjoying a novel when there was a knock at the door. At her bidding, James came in.

"I apologize for disturbing you, Your Grace, but Lord Gorling is here, and he says it is extremely important that he speak with you. Are you at home?"

Alys set aside her book. "Yes, thank you, James. Do send his lordship up."

As soon as he'd left, she popped up and stole a glance at her reflection in the window. It was daylight, so she couldn't see very well, but enough to see that her hair was all still in place. She was just brushing out the wrinkles of her morning dress when James knocked again.

"Lord Gorling, Your Grace," he announced before bowing and leaving them alone.

His lordship came forward and took her hands in his own. "Duchess, thank you so much for seeing me."

"Of course. What is it? What's so urgent?"

"Urgent? Nothing. What I wanted to speak with you about isn't urgent, merely vitally important," he said, smiling down at her. His blue eyes twinkled with mischief.

She looked at him in askance. "Vitally important," she repeated back, not entirely believing him. "Well, then, if it's not urgent, why don't we sit down and make ourselves comfortable. May I offer you a glass of wine?"

"Oh, yes, thank you. You wouldn't happen to have any brandy?" he asked, taking a spot on the sofa.

"Yes, I believe I do." She opened up the sideboard and pulled out the decanter that had hardly been touched since her husband had died three years ago. She poured him out a glass, and another of madeira for herself. She didn't partake very often, but it was nice to do so every now and then.

"Thank you," Lord Gorling said, taking the glass she offered him. He then patted the seat next to him, indicating she should sit close.

She didn't see any reason why she shouldn't since they were alone, so she sat where he'd indicated.

He raised his glass. "To the loveliest woman in London."

She giggled. "To the smoothest talker in London."

"I'll drink to that," he said with wink. He took a sip from his glass and then set it aside. He helped her place her own glass on the table nearby as well, and then took both of her hands in his own.

"My dearest duchess..." He cocked his head at her. "May I have your permission to address you by your given name?"

She suppressed another giggle. "Yes, you may. It is Alys, in case you didn't know."

"I did, and I think it's lovely." He started once again, holding her hands and looking deeply into her eyes. "My dearest, sweet Alys. The reason I needed to see you this afternoon is because I don't think I can possibly live for much longer without you."

Alys laughed. "What do you mean? You see me all the time."

"At parties and such," he said dismissively. "I want to see you every morning when I wake up and every evening just before I close my eyes and drift off to sleep. Marry me, my sweet Alys."

The duchess's jaw dropped, and her eyes widened. "Marry you? How... I mean, why?"

"Why? Didn't I just say? I want to be with you all the time. Why ever not?"

"Well, I don't know," she said honestly. "Truly, I hadn't thought of marrying again." She removed her hands from his and sat back. "I had a very happy marriage," she told him.

"So you've said."

"And I enjoy my position in society."

"Which would be ever so slightly lower, I do understand and apologize that I am not like your esteemed late-husband. I am merely an earl."

She waved off his apology. "I am not so attached to my title, truly, merely my position. I've worked hard for it. I'm well-respected." She turned toward him. "You might not realize it, considering my recent behavior, but I've always been a rather sober person."

"Sober? You? But you love to laugh!"

"I do—with you. You are so amusing. But before this... Well, I was quite the serious sort. I suppose it's because my husband was. He was an esteemed member of Parliament, and while we did enjoy each other's company a great deal, he wasn't...funny or light-hearted in the same way as you."

"You might say I make a nice change?" he asked, fishing for a compliment possibly.

She laughed. "Yes, I suppose you could say that."

"But you would prefer to be married to someone more sober?" he asked, losing his smile.

"Well, it's what I'm used to. Kendell was a politician. I would organize dinners for him and the other men he worked with and their wives, of course. But we would have deep, involved discussions of the current issues of the day. We would spend hours debating the pros and cons of various pieces of legislation being considered in the Lords."

Lord Gorling only smiled. "I could offer you such things, but I thought you would find debate dreadfully dull."

She remembered what Lord Colburne and Welles said the previous week when she saw them at a party. "I've heard that you are politically active."

He nodded. "I am. I have taken my seat in Parliament."

"That's good."

"Does it make you more inclined to accept my offer, then?"

Chapter Thirty-Three

"**I**t does, actually. I do so miss Kendell and the wonderful discussions we would have," Alys admitted.

"I can certainly offer you that. But much more importantly, I offer you laughter and joy." His smile was so warm and filled with kindness that Alys was having a very hard time trying to remember why she shouldn't just say yes.

In fact, now that she thought about it, why *shouldn't* she accept his offer?

Margaret. That was why, of course.

She leaned forward and picked up her glass. "I will accept your offer, my lord, because goodness knows I need laughter and joy in my life, but there is one condition."

He too took up his own glass preparing to toast to them, perhaps. "What is that?"

"That we wait until my protégé, Lady Margaret, is settled. I have promised her brother, the Duke of Warwick, that I would see her thus before the end of this season."

He nodded, his eyes shifting off toward the floor. "I would have said that might take longer than this season, but recently she's quite come out of her shell, hasn't she?"

"She has, I'm happy to say. She's had quite a good bit of interest from a number of eligible gentlemen."

"Very well, then. We will wait until Lady Margaret is settled."

"Thank you. So, we'll just keep this between ourselves?"

"What? I can't even announce my joy and happiness to the world?" he asked, sitting back a little.

"I would appreciate it if you did not. We'll just keep this between ourselves for now. I don't want to put any undue pressure on Margaret, not when she's just begun to put herself forward with more confidence."

Lord Gorling sighed dramatically. "Very well. It will be our little secret."

"You may tell your children, if you wish, of course. I don't imagine they will spread the news if you ask them not to," she said, thinking of whether she could keep the secret from the Ladies' Wagering Whist Society. Those women were too observant by half.

"Ah, very good. I appreciate that. I think it might be hard to keep such news from Henry. But what about Lady Margaret? You won't tell her?"

"No. That I won't. As I say, she might not do well with such pressure."

"All right. I'll be sure to tell Henry not to discuss it with her."

"Thank you."

"Now, may we drink a toast to us?" Lord

Gorling asked, raising his glass again.

"Most definitely," Alys said with a little giggle. "To us."

Before she could lift her glass to her lips, however, his lordship leaned forward and placed his own lips very gently on hers. Alys was startled at first, but as she became accustomed to it, she found it to be much more pleasant than expected. She hadn't been kissed for so long... She could barely remember the last time. Oh, yes, this was a great deal more pleasant than she'd remembered.

~May 13~

Alys didn't know whether she should share her news with the ladies or not. She'd told George, Lord Gorling, that they shouldn't make their engagement public, and yet she just couldn't imagine not sharing such momentous news with her closest friends.

She determined not to say anything unless someone asked. But no matter what, she simply could not keep her joy from showing when she walked into Lady Ayres's drawing room Wednesday afternoon.

She'd already had the most difficult time keeping herself calm and collected around Margaret; she didn't want to have to continue to control herself with her closest friends as well.

"Good afternoon, ladies," she said to those already assembled.

Ladies Ayres, Blakemore, and Moreton looked up from where they were sitting around the tea tray. Mrs. Aldridge was trying to feed her dog a piece of cake on the sly.

"Good afternoon," they said nearly in unison.

"I passed Ladies Welles, Sorrell, and Colburne

walking up the street on my way. They should be here momentarily," she informed them, helping herself to a cup from the sideboard and then joining them around the tea tray.

"Excellent, then we'll be able to get started," Lady Blakemore said with a nod.

Lady Moreton looked at the duchess with her head tilted ever so slightly. "Is there something different… Did you do your hair differently, Your Grace?"

Alys widened her eyes. "No."

"There's something… I can't put my finger on it," she said.

"You seem happier than normal," Lady Ayres commented. "Your smile is brighter. Is it possibly due to relieving yourself of your secret last week? I know I felt immensely lighter after doing so."

Alys gave a little laugh. She would have responded except the three younger ladies chose just that moment to join them. There were greetings all around.

"You're looking particularly well today, Your Grace," Lady Welles commented.

"We were just discussing that when you came in, and I believe the duchess was about to tell us why," Mrs. Aldridge said, giving Alys a broad hinting smile.

"Well…" Alys started. "Since you asked, I do have some news, but it's similar to when we share our secrets—it cannot leave this room. Not until we make it public."

"*We?*" Lady Colburne asked meaningfully.

"Yes, we," Alys said, turning a bright smile onto the lady.

"Oh my goodness, has Lord Gorling proposed?" Lady Welles asked, clapping her hands together lightly.

Alys giggled. "Yes, he has! How very clever of you to have figured it out right away."

"I knew it! I knew it," Lady Welles said.

"I think we were all aware it was going to happen sometime before the end of the season," Lady Blakemore said with a broad smile. "Congratulations."

"Thank you," Alys said as the other all chimed in with their words of support and congratulations as well.

They were interrupted, however, by the footman coming in and clearing his throat loudly. "I beg your pardon, my lady," he said over the women's voices. "There is a gentleman caller who insists he has a very important matter he needs to discuss with the Ladies' Wagering Whist Society."

Everyone quieted down and turned to Lady Ayres to see her response. The lady in question looked around for consensus. They all nodded or otherwise gave indication that they were willing to entertain the gentleman, whoever he might be.

"If our assistance is needed, of course we will give it," Mrs. Aldridge said speaking for everyone.

"Yes, Thomas, show the gentleman in," Lady Ayres told the footman.

He bowed and returned a few minutes later. "Lord Wickford," he announced.

His lordship came in and bowed to all the ladies who stood to greet him.

"Welcome, my lord, please come in. Would you care for some tea?" Lady Ayres asked, making room for him around the tea tray.

"Thank you, my lady, but no to the tea. I have come to ask for your help, I'm afraid."

"No need to be afraid, my lord, we are more than happy to help. What sort of assistance do you need?" Lady Colburne asked.

"It is with a romantic endeavor," he informed them. "Your success at being able to see two people happily connected is becoming quite legendary."

Lady Welles' smile broadened. "Who is the lucky lady, my lord?"

The man started. "Oh, it's not for me but for a friend."

"*Really*?" Mrs. Aldridge said, clearly not believing him.

"Yes, truly," the gentleman replied widening his small, oddly light eyes. "I believe I heard once that your group specializes in secrets?"

"We play for them," Lady Moreton said, her voice quiet as if she were divulging a secret herself.

"Yes, while most people gamble for pennies or even pounds when they play whist, we gamble for secrets," Lady Ayres clarified.

"Do you have a secret, my lord?" Lady Blakemore asked.

"I do, but it's not mine to tell, which is why I must ask for the utmost discretion," he answered.

"This is becoming more intriguing by the moment," Lady Sorrell commented.

"But before I say another word, I would need your assurance that what I say here will not leave this room," Lord Wickford said, looking from one lady to the next.

"You absolutely have our word," Lady Ayres said without hesitation. She looked around the room to confirm with the others. Everyone agreed readily.

"This is extremely important because I've not told the gentleman in question that I'm here. He doesn't even think he needs help, but I..." He paused awkwardly.

"You know otherwise?" Alys finished for him.

"Yes." Lord Wickford took in a deep breath and began. "A very close friend of mine who I went to school with is... Well, he's working for you, Your Grace." He turned to look directly at Alys.

She started, shocked by his announcement. "For me? Who is it?"

"You know him as your footman, James. His name is James Douglass—"

"Of course! James is a fine footman," Alys said immediately. She then recalled the unfortunate conversation she'd had to have with him. "He has had moments..." she started hesitantly.

"He is the Marquess of Rossburke," Lord Wickford said, interrupting her.

"What?" She nearly jumped from her seat.

"The duchess's footman is a marquess?" Mrs. Aldridge asked, clearly as shocked.

"Were you aware of this, Your Grace?" Lady Welles asked.

"Clearly, I was not," Alys answered, quite shocked by this information. "Why in the world is a marquess working as a footman—and not informing his employer of his status?" she asked Lord Wickford.

"He is...or was attempting to make it as an

artist here in London. He's leased the land around his estate in Scotland and was trying to establish a career. He didn't want it known that he was marquess for fear it might impact this endeavor. Er, he's never really spent very much time in London, so it would be the rare member of society who would recognize him. Sadly, he wasn't able to earn anything as an artist, so he turned to being a footman just to keep from starving."

"But what about the income from his estate?" Lady Blakemore asked.

"He said it was leased," Lady Sorrell said.

"Yes, and he is putting all of those earnings into revitalizing the house there which has fallen into sad disrepair. Neither his father nor his grandfather were able to make a profit with the estate, and I believe there were some bad investments along the way as well," Lord Wickford explained.

"So he is an impoverished nobleman," Lady Moreton said.

"Sadly, so," Lord Wickford agreed.

"Who was trying to support himself by becoming an artist?" Lady Welles asked. "Why not just marry a wealthy young lady as most impoverished gentlemen do?"

"I suggested the same thing, but he felt that it would be unfair to the young lady in question," Lord Wickford said with a little shrug.

Alys had been thinking back on her recent interactions with James. It was all becoming startlingly obvious that he *was*, in fact, a nobleman. If she'd known, she would have seen it right away. Since the thought never occurred to her… "My goodness!" she exclaimed involuntarily.

Everyone turned toward her. "I'm sorry, I was just remembering an encounter I had with James recently. I-I told him he was taking on airs, behaving as if he understood society when giving advice to Margaret and speaking to her as if she were an equal. How very embarrassing! He *is* her equal and *does* know how one should behave!"

"Er, yes," Lord Wickford said, suddenly finding the floor rather interesting. "I'm afraid that was the last straw for him. He was... Well, he wasn't happy at being told to remember his place."

"I should say not!" Lady Blakemore exclaimed.

"But how could I have known?" Alys asked, feeling just awful now for all the things she'd said to the man.

Chapter Thirty-Four

"You couldn't have, and truly, Rossburke doesn't blame you. If he'd been an ordinary footman, you would have been absolutely correct to reprimand him so," Lord Wickford said, trying to reassure her.

"But if he'd been an ordinary footman, he probably wouldn't have spoken to Lady Margaret or been able to give her such good advice," Lady Moreton pointed out.

"That is correct as well, my lady," Lord Wickford said, giving her a smile.

"So, we have established James's or Lord Rossburke's identity. Now how do you need our help?" Lady Ayres asked, bringing them back to the point.

"Ah, yes. Well, er, Her Grace pointed it out already, James and Lady Margaret have grown rather close," Lord Wickford said with some awkwardness now that it came right down to it.

"They have," Alys agreed. She also immediately saw where this was leading, as did most of the other women in the room.

"He's fallen in love with her, but I can't imagine she has the same feelings for him since she thinks he's a footman," Lady Colburne said.

"You are probably right, my lady," Lord Wickford said. "But we do know that Lady Margaret *does* have feelings for him. Yhe thing is, she doesn't know it."

"I don't understand. Could you clarify, please?" Lady Blakemore asked.

"Naturally," Lord Wickford said with a smile. "If you'll remember my Venetian ball, Lady Margaret spent the entire evening in the company of one gentleman."

"Don't tell me—" Lady Welles gasped.

"Indeed, my lady. That was Rossburke," Lord Wickford said with a laugh.

"No wonder she hasn't been able to discover his identity!" Alys said.

"Precisely. She couldn't possibly because no one knows that he's here."

"JR—James Rossburke," Mrs. Aldridge said, just getting it.

"Well then, that changes everything, doesn't it?" Lady Ayres said.

"It sounds to me like all we need to do is to have an occasion where Lady Margaret can re-meet Lord Rossburke as himself," Lady Colburne said.

"That is precisely what we need. The difficult part is that Rossburke has no intention of admitting to anyone his true identity," Lord Wickford said. "In fact, he's mentioned that he's thinking of simply disappearing from Town altogether and returning to his estate. We need to do something before he does so."

"But what about Lady Margaret? Does he not have feelings for her?" Alys asked.

"He does. Extremely strong feelings, but he

believes it wouldn't be fair to her to marry such an impoverished man," Lord Wickford explained.

"But if she loves him..." Lady Welles started.

"Naturally, *you* see the fault in his logic as do I, but he, sadly, does not. He is completely besotted and intractable in his ideas of right and wrong." Lord Wickford's smile was just a slight lift of one corner of his mouth. Clearly, he'd had this discussion with Lord Rossburke and came away unable to convince him of the folly of his decisions.

"He sounds most noble," Mrs. Aldridge said with a little sniff.

"I have an idea," Lady Ayres said, a small smile growing on her face.

"If you can figure out a way to get Rossburke and Lady Margaret together in a room where they can meet as equals, I might be able to reveal his true identity," Lord Wickford said, turning to Lady Ayres. "Er, without being the one to actually do so because I do value our friendship."

"It sounds as if the two of you are very close, my lord," Lady Moreton said with a tilt of her head.

He turned and gave her a smile. "We are—ever since he saved my hide from numerous beatings from the other boys at school when we were children."

"Nobler and nobler," Mrs. Aldridge said quietly.

~May 14~

Jamie had tossed and turned each night, thinking about what he was going to do. He knew that quitting was absolutely the right thing for him to do, but to return to Rossburke? Was that right? He'd said it at the spur of the moment when he'd had, perhaps, too much to drink.

But he *hadn't* had too much to drink—not at that point, anyway.

Still, the words had popped out of his mouth before his brain had even had a moment to contemplate the wisdom of them. Now that he'd thought about it some—just about every waking minute, and quite a few non-waking ones as well—he knew in his heart that it was what he needed to do.

He loved painting. It was his passion. Happily, he had a talent for it as well, but it wasn't what was going to support him through his life. And it wasn't what his father, grandfather, or even great-grandfather had meant for him to pursue.

He supposed his father had known that. It was why he tried his hardest to run their estate even though Jamie knew his passion lay in creating beautiful sculptures—their house was full of those he'd made when he'd been a young man. But then his father had married and settled down and done his best for the estate, for their family.

Jamie would do the same.

He wasn't so sure about the marriage part, though. He knew how very unhappy his mother had been living in a run-down, falling-down old house. He needed to get the estate profitable, or at least on the road to profitability. He needed to fix the house and make it livable. Then he would turn his mind to finding a woman with whom he could share his home and his life.

He knew that Lady Margaret couldn't wait for him, if she didn't want to lose her own inheritance, so it would have to be someone else. Perhaps a Scotswoman, he thought. No one would ever be able to take Margaret's place in his heart, but it was because he loved her so that he had to let her go.

But first, before he did anything else, he needed to quit this position, which led him to knocking on the drawing room door early Thursday morning after sleeping on it for two nights. He'd tried to wait for Wickford to come through with whatever his plan was, but Jamie just didn't have the patience to wait any longer.

"Come in," the duchess called through the door.

Jamie walked into the room, immediately noted that Lady Margaret was there as well, and bowed.

"Yes, James?" the duchess asked. She'd been looking at him oddly ever since the previous afternoon. Did she perhaps know that he was thinking of leaving?

"Your Grace, may I have a word?" Jamie asked. He wasn't sure he wanted to do this in front of Lady Margaret. He knew she'd find out sooner rather than later, but having her there would make it all the more difficult.

"Of course." The duchess set aside her stitching and looked up at him expectantly.

He supposed he had no choice. "Your Grace, I am extremely saddened by this, but I'm afraid I must give my notice."

The lady's eyes widened. "What? You are leaving us?"

"I'm afraid so."

"Why?" Lady Margaret asked, looking up from her book. Did she look upset or was that just his own wishful thinking?

"I, er, I need to go home," he said. It was the truth.

"Immediately?" the duchess asked.

Jamie *had* thought he'd leave right away, so he gave a nod. "If it wouldn't be too much trouble."

"Well, it would," she said in a huff. "I would be less one footman. Who would watch the door?"

"I'm certain Harold is more than capable..."

"I don't know that he is," she said.

"Mr. Holton—"

"Mr. Holton does an admirable job, but we've been relying on you to do yours for some time now. No, I'm sorry, but you cannot leave immediately," the duchess announced.

"Your Grace?" Jamie asked. If he didn't leave immediately, he worried that he wouldn't be able to leave at all, that he might rethink his determination to learn how to run his estate. It hadn't been an easy decision to come to.

"You may go next week," the lady said. "A week from today. Does that suit you?"

Did it suit him? No, it didn't, but he couldn't very well say so. What would suit him would be to get out of this house as quickly as possible. Make a clean break. But he supposed he didn't really have a choice in the matter. If she needed him...

"Very well, Your Grace, if you insist," he answered with a bow.

"Good. Thank you, James," the duchess said, picking up her embroidery once again.

Jamie bowed again and left the room. He hadn't gone far before Lady Margaret caught up with him.

She pulled him to a stop with a hand on his arm. The heat of it seared through his coat, and it took all his willpower not to immediately pull her into his arms. Instead, he took a step back but remained facing her.

"Why are you leaving? Really?" she asked, looking up him.

The tears in her eyes startled him, making it even harder to keep himself aloof.

For a moment, all he could do was to stare into her large, shining, blue eyes. He found himself swallowing hard.

"As I told the duchess—"

"You have to go home? Is...is someone ill?" Lady Margaret asked.

"No, it's just..." He hated lying to her. No, he couldn't do it. "I'm needed there," he said.

"But you're needed here as well." She paused and looked down at her hands clasped in front of her. "I need you."

He could only smile and clasp his hands behind his back to keep them from dragging her against his chest. "No, you don't. You're doing very well. Look at how you've grown in just the past few weeks. You now have gentlemen sending you flowers, and visiting, and taking you out for drives in the park. You don't need me."

Her gaze flew up to his once again. "But I do! You give me strength to do all that. I don't know that I'd be able to do anything without you here supporting me."

He reached out and took one of her hands in his. He simply had to touch her. "Yes, you can. You're strong now. You're brave and you know just what you should do. I know you can do it without me. I know it for certain."

"I don't," she said in a small voice, holding onto

his hand as much as he was holding hers.

He gave her hand a squeeze. "I have faith in you." And then he did the hardest thing ever. He walked away.

Chapter Thirty-Five

~May 16~

Margaret was very excited. Her brother had finally decided to hold a party for the unveiling of her portrait. Actually, she was pretty certain it was Tina who she would need to thank for pushing her brother into doing something. It wasn't going to be a very large party—it was, after all, simply to show off James's wonderful painting—but she was sure it would be a very pleasant evening.

What made the evening even more enjoyable was the fact that Warwick, or maybe Tina, had prevailed upon James to join them.

He was wearing his best and looking more handsome than Margaret had ever seen him. He had always made her heart beat a little faster, but this evening with his blond hair tickling the collar of his black coat and a stark white cravat tied just so, he looked incredible.

"Mr. Douglass," Tina greeted him, as they arrived together. The duchess had been so kind as to take him up with them in her carriage.

"Your Grace," James said, bowing to her. "Thank you so much for your kind invitation."

"Of course! How ridiculous would it be to have an unveiling of a portrait without the artist being present." she said with a laugh.

He smiled.

"And as you see, we have hung it in the place of honor." Tina turned, indicating the painting on the wall above the fireplace. It looked wonderful. Margaret was a little anxious at her likeness being hung so prominently, but at the same time proud of the beautiful work James had created.

"It does look good there," James nodded.

"You have captured my sister perfectly." Warwick joined them, coming up and shaking James's hand.

"Thank you, Your Grace. I'm very happy that you are pleased with it," James said with a slight bow.

"Truly, we couldn't be happier." Tina gave both him and Margaret a smile.

"Come, have a drink." Warwick motioned to a footman standing nearby with a tray of champagne.

Margaret laughed. The footman was being waited upon by a footman, and yet, oddly enough, James seemed to be very comfortable in his surroundings. He didn't seem overwhelmed, as Margaret remembered Tina being the first time she'd come into Warwick's home. How strange. She supposed he was used to grand homes, although more as a servant than a guest, but still.

The duchess joined them, and they all raised a glass to the portrait and the artist.

Very soon more guests began arriving. There were, of course, the ladies of the Wagering Whist Society and then others.

"Lord Wickford, what a lovely surprise to see you here, this evening," Margaret said, soon after he came into the drawing room, which had been opened up and most of the furniture pushed to the walls. She hadn't known why they'd allowed for so much space, but now that more guests were coming, she realized it would, in fact, be needed.

The gentleman bowed. "Lady Margaret, what a pleasure." His smile grew when he took in the portrait just behind her. She'd deliberately worn the same dress this evening as she had for the sitting.

"You look beautiful as always, and may I say the portrait, while excellent, does not do you justice?" he said.

Margaret laughed. "Well, I should hope I have a little more life in me than a painting."

"Indeed, you do," he laughed. "And where is the artist?"

Margaret turned around and scanned the room. She was surprised to see James laughing at something Lady Blakemore was saying to him. "There he is," she said, indicating him. "Standing next to Lady Blakemore. He's the gentleman in black."

"Ah, yes." Lord Wickford raised a hand, getting James's attention.

James gave Lady Blakemore a slight bow and headed toward them.

When he reached Margaret's side, she said, "James Douglass, may I make you known—"

"We are already acquainted, Lady Margaret, but thank you," Lord Wickford said, interrupting her. He gave James a broad smile. "I do like the portrait," he said to James.

"Thank you," James said. He didn't have a chance to say anything more because two other gentlemen who Margaret didn't know joined them just at that moment.

"Rossburke!" a very tall man said with enthusiasm.

"Rossy, old boy, damned good to see you!" the shorter man said but with equal joy. He slapped James on the shoulder and grabbed his hand.

"Thandler, Ormonde! What the devil?" James said, looking a little stunned.

"Just got into town," the shorter man said. "Wick told us you were painting now. Couldn't miss this, now, could we?"

"The duke was kind enough to extend an invitation," the taller man said with a broad smile before turning toward Margaret. "Is this...?" he wiggled his eyebrows while looking between James and Margaret.

"Oh! Er, Lady Margaret, may I present the Viscount Thandler and the Earl Ormonde," James said, making the introduction.

The two gentlemen bowed.

"Ah, you're the subject, er, the duke's sister?" Lord Thandler asked.

"Yes," Margaret said. "May I ask how you know James?" she asked, unable to contain her curiosity.

"James, eh?" Lord Ormand gave a little chuckle and then added, "Went to school together."

"Rossburke here, Wickford, Ormand, and I were classmates. The closest of friends," Lord Thandler added.

"Well, not as close as Rossy and Wick," Lord Ormonde corrected his friend.

Lord Thandler gave a laugh. "No one was as close as Wickford and Rossburke, but they roomed together for what, six years?"

"Something like that," Lord Wickford agreed.

Margaret couldn't believe it. She looked at James who had the grace to look embarrassed. No wonder he didn't have any sort of accent. He was…what? The son of a cit? He couldn't be a nobleman, but then… They were calling him Rossburke when Margaret knew his family name was Douglass. Which meant… "*Lord* Rossburke?" she asked.

He gave an uncomfortable tug at his cravat.

"Of course Lord Rossburke," Lord Ormand said with a laugh. "It wasn't Eton, but it wasn't too far below."

"It was a pretty good school…"

Margaret couldn't stay and listen to any more. She needed some air. She quickly excused herself and walked away. Her feet took her into onto the balcony, but she hardly paid any attention to where she went. She just needed some space.

He was a lord? A nobleman? But he was a painter! A footman! She couldn't imagine *any* nobleman waiting on others. No, they had to be funning. They had to—

"Lady Margaret," James's voice called from behind her.

She turned to see him walking toward her, but she wasn't sure she wanted to speak with him just now, so she turned away again.

"Margaret," he said, pulling her to a stop. "I'm sorry."

"Sorry? Sorry for what? For helping a silly girl learn how to put herself forward in society? You did that and I always rather wondered how you were so knowledgeable about how I should behave. Only I never questioned it because…because…"

"Because you didn't want to?"

She spun around. "Because the idea that a nobleman would pose as footman was ridiculous! No one would do that." Was there anger in her voice? Yes. Yes, there was! She was angry!

He nodded. "It's true. No one in their right mind *would* do that. But I wasn't posing. I actually was a footman. I needed to be."

"Why?"

"Because I have no money and I learned that I rather like eating and having a roof over my head."

She scoffed. "I'm sure you've got a very nice roof somewhere."

He just smiled. "It's actually in disrepair and leaks in places."

She started to turn away again. She didn't know what to think of this man.

"I'm sorry. I'm an impoverished nobleman. My father and my grandfather both were horrible farmers and estate managers. They lost more money than they earned and I… I never learned how to run our estate either. I thought I would do better leasing the land and becoming the painter I'd always wanted to be."

"But you couldn't sell your work?" she asked reluctantly, her anger dissipating just as quickly as it had flared.

"No, I couldn't." There was a moment of silence before he added. "I was starving. I needed to eat, so I wrote myself a letter of recommendation and found a job doing something I thought I knew how to do, thinking I could paint on the side." He gave a little laugh, but there wasn't really any humor in it.

"I never realized how much work it is being a footman. I would fall into bed absolutely exhausted every night. I'd wake up every morning, aching with nothing but another day on my feet to look forward to. I had no time to paint—until the duchess hired me and allowed me to work at the front door, which allowed me a little time to sketch."

"And then you got the commission from Warwick," she put in.

"Yes, and I met my old friend Wickford. Honestly, I'd had no intention of dragging him into my sorry life, but he insisted. He sold a few of my paintings as well."

"That was kind of him."

"It was extremely kind of him. He's a good friend...except when he invites our old school mates to a party without telling me."

She laughed. "So, you are *really* a nobleman," she said, finally looking up at him.

"A marquess."

"That is impressive."

"I can't imagine how it could be to the sister of a duke," he said with a chuckle.

"It is."

"All right. I'm an impoverished marquess, then." He made an elaborate leg. "My lady, may I present the Marquess of Rossburke."

She smiled and curtsied. But then she remembered... "Are you really leaving?"

He stood straight again. "I am."

"May I ask why?" Her stomach hurt just thinking about him not being in her life.

He sighed. "I realized that marquesses don't

make great footmen. It's not the life I was cut out for. I'd rather face my crumbling estate and try to learn how to be a farmer."

Margaret could feel the tears welling up in her eyes. She couldn't bear the thought of him leaving. Whether he was a marquess or a footman, he was still her friend—her closest friend. She had such feelings for him, she realized, as she thought about it. Feelings that probably went well beyond friendship, but... It was for naught.

"Margaret," he whispered as a tear slipped from the corner of her eye.

She quickly swiped it away with the back of her hand.

He handed her his handkerchief, and she used it to dab at her eyes. "I don't want you to leave," she said, holding his handkerchief to her heart. She looked down, wondering how she could convince him not to go. The black embroidery on the corner of his handkerchief caught her eye.

She gave a sniff as she flattened the material to look at it, and then gasped. "JR!"

He gave an embarrassed little laugh. "The tailor who made my clothes did that. It's silly. asked how I fashion my initials—I usually put in the D for Douglass."

"But that means... That means *you* are the gentleman from the Venetian ball!" she said, widening her eyes and looking up at him.

His smile broadened as he nodded. "It was the most wonderful night of my life. I didn't ever want it to end. I wanted to dance with you again and again, or even better, spend more time with you out on that balcony." He sighed. "But then midnight came."

"And you left! You left me standing alone in the middle of the floor!"

"I'm very sorry about that, but I couldn't reveal myself, and everyone was about to remove their masks. I had no choice."

"I searched for you!" She then thought of something else and hit his shoulder. "You let me think it was Lord Roseberry!"

"Well, it made sense. His initials are JR," James said, rubbing his shoulder. "And I couldn't tell you it was me."

"But I fell..." Margaret stopped herself just in time, biting the inside of her lip.

"You fell?"

She swallowed. Taking a deep breath, she looked down at her hands again, playing with the handkerchief. "I fell in love with you that night."

His calloused fingers brushed down her cheek and then lifted her chin, so she was forced to look at him. "I fell in love with you the moment I met you. It was made even worse when we were alone while I painted your portrait. What sweet agony those afternoons were—being with you and yet..."

"Oh, James," Margaret breathed.

"You know what I wanted to do?"

She shook her head.

"For so long, for so very long, I've wanted to do this." He bent his head down and gently brushed his lips against hers. When she didn't pull away, he kissed her again, his lips fully taking possession of hers. She found herself in his arms, her hands pressed up against his chest.

She felt safe. His warm, solid, strong body was tight against hers. She felt...loved.

Chapter Thirty-Six

"I sincerely hope your intentions are honorable," the duke's voice cut in between them like a knife.

They jumped apart.

"I understand from Lord Wickford that you are not who you've presented yourself to be, Lord Rossburke," Warwick said, putting his hands on his hips.

"Er, no." James had the grace to look slightly guilty, although Margaret wasn't sure if it was because he'd lied about his identity or because he'd just been caught kissing her.

"Well, then, I expect I'll be receiving a request very soon?" Warwick asked.

"A request?" Margaret repeated.

"For your hand," her brother spelled out.

"Oh."

"I wish I could." James turned to her. "I would love nothing more than to propose to Margaret." He turned back to Warwick. "I love her more than I'd ever imagined I could love another."

"But?" Warwick asked, lowering his brows and glaring at James.

"But I have no money. I have an estate in Scotland that is falling apart. I've leased the land,

and well, I don't know if I can get it back, although I am certainly going to try. It will depend on the good graces of the men to whom I leased it," James admitted.

"I could probably assist you with that. I employ the finest solicitors in London," Margaret's brother said, lowering his hands.

"That's very kind, but even if I get it back... I need to learn how to farm it. If it's even possible to make it profitable. Both my father and grandfather failed miserably. I don't know... I mean, I hope I can do better, but honestly..."

"I've got people for that as well. Estate managers who can assess the land and its potential," Warwick stated.

"But I haven't the wherewithal to pay them," James said, shaking his head.

"I already do so," Warwick pointed out.

"And you could...lend them to me? I would repay you as soon as I could. I just don't know..." James stammered.

"If they can make your estate profitable, then you'll be able to pay them. It's in their interest to make it so," Warwick explained. "And don't worry about repaying me. Consider it a wedding gift," he said with a quirk of his lips.

"My word." James just shook his head. "And they would be able to teach me how to manage on my own?"

"They would. Or they could advise you on who to hire to assist you, so you could have some time to spend with...your wife?" Warwick looked questioningly at Margaret who nodded hopefully.

"And I've got a sizeable dowry that you can use to get started," she added. "If...if you're interested."

James turned to her and took her hands in his own. "I would never use your money for my own ends. That is yours."

"If the two of you married, it *would* be yours," Warwick pointed out.

"Legally, yes, but I wouldn't want to spend Margaret's money. What if someday she needs it, or wants to give it to her children?" James asked. "My father married for money. He and my mother got along well enough, but... He spent every cent she brought to their marriage, leaving her with nothing. She regretted the fact that she had no money to leave our home, to travel, to visit her family in England. She had nothing because my father poured it all into the estate and investments that never earned back what he put into them. I won't do that to my wife. It's why I refused to put myself on the marriage market for an heiress and instead tried to make my way as an artist."

"That's very noble of you," Warwick said. "Perhaps you can establish trusts. One for Margaret to use as she wishes, another for your children, and then you can set aside some to bring your estate back in line."

"Is there enough...?" James started.

Margaret smiled. "If I marry by the end of the season, there will be more than enough."

Warwick nodded and smiled. "Our father did very well with his estates."

"Well..." James started. He turned toward Margaret and was about to speak when the duke said quietly, "I'll just leave you alone for a few moments, shall I? I expect to see you inside within ten minutes, however."

Margaret heard him leave, but she just couldn't

take her eyes from James.

He glanced over to where her brother had been standing, then turned back to her with a mischievous little smile on his lips. "We can do one of two things with the next ten minutes. Either I can return to kissing you, which would be lovely, or I can tell you how much I love you, detailing every single thing you do that makes me love you even more every single day, or—"

"What you need to do," Margaret interrupted with a giggle. "What you need to do is ask me to marry you because you haven't done that yet."

"Ah, no, I haven't, have I?" He slowly lowered himself to one knee. "Lady Margaret would you make me the happiest man alive and honor me with your hand in marriage?"

She laughed. Never had she imagined that she could be so happy, feel so comfortable with a man, feel so wanted, cherished, admired, and yes, loved. With her heart feeling as if it would simply burst with joy she smiled down at the one man with whom she truly wanted to spend the rest of her life with. "I would, my lord, I would be very, very happy to do so."

~*~

Margaret had been thoroughly kissed by the time they started back to the drawing room—so much so, that she'd gone instead to the ladies' retiring room to fix her hair. Jamie, however, wanted a word with his dear, old friend Wickford.

It took a little searching, but he found him in the far corner of the room, speaking with Lady Moreton. "Good evening, Lady Moreton," Jamie said, bowing to the lady.

"Lord Rossburke," she said, curtsying.

He quirked up his lips. "I see you've been informed."

"Oh! Er, yes," she said momentarily flustered.

He gave her a kind smile. "It's quite all right. I am afraid I will need to steal Lord Wickford away from you for a moment. I do apologize."

He took hold of his friend's arm in a firm grip and led him back out onto the balcony, smiling and nodding to other guests along the way.

When they were finally alone, Jamie let go of his arm and faced his best friend of nearly twenty years. He crossed his arms over his chest and waited.

Wickford looked him in the eye at first, then had the intelligence to look down and find his shoes very interesting.

"I'm waiting for an explanation if it wasn't clear," Jamie said in a no-nonsense voice.

"Er, yes, I guessed as much." Wickford scratched at the back of his neck and then ran his hand up and over the tight curls of his hair. Finally, he took in a deep breath and said, "Well, I *had* to do something! You were being such a bloody, obstinate idiot!" He gave Jamie a pleading look and then said, "Come on, Jamie, you were about to return to Scotland, having never told her the truth. You would have never even given her the option of knowing who you really were. You would have left her to wonder who that man was at the Venetian ball for the rest of her life. Is that fair? Is that right? I think not!" he said, answering his own rhetorical question.

"You talk about giving her a choice, but you didn't give *me* a choice. You simply ensured that I would be exposed by inviting Thadley and Ormonde." Jamie was trying so hard to keep his calm, but the gruffness of his voice gave away his anger.

Wickford opened his mouth, perhaps to deny it, then closed it again without speaking.

"You can't deny it," Jamie growled.

"No. I can't. But I say again that I had to do *something*. I couldn't just let you leave."

"You *could* have. You could have minded your own damned business."

Wickford looked at Jamie, and his eyes widened. "And when have I ever done that?"

That took the hot air out of Jamie. "Never."

"Not when it came to your happiness. No, never. You are such a stubborn fool you don't know half the time what you need, and if you do, you *still* won't admit to it. Now tell me that you aren't happy? Tell me that Lady Margaret, upon learning your true identity, has told you to get lost, go back to Scotland, and stay out of her life because you lied to her." Wickford was the one crossing his arms over his chest accusingly this time.

Jamie frowned. "She's accepted my proposal of marriage. We are going to move back to Scotland, and her brother is going to send solicitors and an estate manager with us to get me out of the leases I signed and help get my estate running properly."

"And you are *blaming* me for letting everyone know that you are a marquess?" Wickford ask incredulously.

"Yes, I am!"

"Are you unhappy, Jamie?" Wickford said, lowering his eyebrows. "Do you not love Lady Margaret? Were you forced into this marriage and all that comes with it?"

Jamie could only sigh. "No. I'm very happy. I love Margaret with all my heart, and I am hopeful I can work with the duke's people and actually get my estate running properly."

"You're welcome," Wickford said and then turned and started to walk away. He stopped a few steps away and turned back. "I'll be expecting an invitation to your wedding and then to your home once it's fixed up," he informed Jamie seriously.

Jamie burst out laughing. "And to the christening of our first child."

"Yes! Don't forget that," Wickford said with a laugh before returning to the drawing room.

Jamie stood outside another moment to take in the evening air and quiet of the night. It had been quite a journey these past six months. It wasn't one he'd ever regret.

"What are you still doing out here?" Margaret asked, joining him. "I thought I'd see you inside."

"I was just thinking," he admitted.

She came forward. "What about?"

"Just how much I love you," he said, taking a step closer.

She smiled up at him. "And I love you, my Lord Footman," she said with a laugh.

Next in the Series
An Affair of Hearts

Can the Ladies' Wagering Whist Society turn back the clock to restore the reputation of a lady maligned?

The lovely, kind Elizabeth, the Countess St. Vincent, is determined to re-enter Regency society now that she is widowed. Despite the years that have passed since her fiasco of a debut, one man still remembers and resurrects old rumors. With her reputation destroyed, so are her hopes. Can a newfound friend be the key to burying the past before the season ends?

Charles Aldridge is a watchmaker and businessman fighting to protect a centuries-old industry threatened with extinction. But he is distracted from his quest when he is dragged into the troubles of the beguiling Lady St. Vincent. Every chivalrous bone in his body insists he do all he can to help her. Yet, following his heart may mean jeopardizing his life's mission.

The Ladies' Wagering Whist Society will have to play a clever hand to settle this Affair of Hearts... before time runs out.

About the Author

Meredith Bond's books straddle that beautiful line between historical romance and fantasy. An award-winning author, she writes fun traditional Regency romances, medieval Arthurian romances, and Regency romances with a touch of magic. Known for her characters "who slip readily into one's heart," Meredith's heart belongs to her husband and two children.

Meredith loves connecting with readers. Sign up for her monthly newsletter at http://meredithbond. com/blog/newsletter-sign-up/ to receive free short stories and get all her news before anyone else. And don't forget to find her on-line:

Website: http://www.meredithbond.com

Facebook: https://www.facebook.com/meredithbondauthor

Amazon: http://www.amazon.com/Meredith-Bond/e/B001KI1SNE

Instagram: https://www.instagram.com/meredith_bond/

Bookbub: https://www.bookbub.com/authors/meredith-bond

Newsletter: http://meredithbond.com/subscribe/

Please don't forget to leave a review wherever you buy books.

Follow all of the women of the Ladies' Wagering Whist Society

1806 Season
A Hand for the Duke
Featuring Christianne Norman, Lady Norman
The Jack of Diamonds
Featuring Miss Lydia Sheffield
The Games She Played
Featuring Miss Diana Hemshawe

1807 Season
A Trick of Mirrors
Featuring Claire Tyne, Lady Blakemore
A Bid for Romance
Featuring Alys Russell, Duchess of Kendell
An Affair of Hearts
Featuring Mrs. Penelope Aldridge

1808 Season
Love in Spades
Featuring Cynthia Montley, Lady Sorrell
coming: Spring, 2021
A Token of Love
Featuring Ellen Aston, Lady Moreton
coming: Spring, 2021
Bonus
The King of Clubs
Featuring Joshua Powell, Lord Wickford
coming: Spring, 2021

Other Books By Meredith Bond

The Merry Men Series
An Exotic Heir
A Merry Marquis
A Rake's Reward
A Dandy in Disguise
My Lord Ghost
My Gentleman Thief
Under the Mango Tree
A Spanish Dilemma
When Hearts Rebel

The Storm Series
Storm on the Horizon
Bridging the Storm
Magic in the Storm
Through the Storm

The Children of Avalon Trilogy
Air: Merlin's Chalice
Water: The Return of Excalibur
Fire: Nimuë's Destiny

Falling
Falling for a Pirate

Chapter One: A Fast, Fun Way to Write Fiction
Self-Publishing: Easy as ABC
"In A Beginning", a short story featuring Lilith

www.ingramcontent.com/pod-product-compliance
Lightning Source LLC
Chambersburg PA
CBHW060232100726
47907CB00003B/598